THE
BLOODY CITY
A MEDIAEVAL MYSTERY

THE BLOODY CITY

A MEDIAEVAL MYSTERY

C.B. HANLEY

The Mystery Press

For P.C.

who, without knowing it, gave me an idea.

First published by The Mystery Press, 2013

The Mystery Press, an imprint of The History Press
The Mill, Brimscombe Port
Stroud, Gloucestershire, GL5 2QG
www.thehistorypress.co.uk

British Library Cataloguing in Publication Data.
A catalogue record for this book is available from the British Library.

ISBN 978 0 7524 9704 4

Typesetting and origination by The History Press
Printed in Great Britain

Woe unto the bloody city!
It is all full of lies.

Nahum, ch. 3, v. 1

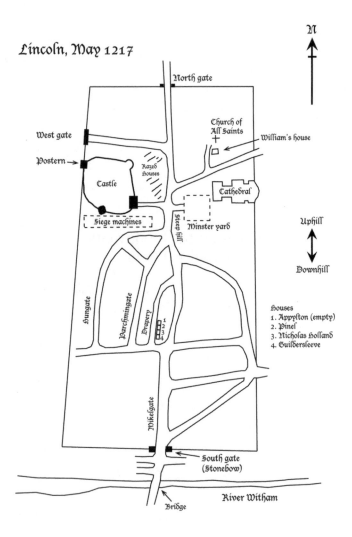

Lincoln, May 1217

North gate

West gate

Postern →

Castle

Razed Houses

Church of All Saints

William's house

Cathedral

Siege machines

Minster yard

Jill steep hill

N

Uphill

Downhill

Hungate

Parchmingate

Drapery

1
2
3
4

Houses
1. Appylton (empty)
2. Pinel
3. Nicholas Holland
4. Guildersleeve

Wikelgate

South gate
(Stonebow)

River Witham

Bridge

Prologue

It was quiet.

Too quiet.

He peered out from his hiding place in the fetid alley and looked up and down the remains of the street. By the faint light of the crescent moon he could see that it was empty, the shattered buildings yawning to the sky and the roadway strewn with rubble. The only movement came from something scuttling through the gutter, no doubt one of the rats which had become fat since the invasion started.

The streets of Lincoln were not a safe place to be, in the spring of this year of Our Lord twelve hundred and seventeen; the French, together with those rebel Englishmen who had joined forces with them, had attacked and taken the city, and there had been burning, plunder, bloodshed and murder. It had fallen quickly, despite the best efforts of the townsfolk to defend it, for they were civilians, not men of war like the seasoned troops who had faced them across the walls and through the bloodied streets. Only the castle had held firm, and the nobility and knights, the real fighting men, were trapped in there, defending the last Royalist stronghold in the region. Meanwhile the invading forces kept the town in a suffocating grip while they sought to capture the castle, by starving the garrison into submission and smashing the walls down with their monstrous siege engines. For weeks the smell of terror had lain over the city like a pall, and the castle walls shivered under the onslaught. And yet through it all the citizens tried to maintain the vestiges of their old lives. They traded when they could; they ate and drank when the means were available. And they sought out old friends.

He was headed towards the northern part of the town, which became more dangerous as he drew nearer to the castle, and the stillness of the night had aroused his suspicions. On previous occasions when he had crept through the streets after the curfew, he had heard the groaning of the engines and the crashing of huge missiles into the walls; he had been forced to avoid gangs of French and rebel English soldiers, stamping about the town in search of disquiet or rebellion, or simply trying to cause some trouble of their own. But tonight there seemed to be nobody around. Where were the invaders? Perhaps they were guarding their siege machinery on the south side of the castle, but here to the north-east they had cleared the area in front of the massive structure and left it empty, with only the ruins of the razed houses thrusting their charred beams towards the night sky.

It was quiet.

There was nothing else for it – he couldn't stay here, so he either had to go forward or turn back. He slipped out of the alley and stole along the street, picking his way through the debris and trying to remain silent. His senses screamed at being out in the open and he tried to keep to the gloom surrounding the ruined houses as far as possible. Gradually he crept nearer to his destination, but still not near enough. He stopped again and crouched in a shadow, considering his position. What if he were to be attacked? What would happen to his family? How would they survive without him? But still he was drawn to continue. He forced himself to swallow the fear and stand up.

He had reached the end of the safe cover and only open space beckoned. He would be expected. She would be looking out for him. He would only be out in the open for a few moments. He must do it. Do it now. His heart was so loud it must be giving his position away anyway. He stood up.

It was at that moment that a figure arose from the shadows behind him and struck him down. He was conscious of the searing, splitting pain in his head for only a fraction of a moment before he fell forward into the darkness.

Chapter One

The pain was unbearable.

Edwin had no idea who had first considered the back of a horse a suitable means of transport, but clearly he'd been out of his mind. Every mile, every yard, every step, was agony. To make it worse, nobody else around him seemed to be suffering in the same way: they all rode as though the horse were a part of them, rising and falling easily in the saddle and even turning to talk and jest with those around them. But then again, most of them were knights, men who had been trained in the saddle and who had probably learned to ride before they could walk, whereas he, Edwin of Conisbrough, was just a commoner who had never ridden further than a few miles on the slowest of nags.

What was he doing here? Just a week ago he had been the acting bailiff on the earl's Conisbrough estate, spending his time organising the work of the villagers and dealing with petty disputes over a few yards of land. But all that had changed when a murder had been committed and Edwin had been set to finding the culprit. He had done so successfully, but in many ways – so many ways – he wished he hadn't. Yet here he was, suddenly promoted, not as bailiff but to an as-yet unnamed position in the earl's personal retinue, as his 'man' – or a useful person to have around, as the earl had put it. He, Edwin, a personal servant of William de Warenne, Earl of Surrey and one of the most powerful men in the kingdom … in his most fevered dreams he couldn't have imagined such a thing, and it still seemed barely real. He hadn't yet become accustomed to the position and wasn't sure what his function was exactly; his only duties appeared to be to keep his eyes and ears open and to wait for the earl to order him to do something. In the meantime he would sell his soul to be able to get off the back of this horse.

They'd been on the road all day yesterday, as they made their way from Yorkshire southwards to Newark, where they were to meet up with the army of the regent. Edwin had only the haziest idea of where Newark might be – once it had passed noon, he was already further from his home village than he had ever thought to be in his life – but anyway, this was not to be their final destination. Once the army was complete, they were to march upon the city of Lincoln, which was held by French forces, in order to recapture it. Presumably this was to be achieved by fighting, something about which Edwin knew nothing, and he wondered how in the Lord's name he was to be of help during the campaign. Still, his place was to serve the earl, no matter what he was asked to do, so he supposed he'd better get used to following orders without really knowing why.

They'd made camp overnight at a place called Retford, and Edwin had been amazed at how smoothly everything had functioned. Everyone – or at least everyone except him – seemed to know exactly what he was doing, and in almost no time a small thicket of tents and campfires had appeared, horses had been fed and watered, and a meal had been cooked. Not that Edwin had eaten any of it: he hadn't been sure where he should go, as he didn't belong to any of the retinues, and when he'd edged diffidently up to the central area of the camp where the earl's personal staff were, he had been told in no uncertain terms by Hamo, the earl's supercilious marshal, that the victuals there were not for the likes of him, so he should begone and seek his meal somewhere more befitting his station. The result had been that he'd wandered hungry around the camp before finding a place to rest, wrapping himself in a blanket and sleeping alone and miserable on the cold ground. And to think it was only a short time ago that he'd envied those who were about to go on campaign while he was left behind. What was it he'd thought in his naivety? *Honour and glory and a chance to see the world*. It wasn't turning out the way he'd expected.

So now here he was after a second day in the saddle, on fire with agony at every step, waiting for the moment when he could dismount and rest. He was hot and sweaty, itching under his clothes, and he was so hungry that his stomach was growling, but he wasn't sure he would have the energy to try and find whatever the correct source of food was supposed to be. Hopefully he could just prepare his horse for the night and then sleep, assuming the earl didn't want him for anything, which hadn't been the case thus far. When was this journey to end? He'd had no idea that the realm could be so vast. He kept his eyes on the road and tried to switch off his mind to the pain, as the movement of the horse went on and on and on.

Finally, as the temperate spring afternoon wore on into early evening, the earl's host rounded a bend in the road and they were treated to the sight of a large encampment spread out before them, outside the walls of a small town. Roused from his stupor, Edwin gaped at the rows upon rows of tents, horse pickets and camp fires. He'd never seen anything like it – how many men must there be in the army? As usual, the numbers arranged themselves neatly in his head as he calculated: judging by the number of tents, and then working out how many men were probably attached to each, would make it …

His attention was distracted by several figures who were approaching from the camp. They rode up and reined in when they reached the earl and the senior members of his household at the front of the host, and began what looked like an animated conversation. Edwin assumed they would probably tell the earl and his men where they could make camp, but apparently this wasn't the case. There was a lot of arm-waving going on, and some sort of argument, with the earl in particular becoming quite irate. Eventually two of the men rode back to the camp, while the earl's horse pawed the ground and his host didn't move. After a short while the men returned, together with a third who looked much more important: he was wearing mail and a surcoat emblazoned with a device Edwin didn't recognise. He too engaged in conversation with the earl, seemingly trying to placate him, and finally the host was waved towards the edge of the encampment, and they were moving again.

Edwin didn't think he had ever been as thankful for anything as for the opportunity to finally get down from his horse, but after so long in the unaccustomed saddle he feared that he wouldn't even be able to move his legs well enough to swing them over the beast's back and dismount. All around him men were slipping easily down from their saddles, smiling at each other at the thought of rest and a hot meal. He must make an effort. Soon he would be the only one on horseback. Come on, move. Wincing, he tried to shift, and eventually succeeded in disentangling his right foot from the stirrup and lifting the leg on to the horse's back, albeit by having to lift it bodily with his hand, and once both legs were on the same side of the horse he slid down to the ground in what he hoped was an unremarkable manoeuvre. It was all going fairly well until his feet touched the floor and his legs buckled underneath him.

He was spared the embarrassment of collapsing in a heap on the ground by a strong hand which caught the back of his tunic and hauled him more or less upright, supporting him until he could feel his legs properly. He turned in gratitude to see that his rescuer was Martin, the earl's squire, who was looking down upon him from his great height with a mixture of pity and amusement.

His voice was deep. 'I forgot that you won't have had much experience at riding; don't worry, it'll get better as you get more used to it.'

Edwin could only nod.

Martin released him, slapped him heartily on the back – making him wince even more – and strode off to attend to his duties. Edwin stood, his face hot. Honestly, a noble child of five would have made a better showing. He risked a glance around, but strangely nobody seemed to have noticed; they were all too busy stretching, talking, leading their horses off or handing them over to grooms or squires. Perhaps he'd escaped humiliation this time, except to himself. The horse was looking at him with what seemed to be barely concealed contempt, so he scowled at it. It flicked its ears at him. He sighed and, hobbling stiffly, led it away to follow the others.

A while later he decided to have a look around the encampment, mainly in order to take his mind off the hunger, but he was soon disappointed. He'd always imagined an army to be a host of knights in glittering mail, but he soon realised that although there were such here, they were outnumbered by the other types of men – foot sergeants, crossbowmen and servants, to name but a few – and the overwhelming sense was one of boredom. Here and there, knights were striding about or greeting friends whom they hadn't seen for a while, but the majority of the men, the common men, simply sat around. They'd erected their tents, so there was nothing to do but await the evening meal. Some polished weapons or played at dice; others spoke in low tones to each other or simply sat still, staring ahead of them. Edwin realised that most of these men probably had very little idea of why they were here – they weren't privy to the details of the nobles' campaigns; their task was simply to obey and to fight and die wherever their lord sent them. It was depressing, especially when he realised that his own situation was similar: they were all owned, like horses or dogs, unable to choose how they lived their own lives. He lost his appetite for looking around and turned back.

As he reached the earl's part of the camp again, he smelled the aroma of pottage cooking and his stomach growled anew. How long could he keep going if he didn't get anything to eat?

But he had no stomach for an argument with the haughty Hamo, so he sat on his own, kicking at small stones and watching other men eat while he tried to quell the pangs in his innards. If only he had someone to show him where to go and how to act, somebody with whom he could share the wonder of his new experiences. If only – but no, the one man who could have helped him was cold in his grave at Conisbrough, and Edwin would never hear his voice or share a jest with him again. Martin was there, of course, but the newly promoted senior squire was fully occupied trying to serve the earl to the best of his abilities. Edwin didn't know the new junior squire, Adam, at all, and besides, the boy was a number of years younger than him. He sighed, lonely, and continued with his gloomy thoughts.

He was disturbed by a tug at his sleeve and turned to see a small boy holding out a steaming bowl to him. It was Peter, an orphan from Edwin's village, who had accompanied the host when it travelled. Edwin had seen him in the company of Sir Roger, one of the earl's knights, but he had little idea of how this had come to pass. Still, presumably the lad was earning his keep, which was better than starving back in the village.

Edwin was a little unsure where the food had come from, but he took the bowl with thanks. Peter, still not used to speaking, mumbled that it was from his lord, and fled. Edwin was a little confused, but his stomach was crying out for the meal so he took out his spoon and shovelled it in before it went cold. As he was finishing it, another man sat down beside him. Edwin started to leap to his feet, for it was Sir Roger himself, but the knight bade him stay seated. Edwin was grateful, for he wasn't sure that his legs would have supported him all the way up anyway. Still, he felt ill at ease sitting next to a knight like this. There was silence for a moment, before Sir Roger looked at him, seeming as always to be pulling himself back from a serene and remote place. The sapphire gaze was piercing and Edwin bowed his head.

'I'll speak to Hamo for you.'

Edwin jerked his head up again. He couldn't have heard that right. But Sir Roger was looking at him with some sympathy. Had he noticed what had happened yesterday? Surely not. He was a knight – why would he care?

But he had underestimated Sir Roger's calling for righting wrongs, no matter how small. 'I know Hamo of old, and he often tries to belittle anyone he doesn't like. I won't let this continue – you're the earl's man and it is right that he should treat you as such. The service you rendered him during the last week was invaluable: these are troubled times, Edwin, and you're the sort of man that my lord is going to need around him. His troubles aren't over: the regent still harbours some suspicions about his defection to the rebel cause and then his return, and he doesn't trust him entirely. There was some debate about whether he should be allowed to join the army at all.'

So that was what the trouble had been about earlier. Edwin supposed that if he was going to serve the earl properly, he'd better keep himself informed about this kind of thing, although he didn't really know how to go about it. He must keep his eyes and ears open.

Sir Roger fell silent and Edwin wasn't sure whether he was supposed to continue the conversation or whether he should take the lack of speech as some sort of dismissal, but fortunately he was saved from having to make the decision by the arrival of two more men whom he didn't know, but who were obviously knights and friends of Sir Roger's. He stood awkwardly while the three men greeted each other, unsure whether he should just slip away, but with calm civility Sir Roger invited him to step forward and be introduced.

'Edwin, these are two friends of mine. Sir Reginald le Croc –' he gestured towards the man on the left, a tall fellow, perhaps slightly older than himself, with long dark hair and merry eyes. Sir Reginald automatically held out his right hand to Edwin, but then winced as he took it, and Edwin realised too late that the hand was bandaged. He started to offer an apology but the knight waved it away, smiling.

Sir Roger continued: '– and Sir Gilbert de l'Aigle.' The other man was older, perhaps thirty years of age or more, and he had a seasoned and weather-beaten look about him. However, he was pleasant and welcoming, greeting Edwin courteously.

Sir Roger now had his hand on Edwin's shoulder, preparing to introduce him to his companions. This would be the great test. How would they react when they knew he was a commoner? Would their smiles melt away? Would they simply refuse to talk and move away from him? How would Sir Roger describe him? He held his breath, anticipating the worst, but Sir Roger presented him in an affable manner, as 'Edwin of Conisbrough, from the household of my lord the earl.' Then he gestured and all four sat down close to one of the campfires, Sir Roger's small party of foot sergeants moving away to a discreet distance.

Edwin could hardly believe that he was sitting with three knights, conversing with them on an equal level. Thank the Lord that his French was proficient enough to support him – his accent might sound a bit odd to these men, who from their names were pure-blood Normans, but they might just attribute this to his being from the north of the country, and he was able to speak fluently. Still, he decided that this was a good chance to learn something about the new world he now inhabited, so he kept his mouth shut while he listened to the others speaking of troop numbers, horses, provisions, the latest developments in armour, possible tactics … as the conversation continued he basked in the glow of the fire with a comfortably full stomach, and almost began to relax.

It was becoming full dark when Martin suddenly hurried up to the fire, calling Edwin's name and shattering his mood of calm. 'There you are! I've been looking for you everywhere – my lord the earl wants to speak with you right now.' Belatedly he stopped and nodded his head respectfully to the knights around the fire.

Edwin scrambled to his feet, almost falling over himself as he tried to rise too quickly. Why would the earl want to see him now? What task might he have? Despite his panic he remembered his manners and took his leave of the others. They waved him away cheerfully, no doubt used to being summoned at will by their own lords and masters and recognising when orders must be obeyed instantly.

As he followed Martin, his stiff legs struggling to keep up with the long strides, Edwin tried to question him, but Martin said no more than that the earl wished to see both him and Sir Hugh Fitzjohn – one of his most experienced knights – immediately. He upped his pace even more. Edwin hardly had time to catch his breath before they reached the earl's tent and he was being hustled inside.

The interior of the tent was close in the flickering light, the air thicker than outside; Edwin stole a glance round as best he could. The place was functional, and yet still much more lavish than he would have thought possible; he should have realised that peers of the realm didn't travel without some of the trappings of their estate. The space was well lit by several torches, and had mats on the floor and hangings suspended from various wooden poles which divided the tent into several rooms. He was standing in the central space, but over to one side he could see into another compartment which contained a wooden box bed, a kist, and, ominously, the earl's gleaming hauberk on a pole, with his shield and sword leaning up against it. It reminded Edwin of why they were all here – for war.

The earl was in conversation with Sir Hugh Fitzjohn, a tough, grey-haired knight who had seen his fair share of campaigns; they were attended by Adam, the earl's younger squire, who stood silently in the corner. He smiled briefly but nervously at Edwin as he entered, not yet being used to his new position in the earl's household. Both men turned to face Edwin and the earl got down to business straight away.

'Weaver, good.'

He jumped. It was still odd being called 'Weaver', for that was his father's name, not his. He would have to try and make himself worthy of it.

The earl hadn't noticed his slight pause and continued without stopping for breath. 'As I've just been telling Sir Hugh, I've been summoned to the regent's command tent to discuss tactics with him and the other senior men in the host. As my most experienced knight, Hugh will accompany me, but I want you to come as well. You will stand with Hugh and listen carefully. Some of the other nobles don't trust me, and there will be doubt and suspicion there. Your quick wits may pick up on something which the rest of us miss, so you will take note of everything which is said and report to me afterwards. Clear?'

Edwin nodded. 'Yes, my lord.'

Before he had time to frame any questions, he was dismissed peremptorily with a wave of the hand.

Edwin left the tent, his head buzzing so hard that he tripped on one of the ropes outside the door. The regent? The nobles of the kingdom? He was to stand in the same place as these exalted men and listen to their counsel? What if he couldn't discern anything in the way the earl wanted? What if ...?

He was interrupted by Martin, who had followed him out.

'Edwin, you're a lucky man. What I would give to be able to accompany my lord into the regent's own tent!' Edwin felt momentarily guilty, but Martin was continuing. 'Still, much better for my lord to have you than me – you're bound to discover something which I wouldn't realise.'

Edwin wished Martin wouldn't do that all the time, but before he could say anything he was struck by another thought. 'Do I look well enough to appear in such company? I'm not a knight, have no surcoat ...'

Martin looked him up and down critically. 'The knights have disarmed now they're in camp: they won't be wearing

their mail or anything, they'll be dressed normally. Still …
hmm …' he put out a hand and span Edwin round as he considered, '… you don't want to look *too* untidy; you might want
to go and put on your best tunic.' He turned and disappeared
back inside the tent.

Edwin gulped. He was already wearing his best tunic.

———•———

Alys had already checked the gate at the bottom of the yard,
but she did so again, unable to help herself. Of course it hadn't
come unfastened since the last time she looked at it, but she
was driven to go over and over everything she could possibly
do to protect her family – what was left of her family.

Eventually satisfied that it was still shut, she turned her
attention to the rest of the yard. The four houses were all close
together, but they were of a fair size, so the communal space
was quite large by Lincoln standards – all the better, as they
needed it for the weaving sheds, as well as the latrine and
the vegetable patches. Her own vegetables and herbs, outside
the kitchen door, were the worse for wear, but she would
have to eke out what remained as best she could. Those of
her neighbours weren't in much better state, and the one at
the end of the block was overgrown with weeds, had been
since the Appyltons fled the city some weeks back. They had
all tried hard to cover up the fact that the place was empty,
for if it became common knowledge it would cause trouble
with pilferers or housebreakers. Fortunately the rest of them
had stayed, with Mistress Guildersleeve on the one side acting
almost as a mother to them all. And although Mistress Pinel,
on the other side, hadn't left her house for weeks, her husband
had been so helpful, especially since …

Tears came to her eyes and she fought hard to stop them.
Crying wouldn't help. She tried to think about something else.
She needed to go out and buy something to eat – that would

take her mind off everything else for a while, for buying food was something of an effort these days and would require all her concentration.

She fetched her basket from the kitchen, checked twice that she had shut the door properly, and walked through the alley that led from the backyard into the street, fastening the gate behind her. In the open space she was immediately wary. Where were the French? Who might be stalking the streets today? She looked about her as she made her way up the Drapery, past the stalls where desperate vendors tried to sell their fabric, aware that hardly anybody had money for any-thing except food these days. She herself hadn't opened the shop for nearly a week now, as it just wasn't worth it: nobody came in, and it meant leaving the front door open onto the street all the time.

She started as a hand touched her lightly on the arm, stifling a scream. But it was just Ralf.

'Miss Alys – I thought that was you. Are you all right?' His face was kind, and she felt a pang of guilt that he'd had to be laid off once it became clear that there wasn't enough weaving to be done until more supplies of wool could be brought into the city. He looked gaunt, but his concern was all for her as he peered at her in that slightly squinting way he had, which came from too many years spent looking at fine patterns.

She mustered a smile. 'Yes, Ralf, I'm fine, thank you. I'm just off to …' she tailed off, aware that it might be tactless to say she was going to buy food, when he'd been deprived of the means of purchasing any. She stood with her mouth open, feeling foolish, waiting until she could think of something to say, but she was saved by the sight of the elderly mayor waving to her from the other side of the street. 'Oh look, Ralf – over there.'

Ralf blinked and peered across the street, but his face didn't register any recognition until Master William was almost upon them.

The mayor nodded at them both benignly. 'Alys, how nice to see you. And it is good to see your father's workers taking care of you in these dangerous times.' He beamed at Ralf before continuing. 'And how is your father?'

This time Alys couldn't stop the tears, and she felt the sting as they poured from her eyes and down her face. She couldn't speak, shaking her head silently in misery. William nodded and gripped her hand. 'And your brothers?' She shook her head again, trying to take control of the weeping before she embarrassed herself in front of the whole street.

All at once a beautiful scent enveloped her, and a soft hand touched her arm. A gentle voice spoke, shushing and comforting her, and admonishing William gently for being so thoughtless. Through her tears Alys looked into a small, delicate face, topped by a widow's cap with a few blonde hairs peeking out from underneath it. She stared in bemusement, immediately aware of how her own face must look blotched and swollen. She had seen the woman about town a few times – thinking how young she was to be a widow and wondering what tragedy might have befallen her – but they had never spoken, so why should she care? She looked to William, who hastened to introduce them. 'My dear, perhaps you don't know Mistress Gunnilda? She lives up in the northern part of the town.'

Alys recollected herself enough to give a small curtsey, trying to brush the tears from her face as she did so. The widow Gunnilda put up one delicate hand to help smooth them away, and brushed back Alys's hair. 'There. It must be a very difficult time for you, even without being reminded of it in the street. I heard what happened to your father and I'm truly sorry for it.' Her voice was soft and comforting. 'Now, could someone not take you back home?'

Alys glanced round at Ralf, but for some reason he looked tremendously awkward, and was backing away while he struggled to get any words out. He stuttered once or twice, turned red, and eventually span on his heel and fled, without having said a word.

There was a surprised silence for a moment before William gallantly stepped into the breach, proposing to escort her home, and Alys wanted nothing more than to take him up on the offer and return to the familiar haven. But she just couldn't. She had responsibilities, two little brothers and a sister to feed, and must keep going no matter what the circumstances. She drew herself up, mustered as much dignity as she could, and bade them good day.

Edwin still wasn't quite sure this was really happening, but he found himself pacing in the dusk behind the earl and Sir Hugh towards the middle of the camp. He was dressed in one of Martin's old tunics – the squire had taken pity on him and opened his own pack, finding a garment which Edwin could wear and saying he could keep it as it was too small for him anyway. Too small it might have been for the huge Martin, but it was still on the large side for Edwin, and he felt awkward. Still, one advantage of it being the ex-tunic of a squire was that it had the small checked blue and gold badge stitched on to it, which identified him as a member of the earl's personal household, so at least that was something: he felt more as though he belonged, at least on the outside.

Any confidence he might have felt evaporated as soon as he reached the huge tent in the middle of the camp, surrounded by guards and by spitting, flaring torches which warded off the darkness. Two awe-inspiring standards flapped heavily above it, visible in the smoky gloom: the red lion of the regent on its green and gold background, and the royal arms, three golden lions on a red field. Edwin swallowed, intimidated by the sort of company he was about to encounter, but there was no time to think as he followed the others through the open mouth of the tent.

Inside there were more torches, and a large press of men. It was hot and airless, with the sharp tang of sweat and smoke, and Edwin felt moisture beginning to form on his brow almost immediately. The earl moved towards the middle of the tent, and Edwin followed Sir Hugh to stand at one side. As they found a position which offered a view of the nobles, Edwin was able to see the most powerful man in the kingdom.

He stood next to a table in the very centre of the tent, surrounded by other lesser men, as a huge oak might be by mere saplings. He was certainly the oldest man Edwin had ever seen – well over seventy years of age, if the tales were to be believed – and the experiences of a long and eventful life were carved into the lines of his face. William Marshal. Edwin could hardly believe he was looking at the legendary figure. Here was a man who had started out as the fourth son of a minor noble, but who had fought his way round Europe, been on a crusade to the Holy Land, become the servant and confidant of kings and queens, and was now the ruler of the whole country, the guardian of the ten-year-old king. Looking at the white-haired figure was enough to make anyone tremble with awe, and Edwin suddenly felt that he could barely stand. The absolute authority which Marshal held was etched into his every line and was easily discernible from the way the other nobles – earls and lords all – deferred to him with great respect. There was no question who was in charge. The regent held all their lives in the hollow of his hand, and every man knew it.

As they stood watching the nobles, Sir Hugh began to murmur to Edwin behind his hand. 'Stand quietly by me and I will try to explain to you what is going on and who is who. Over there are some of the most powerful men in the land. The regent, obviously, and next to him his son, William Marshal the younger. Our Lord William de Warenne. Then William Longsword, the Earl of Salisbury; William Ferrars, the Earl of Derby; William the Earl of Albemarle; the Lords William d'Aubigny, William de Cantelou and his son William.' Edwin wondered briefly if some law had been passed on the naming of nobles of which he had previously been unaware, but he had no time to go on with the thought as Sir Hugh was continuing. 'And on the other side of the table, Falkes de Breauté; Peter des Roches, the Bishop of Winchester; John Marshal, the regent's nephew and Ranulf de Blundeville, the Earl of Chester.'

Edwin looked with particular interest at the last two whom the knight had named. The Earl of Chester, the second most powerful man in the kingdom, stood slightly apart from the others, listening to their conversation with an ill-disguised temper. He was shorter than most of the other men there, but had hugely broad shoulders and a look of immense physical power. How men must quail at the thought of facing him across a battlefield! The earl's gaze turned from the nobles to sweep the rest of the tent, and Edwin looked away hastily lest he be caught staring. He looked instead at the lord Sir Hugh had named as the regent's nephew. He had never heard the name John Marshal before, but he recognised the man as being the one who had come out to meet their party earlier when they had arrived; the one who had finally let them join the encampment. He was neither the oldest nor the youngest of the men around the table, being perhaps of an age with Edwin's own lord, maybe a bit younger, his dark hair just starting to be flecked with grey. Now that he wasn't wearing his mail, Edwin could see how slight he was, not tall, and easily the lithest of the men around the regent. He was listening to the conversation around the table with interest, his eyes darting back and forth from one lord to the next, his movements quick and restless as he was seemingly unable to keep still. He kept looking as though he wanted to interrupt, but he didn't speak.

Sir Hugh murmured again, encouraging Edwin to watch and to listen to what was happening, and then he fell silent as they turned their attention to the talk of the men around the regent.

The first thing which struck Edwin was the noticeable distrust and lack of warmth with which most of the other nobles were regarding his lord. He stood at the outermost edge of the group around the table, even though he was one of the highest ranking there; others turned their shoulders to avoid him, and some looked at him with open suspicion. One of these was the Earl of Chester, who took no trouble to conceal his dislike. Edwin was worried. He whispered to Sir Hugh, to see if his opinion of the situation was shared; the knight nodded sombrely.

Edwin began to listen more carefully to the talk of the nobles. They were looking at a map, and the discussion seemed to centre on the route they would take to Lincoln. Edwin had no idea at all of the relative situation of the towns they mentioned, or how far away they were, but the consensus seemed to be that they should avoid taking the direct road to Lincoln, which would bring them to the side of the town on which the French were encamped. Well, that sounded fairly sensible, even to him. Instead they were to travel via a different route, which would mean camping overnight at somewhere called Torksey, and then moving on to Lincoln to approach from the west, the side where the castle was situated. There might then be some possibility of communicating with the besieged men in the castle. Men? Edwin's ears caught a new name, and he was amazed to discover that the stronghold was apparently being held by a woman, Dame Nicola of something.

While he was considering this startling piece of information, the conversation turned to the number of men that each lord had brought with him. Each was giving the regent a figure of knights and crossbowmen; nobody seemed particularly interested in foot sergeants or servants, but surely they'd be important as well, wouldn't they? Edwin didn't dare open his mouth to say anything out loud, so instead he watched as a harried-looking clerk wrote all the numbers down.

The numbers kept coming. Edwin had no idea whether all of this constituted a large host or not or whether there would be enough of them to raise the siege, but he listened with interest. The great men, the earls, each had many knights in their retinues; some of the lesser lords had fewer knights but more crossbowmen. Once the final lord had given his figures – William d'Aubigny supplying ten knights and thirty crossbowmen – Edwin turned without thinking to Sir Hugh and whispered, 'Four hundred and six knights, and three hundred and seventeen crossbowmen. Will that be enough?'

'Who said that?'

The regent might have been old, but there was nothing wrong with his hearing: pausing in the very act of asking the clerk to reckon the final tally, he had whirled and snapped out the question. His eyes swept the tent.

Edwin found himself standing in the middle of a growing space as men melted away from him. He stood exposed and petrified, his face burning, breathless, knees trembling, wishing the ground would open so he could sink into the earth and hide. He had interrupted the council of lords! What punishment was to be his? He couldn't speak and dared not meet the eyes of his lord, whose temper was legendary.

The regent was addressing him. 'You there.' Edwin forced himself to look up and meet the gaze, quaking. He was face-to-face with William Marshal. Oh dear Lord. How had his life come to this? He cowered and awaited his fate.

The regent noticed the badge on Edwin's tunic and raised an eyebrow. 'One of yours, Warenne?' The earl nodded without speaking, and Edwin winced at the thought of the conversation they would probably have once this meeting was over. The regent spoke again, but thank the Lord he sounded more interested than angry. 'How did you reckon so quickly?' Without waiting for an answer, which was good, as Edwin didn't have one, he turned to the clerk. 'Is he correct?' The clerk was still frantically scribbling on his list. 'Hurry up, man!' After a few moments of pained silence broken only by the scratching of a pen, he finished writing, wiped the sweat from his brow, and looked up.

'Yes, my lord. Four hundred and six knights, and three hundred and seventeen crossbowmen, as *he* stated.' He looked spitefully at Edwin, obviously feeling that he had been made to look a fool.

Edwin shivered as the regent looked over him appraisingly, but all he said was, 'Well done. It is good to have men around us with quick wits. Warenne, I compliment you.' He moved back to the table.

It was over. Edwin's legs had turned to water and he wanted nothing more than to sink to the ground, but he could not, would not, while he was still in here. The feeling of being hot carried on as the glances of other men fell on him, but at least he was no longer the centre of attention as the discussion at the table continued.

He didn't take in much of the rest of the conversation – something about scouting and being able to speak with those inside the besieged castle – so concerned was he with his determination to stay on his feet, but soon enough he was following Sir Hugh out of the tent and into the cool night air. The freshness, after the heat and humidity inside, revived him and he began to look around him again. The knight, after several quips from others, nudged him. 'Well, well, coming to the attention of the regent himself, eh? We'd all better look out for our positions!' Horrified, Edwin started to deny any intent, but Sir Hugh merely chuckled into his beard. 'Have no fear, boy, I'm jesting with you.' He slapped Edwin on the back.

The knight set off back to their part of the camp. Edwin followed him and then asked whether they should wait for the earl, who had not yet issued forth from the tent. Sir Hugh looked more serious. 'No. Didn't you hear? The lord regent wished to speak with him alone. I don't think this bodes well at all.'

They were both sombre as they returned to the camp.

It was deep into the night when Edwin was awakened by Adam. He groaned as the boy shook him, trying to rid himself of the fog of sleep, but eventually he threw off his blanket and stood, stretching his muscles after they had stiffened even more on the hard ground. In a daze he followed the squire towards the earl's tent, unsure of why he had been summoned but certain that it was not to hear any good news.

As he entered the tent the first thing he saw in the dancing light was the shadow of the earl as he paced up and down, muttering furiously to himself. The shadow stopped as he turned, and, seeing them enter, made a physical effort to calm himself.

The earl spoke first to Adam. 'You look dead on your feet. Go now, and sleep – I won't need you again tonight.' Adam bowed gratefully and moved around to one of the curtained-off parts of the tent. Edwin heard him thump down on to a straw palliasse, and then there was silence.

The earl turned to Edwin and ran his hands through his hair, which was already tousled. He too looked exhausted, his eyes hollow with troubles, but Edwin didn't dare say so. He waited respectfully for his orders, but the earl resumed his pacing again for a few moments, his movements tight and controlled. Eventually he stopped and splashed some wine from a flagon into a cup, which he drained in a single gulp before replacing it on the table. He filled it again, and then, to Edwin's astonishment, filled another and handed it abruptly to him, so that some of the red liquid slopped over the side on to his hand, dripping like blood. 'Drink this.'

Edwin was so amazed that he barely heard the earl's next words, spoken under his breath as he sat on the one fine chair and motioned towards a low stool for Edwin to do likewise. 'I think you're going to need it.'

It was even deeper into the night, the first glimmerings of a pre-dawn light showing on the horizon, and Edwin couldn't sleep. He sat wrapped in his blanket, staring at the embers of a fire, going over and over in his mind the conversation he'd had with the earl. What was he going to do? He had no choice but to obey, but he could see very little chance of coming out of this alive.

Chapter Two

The sick man groaned and stirred in his sleep. Alys dipped the rag once more into cool water and applied it to his forehead, hoping to soothe him a little, but she knew that it would be of no avail. Since her father had been found three days ago, lying in the street with the back of his head crushed, the world had been a different place. Master Pinel and the other neighbours had managed to get him home – for miraculously he was still alive – but there was nothing she could do for his injury, and he had developed a fever on the brain. Father Eustace had come when he could to offer comfort, but with so many others in the town in need his time was scarce, so there was nothing to do but try to ease her father's pain and wait for him to die. And if she ever managed to take her mind off him for a moment, the torment over her missing brothers took over. Thoughts of what might have happened to them sickened her. It was as though she had a stone in her belly, a stone which became heavier with each new worry. And in the meantime the children were hungry and she had very little to offer them. They huddled in the corner, huge-eyed, looking fearfully at the stranger in the bed, the father who no longer knew them.

Eventually Alys realised that it was late into the evening, and they'd had nothing to eat. She called her sister to her, and Margery extricated herself from her sleepy brothers and crept over.

'Margery, I want you to go down to the kitchen. There's still some bread left, so take the boys in there and share it with them. If you can find any other food there, you can have that as well.'

Margery nodded and hauled Edric and Randal to their feet before leading them by the hand out of the room to the staircase. Alys sighed, looking after them. That she should have to rely on a ten-year-old to help her to mother the others was unfair; the strain was too much, and Margery had been growing paler and paler as time went on. She had barely spoken since their father's accident, and was becoming ever more withdrawn. The boys were not yet at that stage, but being younger their minds were more concerned with filling their empty bellies. She tried to think. What was she going to do? Papa would die, that was for certain, so the task of keeping the family alive would fall to her, at least until either of her brothers came home. Fortunately there was still some of the hoard of pennies left – even before his accident, Papa had known that something might befall him, so he'd shown her where he'd hidden the money to keep it safe. Before the siege the cloth business had been good, and by living carefully he had managed to save a good deal against the possibility of an uncertain future. She gave thanks every day for his foresight, but although she still had some money, it was no use if there was nothing to buy, and food supplies were short in Lincoln. What was she to do? She sighed and turned back to her father. While he was alive, she must care for him to ease his passage into the Lord's grace.

He stirred and mumbled something incomprehensible. Occasionally this had happened – he'd seemed almost on the verge of regaining consciousness, but then he'd either murmured or even raved for a few moments without waking, before subsiding back into the dark world he now inhabited. She dipped the rag and tried to cool him again.

As she turned towards him, she started as she realised that his eyes were wide open and staring at her.

'Papa?' She reached out to him gently, but he didn't respond.

He continued to stare silently, but after a few moments a hoarse whisper came from his lips. 'Edith?'

Her mother's name. Alys's eyes filled with hot tears. 'No, Papa, it's me, Alys.'

She had little hope that he would understand her, but to her surprise he seemed to focus on her coherently. 'Alys.' He twitched his hand and she took it, holding the gaunt pale fingers in her own. He continued to whisper, his wits somehow returning. 'You brought me home?' She nodded. 'Proud of you. Proved yourself.' His hand was so cold. She held it to her face, and he moved his fingers to touch her cheek. His voice was hoarse. 'You must do something for me.'

She thought she knew what was coming. 'I've looked after the little ones, Papa, I'll make sure no harm comes to them.'

He tried to move his head and whimpered. It was a moment before he could speak again. 'Yes ... but ... something else you have to do. Someone you must talk to.'

He was raving again, surely.

'Come closer, child, and I will tell you. You must do this, for all of us ...' She bent her head closer and listened to the rasping whisper. So that was what he'd been doing! She sat back in shock.

His strength was failing, the words slow, laboured. He gripped her hand. 'You must ... promise me.'

She couldn't stop the tears. 'I promise.'

'Good ...' the whisper tailed away in a rattle, and he breathed no more.

She sat looking down at him for a long moment before releasing his hand, placing it on his chest and gently closing his eyes. Of course she'd promised, for how could a dying man be denied? But how was she to carry out the task? She had little idea of how to begin, never mind how she would do it while looking after the children. The children! They were orphans now and they must surely be her first priority. She had to keep them safe – she must see to her home and family first, ahead of any other considerations. But her father's urgency haunted her. What if she were to fail

to heed him in order to keep the children, and they
die anyway because of the siege? And what happe
those who broke a solemn vow to the dying?

Dizzy and faint, she tried to seek comfort in p
Her father had at least been shriven that morning, so he
pass into the Lord's grace. She bent her head to pray fo
soul. *Requiem æternam dona ei Domine …*

She was thus engaged, and it was becoming full dark, w
she heard the sound of footsteps on the stair. She loo
towards the door to see Mistress Guildersleeve enter t
room, her kindly face concerned. 'Alys. How is he? The ch
dren said …' She looked towards the bed and her voice fade
'Oh, my dear …' She stepped forward and swept Alys into a
embrace. For a moment Alys allowed herself to be comforted
sinking into the motherly hold. Oh, how fine it would be to
have someone to take the responsibility away from her, a real
adult … but it was her duty and she must do it. She pulled back
and tried to compose herself. 'Thank you for coming, Mistress.'

Her neighbour looked at her. 'It was no trouble, my dear
– I found that I had some broth left after Gervase and I had
eaten, so I brought it over for you. You've been getting thinner,
and you've hardly left this room for a week. Come down now,
and take some.'

Alys could feel her stomach groaning at the mention of food,
but how could she? She spoke dully. 'Give it to the children.'

Mistress Guildersleeve looked at her for a moment and
then, surprisingly, stepped forward and grasped her by the
shoulders with some force. 'Listen to me! You must eat. I know
that you've been giving whatever you can find to the children,
but it won't do them any good if you starve, will it? Who will
care for them then? Like it or not, you're their mother and
their father now, and they need you to be strong. I don't care if
the food sticks in your throat, but you will eat some!' There was
a pause then she slackened her grip and spoke more softly.
'I'm sorry, child, I didn't mean to frighten you – I'm just upset.

I've been your neighbour all these years, seen your mother die and now your poor father – I don't want anything to happen to the rest of you. So please, come and eat something. Come.' She moved towards the door.

Alys was shocked at such an outburst, for Mistress Guildersleeve was normally a placid woman, but she realised that her neighbour was right. How would she look after the children if she didn't have her own strength? She must stay alive and well until the siege was over, until Thomas came back to tell her what to do. Oh Lord, she was already thinking as though Nick would never return. She needed to stop that right now. There was just too much to take in. She took a deep breath and followed the older woman out of the room.

Downstairs they moved from the shop towards the kitchen at the back of the house, where a tiny fire burned in the hearth, giving out little heat but sending shadows around the room. There the three children were sitting, the boys wolfing down some unappetising-looking cheese while Margery watched, nibbling on some bread. There was a bowl of broth on the table which none of them had touched, and Alys's heart melted at their restraint. She took a spoon and began to sip it slowly, appreciating the thick warm liquid. She began to feel stronger.

'Where is my son?' Mistress Guildersleeve looked about her. Alys looked up; she hadn't known that Gervase had accompanied his mother. Unconsciously she patted her hair and smoothed her apron. Seeing that the boys were not about to reply, Margery finished a mouthful and stood. 'If you please, Mistress, he went out the back.'

Alys looked towards the door, which was open, and heard the sounds of a scuffle. Alarmed, she rose and moved towards it, but was stopped by the sight of Gervase entering, dragging another man by the collar. As they came in, she recognised Aldred, the second journeyman weaver who worked – had worked – for her father.

Gervase spoke. 'I found him loitering outside.' He shook the other before letting him go, but stood ready in case of further trouble.

Alys looked at them. She didn't want to have to deal with this. 'Aldred, what were you doing?'

He ran a dirty finger around his collar before replying, 'I need some food.'

She looked at him. The contrast between the two young men could hardly have been greater. Gervase, although not richly dressed (for who was in Lincoln these days? It was an invitation to trouble), was smart and clean in his broadcloth, tall and handsome. Aldred was shorter – like a lot of weavers, he stooped – and was filthy in his old twill tunic. She wondered if he'd washed at all since he left the household.

'I've told you before, we've none to spare. Since the siege began we've had no business. There's no work to do and so we can't pay you.'

He almost grovelled, 'But I'm so hungry!'

How could she not feel sorry for him? No matter that she had always disliked him and even feared him a little as he skulked around at his work – here was someone, another of God's creatures, who had nothing to eat. She wavered. 'Perhaps …' But then, as she looked at the table and saw Edric and Randal, gaunt of cheek, and Margery so pale, she hardened again. Anything she had was for them, not anyone else. 'I have told you, there is nothing.'

He cast her a look which was filled with daggers. 'Perhaps, *Miss* Alys, I could speak with your father. He will have more pity on a hard-working man.'

She was on the verge of blurting it out when she remembered the children. She ignored him and stepped towards them, reaching out her arms. They came to her and she held them all close. 'Children, I'm afraid I have to tell you some bad news. Papa has died. He has gone to the Lord.' There was no other way to say it, no way to soften the blow. Little Randal started crying.

Edric, a year older and trying to be manly, sniffed back his tears. Margery looked like a ghost, but said nothing.

Gervase looked on with sympathy, while Mistress Guildersleeve clucked around them like a mother hen. 'Now then, have no fear! Alys is here to care for you all, and Gervase and I are only next door, and Master Pinel the other side; we will all be able to look after you. You will be safe, and all will be well.' Alys thought that she didn't sound convinced, but the children seemed comforted. Mistress Guildersleeve turned to her again. 'I forgot to ask you, Alys, did your poor father never regain his wits before he died?'

It was a simple question but a little warning chimed in Alys's head and something – perhaps it was the sly way Aldred was looking at her? – kept her from telling the truth. For the first time in her life she told a deliberate lie. 'No, Mistress, he didn't. He just slipped away in his sleep.'

Mistress Guildersleeve crossed herself. 'May God bless him and take him into His kingdom.'

Alys looked at everyone in the darkened kitchen and decided it was time that she started to undertake her responsibilities as head of the family. She spoke with as much dignity and as little wavering as she could muster. 'Children, wash yourselves and come upstairs to say goodbye to Papa. Mistress, perhaps you would help me prepare him? And Gervase, would you be so good as to ask Aldred to leave?' To her surprise they all acquiesced, although Aldred looked less than pleased at being shoved roughly out of the house. With a sinking feeling, Alys realised that she probably hadn't heard the last of him. Well, she had more pressing matters to worry about at the moment. She lit one of the remaining precious candles, so that her father should not go to his rest in the dark, and led the way upstairs.

There she watched as the children each kissed their father on his cooling forehead. Margery took the boys away to put them in bed, and Alys and Mistress Guildersleeve turned themselves to the task of preparing the body for burial, washing and straightening the limbs and wrapping him. Later Gervase returned with Father Eustace, who said the prayers for the dead and promised to return on the morrow; once he left, Mistress Guildersleeve and her son departed with many promises of help and support – Alys should call if she needed anything or if there was any trouble – and finally Alys was left alone. She barred the kitchen door behind them and checked twice that the shop was locked, before returning upstairs to settle herself and begin a lonely vigil over the body until dawn.

———

Snatches of the earl's words played in Edwin's head as he looked at the fire. 'The other nobles distrust me, as I returned to the Royalist cause so recently … the regent doesn't want me on this campaign … he's told me to keep my troops in reserve … we won't join the host as it makes its way to Lincoln …' To start with, Edwin had wondered why he was being favoured with this information, rather than Sir Hugh or Sir Roger or any of the other knights. The earl was obviously concerned, but what was it to Edwin that they should pack up and leave, and not put themselves into danger? He wasn't the one who would order the camp to be broken. But the earl hadn't finished, he continued with words that now burned in Edwin's mind. 'I need to get myself back into favour with the regent; he will surely win this war, and if I'm not of his party then all will be lost. I had to do something … he noticed you particularly, said you were a man of quick wits … the plan is for a small party to approach the town ahead of the rest of the host, to try to gain access to the castle to find out what's going on and to report back before the attack is carried out … a group will be noticed, but one man might be able to get in … I've volunteered your services, assured the regent that you're an able man who will find a way to help, who will discover something which can be used to our advantage …' The words tailed away as Edwin stared again into the glowing ashes. He was to leave the rest of the earl's household, leave Martin, Adam, Sir Roger, everyone whom he knew even slightly, and was to travel with the host of strangers towards Lincoln, where he would ride forward with an advance party and try to gain access to the besieged castle – the castle which was surrounded by hundreds of French and English troops, all ready to kill him on sight. Even if he did get in he would need to find some piece of information, some crucial tactical advantage which would aid their cause, for without this they might fail – the nobles all agreed that their forces were outnumbered by their enemies. How was he to manage? What was he to do? How would he face the earl if he failed? He tried to pass quickly over the bleak thought that if he did fail, he would have no need to confront his lord, as he would be dead and facing a far greater judge.

He shivered, remembering the most chilling words of all. The earl had leaned forward and gripped him by the shoulders, his face close to Edwin's own as the slate-grey eyes bored into him. 'My reputation, my future, your livelihood – everybody's lives – might well depend on this. Don't let me down.'

———◆———

It was dawn but Edwin hadn't slept. At least, he'd managed a couple of hours of restless dozing, but he didn't feel as if he'd gained anything from it. His head was heavy and his eyes were full of sand. Added to this, the farewells were turning out to be more difficult than he'd anticipated … after the events of the previous week he'd thought it impossible to say any more affecting goodbyes, but here he was again. At least he'd eaten a fine breakfast – Hamo hadn't been able to do enough for him that morning – so he had the strength to endure the earl wishing him Godspeed, Sir Roger and Sir Hugh clapping him on the back, Adam offering shy good wishes, and Martin shaking his hand with a bone-crunching grip as he bade him take care of himself. Even the taciturn squire seemed to feel some of the emotion as he shook hands and clasped Edwin about the shoulder. He bent his head to speak quietly but earnestly; 'I've lost too many companions in these past days. Make sure you don't join them.' Edwin could barely reply, managing only a nod. So consumed had he been by his own feelings that he'd forgotten that Martin too had lost much. Martin also appeared lost for words after his speech, and turned away.

And then they were leaving. The earl's host mounted and rode away from the encampment, leaving Edwin staring forlornly at the backs of the last group of people from his home. He was now totally alone in a host full of strangers. The morose thoughts returned. Surely he would never see them, or his home village of Conisbrough, again. He would die in this insane endeavour to penetrate the besieged city, and his body would lie forever in this alien place. What would happen to his mother? He would like to think that somebody would look after her but times were often hard, and what if she were left by herself? Would she starve?

So engrossed was he in his thoughts that he barely registered the fact that he too was mounting and riding away from the main host. He was now in a small but diverse retinue led by John Marshal, the regent's nephew, who would command the party that would attempt to infiltrate the castle at Lincoln. Blindly, Edwin sat on his horse and followed the man in front, noticing neither his companions nor the distance he travelled. He sank further into his solitary reflections.

After some time he became aware of a man riding close next to him. He looked up and saw that it was Sir Reginald, whom he'd met the previous evening, with his friend Sir Gilbert on his other side. The younger knight looked at Edwin and smiled sociably. 'You seem deep in thought, my friend.'

Edwin didn't know how to reply. These knights would be used to leaving friends and family behind; it was what they did all the time. He would sound stupid if he tried to explain his concerns to them, so he said nothing.

The more serious Sir Gilbert edged his horse forward slightly so that he could look past his companion to see Edwin. 'Let me guess. You're worried about what lies ahead of us, and your worries have been made worse by the fact that the people you know are not accompanying you and you've been left among strangers. Am I right?'

Edwin nodded miserably. Was it that apparent? What ridicule was about to come his way? But he had misinterpreted again, for both knights were nodding.

Sir Gilbert continued. 'It's always the way. The first time I rode on a campaign I was numb with fear. And as for Reginald here, I could barely get him on his horse.' Half a smile flickered across his face as his friend started a mock protest. Then, serious again, 'And possibly this is all made worse again by the thought of someone you have left behind at home?' Edwin nodded again. 'A wife? Sweetheart?' At these words Sir Reginald, still riding between them, smiled at him slyly.

Here Edwin felt that he had to correct the knight. 'No, my mother.'

Sir Reginald seemed to bite back whatever comment he had been about to make, and spoke seriously. 'Ah, yes – Roger said that you lost your father last week. My condolences – it must be a terrible thing.'

'It is.' Edwin couldn't think of anything to say as a lump rose in his throat.

Sir Reginald continued. 'Thank the Lord, my father continues to enjoy excellent health, but Gilbert here lost his some years ago, so he'll understand.'

Edwin looked at the other knight, who sighed. 'Yes, it's a difficult time, although it's the natural way of things. More difficult when you have to take on the responsibility for your lands and family. I was young, but fortunately my father had given me good advice and guidance, so I was able to take over as he would have wished. When I struggled with problems to start with, I was able to think of what he might have said or done had he been in my place.'

All of a sudden Edwin was awash with memories of his father, the things he'd achieved, the problems he'd solved, the tasks he'd carried out, and the advice he'd constantly issued – even if it hadn't seemed so at the time, disguised as it might have been as a throwaway remark. What had his father taught him? Always to think about a situation before rushing in headlong, for that was why the Lord had given him a mind to differentiate him from the beasts of the field. Things are often not as they seem. People are often not as they first appear. Look not just at what has occurred or may occur, but *why*. As the recollections continued, the day seemed imperceptibly brighter. Perhaps he wasn't in an impossible situation. It would be a fine thing to survive and return to the earl in triumph.

Perhaps noticing that he had cheered somewhat, Sir Reginald changed the topic. He said he'd heard something of Edwin's role from Sir Roger the previous evening, and was interested to learn more. He quizzed Edwin about the events that had led to his promotion, and seemed impressed by the tale, although Edwin certainly didn't feel like boasting.

The knight had a question, though. 'But while you are doing all this work with your mind, how do you find the time for weapons training?'

Edwin was nonplussed. 'Training? I practise with my bow, as do all the men in the village, but my work involves letters, pen and ink, not weapons.'

'But, I mean, never? You never train?'

Edwin wasn't quite sure what he was getting at. 'No.'

'So you mean – you don't use weapons at all? How will you fight? How do you defend yourself?'

Edwin realised he was talking to someone who came from a different world. He would have to be clearer. 'Fight? If you gave me an axe or sword I would be more likely to cut myself than to do any damage to anyone else. I have never even picked one up.' He smiled, but was then struck by a thought. 'As to defending myself, I've never had to.'

The knight was aghast. 'But we're going into battle! Jesu, you're going to get yourself killed! You must – I – we – what I mean is, when we encamp today I'll have to give you some lessons. You must at least be able to look after yourself and get out of trouble.' He shook his head and spoke more to himself. 'I can't believe it. How can anyone …' He shook his head again and looked to Sir Gilbert for support: the other knight had been watching the exchange with interest, but he merely spoke in an inscrutable tone. 'That's a good idea, but I suggest that you remember to wear your gloves this time.'

Sir Reginald held up his hand and looked at it. 'Curse you, Gilbert – I'd just managed to forget about it, but now you've reminded me of it, all the pain has come back.' He explained to Edwin that one day not long ago he'd been so keen to practise that he'd started sparring before anyone could fetch his gloves, and the result was a broken hand. He dismissed the injury. 'It'll heal. Have no fear, it certainly won't stop me fighting once I get to Lincoln, even if I can't hold my sword properly! And it won't stop me teaching you, for if you don't learn something quickly, you'll never get through the battle alive.'

Edwin rode on in silence.

It was the middle of the afternoon when they arrived at Torksey. Edwin awoke from his daze and looked around him: he had travelled so little that any new place was of interest to him. He couldn't decide at first whether the place was a large village or a small town: it was bigger than Conisbrough, certainly, but smaller than Newark. A river ran through the middle of it, filled with loaded craft making their way upstream, and the whole was overlooked by a small castle which stood on a motte on the eastern bank of the river.

As their retinue had outstripped the pace of the main host, they had arrived first and had their pick of the area for making camp, so they moved down towards the river to pitch their tents in the open space there. Edwin again had nothing to do, so once he had dismounted stiffly (was it his imagination or was that slightly easier than it had been yesterday?) and dealt with his horse he was free to look around him. He wandered along the riverbank, looking over at the edge of the town. There was no wall enclosing it, and the neater and compact streets gave way to a straggle of untidy dwellings which stretched out alongside the water. Here he was upstream from the town, so the river wasn't fouled and full of refuse, as it might have been further down; nevertheless there was a certain smell attached to it which wasn't particularly pleasant. He was wondering about this when he saw a man on one of the boats throw a pile of rubbish overboard: some of it sank but the rest floated towards the water's edge and became entangled in the weed there. A couple of small and very ragged children were wading in the shallows, and they dragged their attention away from the wandering stranger long enough to go and investigate the debris.

Edwin looked further out into the middle of the river and gazed with interest at the boats on it, being unfamiliar with large waterborne craft – Conisbrough wasn't a port. The people on the river stared back at him suspiciously, watching the military encampment being set up. Edwin could understand their anxiety – it would have been the same in his home village if a strange host had suddenly arrived. Folk were concerned to protect their own homes and families, whatever the concerns of the great men of the kingdom might be.

A thump on the shoulder distracted him: it was Sir Reginald. Lord, but he wished people would stop doing that. He rubbed it.

'Come, no time to waste! Let's begin your lesson.'

Edwin felt awkward again. 'Really, there's no need ...'

The knight snorted. 'No need? You're about to go into enemy territory, man! Granted, we'll have to keep you out of the actual battle if we can, but you never know when you might need to defend yourself, or someone else. Now come.'

There was no sense in arguing, and Edwin conceded to himself that Sir Reginald probably had a point. He hadn't really considered what he would be doing in the castle or the city if he did, by some miracle, succeed in getting in. The mere idea of gaining entry seemed so huge and impossible that he hadn't thought past it. But what would it be like? What would he do? He had never even been in a city before, never mind one that was overrun with enemy soldiers.

They found themselves an open space at the edge of the encampment where they wouldn't be observed by too many people. For this Edwin was profoundly glad, being certain that he was about to embarrass himself in some way.

Sir Reginald had brought a selection of weapons which he tossed on the floor. They all looked unfamiliar and menacing to Edwin, but the knight crouched and looked them over appraisingly like a carpenter choosing the best tool for a job. He looked up at Edwin. 'This is going to be interesting. I've never trained anyone from the beginning before, or at least not a grown man. The only people I've taught who have been so inexperienced have been small boys with years of instruction ahead of them.' He ran his eye over the weapons again. At last he sighed and picked up a dagger. 'There's no point in teaching you to use a sword, or at least not until after all this is over. You'll never have the time to gain a correct technique or understanding in a few short hours. Besides, if you're going to be in a city then any fighting you might need to do will be in a confined area, so you're better off learning something which you can use without needing too much space.' After carefully donning a pair of gloves and instructing Edwin to do the same with a second pair, he handed the weapon over, and drew the dagger which was at his own belt. 'Now, let's begin.'

The change in his demeanour was immediate. Up until now Edwin had seen him only with an affable, carefree manner, but as soon as he drew a weapon all of that vanished and he was in deadly earnest. Abruptly Edwin realised why knights were so feared on the field of battle. The man was wearing no armour, had no weapon but his dagger, and had no serious intent to hurt him, but he still felt a shiver of fear. When Sir Reginald grasped the weapon and raised it over his head as if to strike down at him, he was shocked by just how terrifying it was to have somebody attack him with a blade. Nothing in his previous experience had prepared him for this. He couldn't help himself; instead of raising his own dagger, he ducked back out of range.

'Good.' Edwin was surprised, but the knight continued. 'You're not exactly the largest of men, and so wherever possible you should try to avoid a close grapple, in case you're overpowered. Staying back is a good technique at this stage.' He continued to circle, dagger held in his right hand. 'Always keep your eye closely on your opponent. Don't let your gaze wander for a moment. And don't watch only the hand which is holding the weapon.' Edwin was surprised by this, for surely that was where the danger stemmed from? But it appeared he was wrong. 'Yes, the weapon will strike, but it doesn't attack on its own, does it? You have to try and gauge the thoughts of the man who is wielding it. What will I do? What's in my mind? Will I try to trick you? Take all this into account.'

Edwin tried to concentrate, his focus narrowing until he was aware of nothing but the man in front of him and the blade which he held. But it was difficult to watch the face and eyes, for he could not help but be constantly aware of the sharp steel blade hovering near him. Sir Reginald made a sudden movement with his right hand, and Edwin's gaze flicked momentarily to the dagger. Instantly the knight pounced, his left hand coming around and seizing Edwin's right, the one which held his own weapon, and forcing it backwards away from his body. He was far bigger and more powerful, and Edwin could do nothing. He was helpless. He flapped ineffectually with his own left hand to try and catch the other in the same way, but Sir Reginald easily eluded him, and in a moment his dagger was at Edwin's throat. Edwin felt cold fear, but the knight spoke calmly. 'You see, this is the sort of thing you need to avoid. If it comes to a wrestle with a bigger and more experienced opponent, you'll be in trouble. Now, let's try again.' He released Edwin and stepped back.

The session went on. Edwin found himself variously with the dagger at his throat, his stomach or his heart, and more than once ended flat upon his back with his opponent looming over him. He ached. But each time he got up and tried to consider what he'd done wrong. Realisation began to dawn on him. He had always believed that combat was something entirely physical, a competition of brute strength – and therefore something he wouldn't be good at – but now he began to see it as something which required thought as well. This insight helped him, and gradually he began to improve, seeing small patterns evolve in the other's moves which he hadn't noticed before. He still didn't manage to land a blow on Sir Reginald, but his own 'deaths' became less frequent.

Eventually the moment came. The knight slipped on the turf and his concentration wavered for a fraction of a moment. Edwin sensed his advantage and lashed out with his dagger. Sir Reginald was still too quick for him, however, bringing his right arm around to parry the blow. Unfortunately for him, Edwin's inexperienced attack did not arrive in the perfect arc he had expected, and his timing was slightly off: the dagger struck him not on his blade but on his broken right hand.

Edwin stepped back in confusion as the knight cursed loudly and dropped his weapon, clasping his injured hand. He began to apologise profusely and stepped forward to ensure that the other was not badly hurt. Sir Reginald managed to regain control of himself – albeit still gripping his hand – and spoke through gritted teeth. 'Good, Edwin, well done. This teaches us two things: firstly, that luck can play a part in any combat. If fortune is on your side, don't hesitate to use it. And secondly, that you must exploit any weakness which your opponent shows. If you're fighting a wounded man, strive to use his injury against him. Here you struck me only a blow to the hand, but the result was that you might easily have killed me. Remember this and use it.' He let go of his hand and shook the glove off. It appeared to have prevented the blade cutting him; it was the force of the blow alone which had jarred the broken bones. That at least was of some comfort.

'I think that's probably enough now.' Unnoticed by either combatant, Sir Gilbert had approached and was looking on, his face unreadable to Edwin. 'Edwin is starting to look tired, and he'll need all his strength for the task ahead. He needs to rest. And as for you, my friend, you need to look to that hand lest it stop you from taking part in the battle. Come to the tent and I'll have Richard look at it for you.'

Sir Reginald nodded, looking slightly sheepish now, like a boy caught out in a prank. Then he grinned at Edwin. 'You still have a long way to go, but it's a start. We'll continue with your lesson after all this,' – he gestured at the camp – 'is over.'

Edwin nodded, secretly glad of the rest, though nothing would have induced him to say so. He sincerely hoped that he wouldn't have to use a weapon in earnest combat in the days to come; although he had slightly more of an idea than he had before, he would still be hopelessly inadequate against anyone who really knew how to fight. He sighed, turned the dagger round and offered it hilt-first back to the knight.

Sir Reginald looked down at it. 'Keep it.' Edwin started to protest but was cut off. 'Keep it, at least for now. You'll need something to take with you into the city, and you appear to have no other weapon. You can return it afterwards if you so wish.' He picked up a scabbard and handed it to Edwin, showing him the loops to arrange it on his belt. Then he looked at the other weapons on the floor and grimaced. 'Come, help me carry these, and we'll try to find something to eat while Gilbert's man looks at my hand.'

Dame Nicola de la Haye, hereditary castellan of Lincoln castle, looked with some distaste at the dry, maggot-infested piece of bread before her. Still, she was lucky to have anything at all: the garrison was rapidly running out of provisions and they would soon be in such dire straits that they must consider surrender as an alternative to starvation. Things were even worse than they had been during the siege twenty-five years ago, when in the absence of her husband, God rest him, she had defended the castle for forty days and nights. That had almost been a good time: they had been young, it was before their son was b– … she stopped and screwed up her eyes against the sudden wet heat. Now was not the moment to think of that.

She picked up the bread, tapped it on the table to dislodge the vermin, and raised it to her mouth as she paced over to the narrow window. She was in the western tower, which looked out not over the town but over the surrounding countryside. Every day she had stood here, scanning the land around to watch for any sign of an approaching force, but every day she had been disappointed. Time was growing short. The French and the rebels had used their siege engines to pound the south side of the castle, and the curtain wall was weakening; it would not last much longer. They had cleared a large open space to the north-east of the castle as well, and she felt that it was only a matter of time before that was also assailed. Thank the Lord for the very narrow gap between the castle's north wall and the walls of the houses still standing on that side. The channel there was so slender that the enemy dare not enter it for they were easily within range of the castle walls and would leave themselves open to attack by archers or by men pouring boiling water or sand on them. In any case the alley led only to the city's western gate, which had been blocked by falling masonry and debris during the initial siege of the town, so it was impassable. Still, although of no use to them, it did at least give them one side on which they didn't face constant attack. Her garrison was thinly spread, and she couldn't afford to cover all the walls at all times; an occasional patrol sufficed on that side.

There was a knock at the door, and at her call it opened to admit Geoffrey de Serland, the knight who commanded the garrison. He looked haggard, as well he might.

She didn't waste any time. 'Well?'

He shook his head. 'Still no word from the city. We've been expecting a message this past week, but nothing, not since …' He tailed off.

She frowned. One of their hopes had been that the beleaguered city might have been able to mount some sort of resistance against the invaders, and earlier information had suggested that this was indeed the case – a man of the garrison had managed to contact his brother outside. However, the brother was now dead and they had received no further word of anything which might have been going on to their advantage in the city. She thumped the wall in frustration. Still, she should have known not to rely on the citizens, for they were only commoners, with no training or organisation – it was no surprise that the city had fallen so quickly, with only the burgesses to back up the small military garrison. They'd had to fall back to the castle and leave the rest of the city to its fate, in order to save the stronghold in the king's name.

And there was another thing. What was the king, or more correctly the regent, going to do? Surely he wouldn't let such an important castle fall into enemy hands? Surely he would send a relieving force? Her frustration at the lack of information rose to the surface again. They must hold out until reinforcements came, but how were they to do so? Within a few days the curtain wall would come crashing down, and her exhausted and starving garrison would have little heart for the battle against the invaders, who had superior numbers and the resources of the city behind them.

She moved again to the window and scanned the countryside as it baked in the afternoon sun. There should be men out there, working in the fields to ensure that crops were growing, but it was empty and barren. Folk were too frightened to leave their homes and who could blame them? She had seen the smoke rising from distant villages and farmsteads as the invaders had plundered in their search for provisions, fodder, and wood to build their accursed siege engines. Those whose homes had survived intact were staying in them and keeping their heads down.

Once more she looked out in vain. Somewhere out in the land there must be a relieving force, but if it didn't arrive within the next three days then she would have to consider the ignominy of surrender. If they came to terms, it was possible some of them might survive; if the castle were to be taken by force, there would be no mercy. Her eyes watered from the effort of trying to look further and further into the distance. Where were they? Where were they?

Chapter Three

Edwin stirred restlessly. Since his combat lesson he'd been lying on a mat in Sir Gilbert's tent trying to doze, or at least to get some rest ahead of what he knew would be another sleepless night, but he couldn't. He was twisting and turning, his mind was wide awake and racing and all he was achieving was a headache. He sat up.

On another mat nearby lay Sir Reginald, fast asleep as though he didn't have a care about what was to come later that day, but past him Edwin could see that Sir Gilbert was also awake. The knight rose from his cot and gestured for Edwin to follow him outside. Once there he spoke in a low tone.

'Sometimes I envy him. I often find that rest doesn't come easily during a campaign, but he sleeps like a child. You're thinking about our tasks later today?'

Edwin confessed that he was and that it was preying on his mind. At this moment, it didn't seem so much like an admission of weakness.

Sir Gilbert continued, pushing a hand through his hair. 'It must be difficult for you – your first campaign, an important task to carry out for your lord, the uncertainty about what you'll have to face ...' he looked at the younger man in some sympathy. 'It probably won't be much comfort to you to know that it doesn't get any easier. Even after many years, the thoughts and doubts are still there. Is today the day I will die? If so, will I die cleanly, or will I receive an agonising wound which will fester and cause a slow death? Will my death have any purpose?'

The words escaped Edwin's mouth before he could stop them. 'But I thought ...' He tried to bite them back, but it was too late. He may as well carry on now, although he was bound to make a fool of himself. 'I am sorry, Sir Gilbert, I didn't mean to be ill-mannered. But … you're a *knight*. Surely knights are destined for combat, and they relish it? Knights are … that's what their purpose is.'

Sir Gilbert smiled, something Edwin didn't think he'd seen before now. 'Don't make the mistake of thinking that all knights are the same, Edwin. If you say "all knights are like this" then you may as well say that "all men who are not knights are like that", when you well know that men come in many different guises. Some are weak, some strong, some wise, some foolish. Knights …' he paused for a moment, 'as knights, yes, we train from our earliest years for combat, for we must keep the peace. But knights are different. Take Reginald and me – although I'm not one of the great men of the kingdom, I own a number of lands, and I have a responsibility for them and to the people who live there. Although I serve my king and my lord when I'm needed, much of my time is spent being an administrator. Others might not have those duties; Reginald is a younger son, and unless something happens to his brother, he won't inherit large lands or properties. In his case this suits him well.'

They both turned and looked through the open mouth of the tent to watch the sleeping figure, happily oblivious to the world around him. Sir Gilbert spoke fondly. 'Look at him. He has no worries about the day ahead, for he lives to fight. Since he was a little boy he's had nothing in his head but arms and combat, and he's never happier than when giving battle or preparing for it. He has no fear of death, for he thinks only of the contest, of pitting his skill against another's to see who will emerge the victor.' His tone turned more rueful. 'I, on the other hand, think about what would become of my lands, of my people, if I were to die tomorrow, and this prevents me from giving myself up entirely to the combat. I'm not married, have no children, and my death would mean a new lord for my people.'

Edwin was beginning to understand that much of what he thought he knew was wrong. He looked again at the sleeping Sir Reginald. It must be a fine thing to know that you were exactly fitted for your allotted place in life. The knight wished to spend his life fighting; so he fought. But Edwin wasn't sure who or what he was, and where he might be going – he felt that he was drifting, powerless, waiting to see where the tide would take him. Were others in the same situation? Perhaps there were as many knights who wished not to fight as there were others who wished they could.

Edwin realised he'd spoken out loud and Sir Gilbert was looking at him, his face serious. Edwin was about to try and apologise, but the knight only said, 'Yes, that may well be the case. But each of us has been allotted our place by God and we must make the best of it, for that is how the worth of a man may be judged. Knights who don't wish to fight have a choice: the cowardly among them seek to avoid combat, while the rest know their duty and strive to fulfil it. A man of whatever station who doesn't do his duty is no man at all.'

They remained in silence until a messenger came to summon them to a council with John Marshal.

Edwin looked at the men around him as he stood in the warm, airless tent. There were about thirty of them, and all looked to be experienced warriors. What in the Lord's name was he doing here among them?

John Marshal was speaking, pacing restlessly in front of a table upon which was a map of the city of Lincoln. Every so often he stopped to stab his finger at a point on the map, but Edwin wasn't in the first row of men about the table and he couldn't quite see.

'We'll move out later this afternoon, and will move close to Lincoln once darkness has fallen. We'll approach from the west, where the castle wall forms the city's outer defence. There's a postern there, so I and one other will steal forward to try and gain entry to the castle. It will be guarded, but I am known personally to the castellan, so we should be admitted if we can get close enough without rousing the French.'

He stopped and looked about him; men were already volunteering to accompany him, but he waved them away. 'Where is Warenne's man?'

There was a murmur at the name, but it subsided quickly as John Marshal made a sharp gesture. His heart in his throat, Edwin stepped forward. John Marshal looked him up and down. 'Good. You'll be the one to come with me. Once inside the castle we may wish to try and penetrate into the city itself, so we need someone who will be able to pass as a citizen.'

Edwin managed to stammer out a 'Yes, my lord,' but the man was already speaking to others. 'The rest of you will stand by, a bowshot away from the walls, and will be ready to support us once we come out. Hopefully we'll have information which will be of use to the lord regent, so it will be imperative that we get it to him as soon as possible. It may be that we will be pursued by the French as we try to leave, so I will need you all to be ready in case we need protection. One of us at least must survive long enough to get a message back to the main host. Understood?'

All the other men nodded grimly. Edwin was amazed at how casually John Marshal was ready to dispense with his own life, as well as those of others, but nobody else was expressing surprise so he schooled his face to look neutral. Then they were being dismissed, with an injunction to be ready to move out as the sun fell to the horizon.

Once outside, Edwin found himself next to Sir Reginald, who thumped him heartily on the shoulder. Honestly, if people would just ...

The knight spoke. 'Going into the city with John Marshal, eh? How I envy you! It'll be a fine opportunity for adventure.'

Edwin didn't quite see it like that, so he said nothing.

Sir Reginald continued, a little wistfully. 'How I wish I'd been chosen. Perhaps if I plead with him …'

Sir Gilbert, who had appeared silently next to them, snorted. 'Didn't you hear what he said? Someone to look like a townsman. One look at you and any Frenchman would know you were no such thing. Besides, there may be men in there who know you. No, Edwin is by far the best choice.'

The other knight's face fell. 'Well, if you must put it like that …'

'I must. But cheer yourself; they may need to be rescued as they flee the place with hundreds of French at their heels, and there's always the battle after that. You're better off waiting to fight properly, not skulking around like a spy.'

Sir Reginald brightened. 'You're right. There'll be plenty of fighting to keep us busy!' He strode off, whistling.

Sir Gilbert shook his head in amusement and turned to the still-silent Edwin. 'Besides, I think you're much more likely to be able to get the information and then bring it out without doing anything stupid.' He moved to speak with another knight just ahead of them, and Edwin was left wondering whether to be flattered or frightened.

———

The sun was touching the horizon behind them as they mounted their horses. Edwin groaned inwardly at the thought of another few miles of purgatory, but somewhat to his own surprise he swung himself into the saddle almost naturally and managed not to flinch too much. He had spent an hour with little to do but contemplate the horrors ahead, and now his innards felt so twisted that he might as well have swallowed a rope. He could feel the cold sweat pooling around him, and the dryness of his mouth. Thoughts hopped and skipped this way and that through his mind and then scattered in all directions before he could catch them. The taste of fear was sharp.

He wanted nothing else but to be running in the opposite direction, to run all the way home to Conisbrough and sleep safely in his mother's cottage, his home, but there was no escape. There was nothing to do but follow the man in front and try to keep a lid on the rising tide of panic.

He didn't know that his two knightly friends were watching him closely as they rode a few places behind.

Sir Reginald spoke first. 'I'm worried for him. He has no combat experience, no idea of how to fight …'

'If all goes well, he shouldn't need to. He'll be there to use his mind, not his sword.'

'But … are we right to be trusting the success of the whole campaign to one such man? A commoner, after all, and one so young.'

Sir Gilbert considered a moment before replying, looking intently at the figure riding obliviously ahead. Then he spoke firmly. 'Commoner, yes. Inexperienced, yes. But there is something about him … he's frightened, but when it comes down to it, he will do his duty.'

They rode on.

As they continued it became darker, and the light had almost gone completely when John Marshal signalled for the column to halt, at the edge of a copse on an upward slope. He dismounted and others followed. 'This is where we must part company, for once we gain the flat ground on the other side of this rise we'll be visible from the walls.' He handed his reins to another knight whom Edwin didn't know, but who was to be left in charge. 'We'll go forward on foot. Wait for us here until dawn. If we haven't returned by the time it is full light, go back to the main host and tell the lord regent that we've failed. In the meantime keep watch for us, and be prepared to ride forward and defend us should the need arise.'

The other man nodded, wishing him Godspeed.

John Marshal gestured to Edwin to join him. Edwin found the reins of his horse being taken out of his hand by

Sir Reginald, who whispered 'May the Lord be with you. If He blesses us, we'll meet again soon.'

Edwin didn't trust himself to speak, but moved forward to stand next to John Marshal. Without further ado, he followed as the man set off silently into the darkness ahead.

———•———

Dame Nicola surveyed the castle ward by torchlight. The bombardment had come again during the day, and she was now certain that the curtain wall would come crashing down within three days, four at the most. Many of the crenellations at the top had been blasted away, smashing down into the courtyard, together with the missiles which had hit them, killing and maiming those who had been unlucky enough to get in the way.

She moved inside the keep to visit the wounded who still survived. In a small room which stank of blood and sweat a number of men lay groaning on pallets, suffering from arrow wounds or from crush injuries. There was very little that could be done for them, other than what had been already: move them out of the way of immediate harm into the strongest building and try to stop their bleeding. There was not even food to give them, although thank the Lord they still had water, else they should all have died weeks ago. Holding her torch high she moved around the room, ostensibly to dispense what comfort she might, but mainly to try and ascertain how many might survive and return to duty. She jumped as an agonised scream came from the next room, but didn't flinch as it went on and on – another poor devil having a crushed limb removed in a futile attempt to save his life. Occasionally someone survived such surgery but most died, either within hours from the bleeding, or lingering for days before being poisoned by the festering of the stump, even if it had been cauterised. The sizzle of burning flesh accompanied by another shriek told her that this was what was happening now. The scream broke off as the man finally lost consciousness. She sighed. Another one gone – even if he survived, he would be no use for fighting.

Downcast, she paced back out of the keep. As she reached the night air, welcome after the fetid and blood-soaked space within, one of the garrison ran up to her, panting.

'Dame Nicola!' He stopped and gasped for breath before continuing. 'If you please, my lady, Sir Geoffrey asks you to come up to the west wall – someone is approaching over the open ground.'

Immediately she thrust the torch at him and hurried as fast as her skirts would allow across the ward and up the steps to the west wall. Once at the top she was met by de Serland, who pointed out into the darkness of the countryside.

'Who?' She was curt. 'How many?' Could this be the long-awaited relief force, or was it some new danger from the French? She stared out over the land but could see nothing, despite the fleeting moonlight. The torch she had been carrying had ruined her night sight.

Fortunately de Serland and the man next to him had been in the darkness for longer.

'It looks as though there are just two men, approaching on foot, my lady.'

Two? Hardly a relieving force, but presumably not an invading one either, unless this was some sort of trick. She ordered archers to the wall to cover their advance, instructing them crisply not to loose until they were sure that those approaching were enemies.

In a very short space of time six men were ranged along the wall, bows strung and at the ready, clothyard arrows with vicious hunting barbs nocked. The two figures creeping through the darkness continued to draw nearer, either unaware of the terrible and imminent death which awaited them, or unafraid of it. Before long, they were almost at the wall, where they stopped. Dame Nicola could now make out their shapes.

A whispered address came from the men outside. 'Hail, the castle! I know there must be men watching us.'

Dame Nicola nodded to de Serland, who replied. Around him, the archers tautened their fingers on their bowstrings and flexed their arms. 'Who are you?'

The reply was terse. 'John Marshal, nephew to the lord regent.'

De Serland stepped back in surprise, but the man without was continuing. 'For the love of God, open the postern! If the French see us …'

The knight wasn't about to fall for that. 'Open the gate? Are you mad? How do I know you are who you say you are?'

The whisper came again. 'Summon Dame Nicola – she and I have met and she will know me. But do it quickly, for all our sakes!'

De Serland turned to Dame Nicola, a hope dawning in his eyes. She nodded. 'I do indeed know John Marshal by sight, but I can't tell from here. We'll have to risk opening the gate to let them in so I can see for myself. Have men ready.'

De Serland relayed the message, and she hastened back down the steps.

Once down she moved towards the small postern which opened out on to the country. Was she about to make a catastrophic mistake? But there seemed genuinely to be only two of them, and at this stage she was willing to take any chance which might help. Besides, even if there were more of them lurking out there, the postern was so narrow that no more than one or two would be able to get through before they were all skewered with arrows.

As armed men lined up on either side, with the archers still above them, she watched as the gate was unbarred and then opened. There was a tense moment as the threat of bloody violence hung in the air, and then two men stepped warily through the open doorway. She held her breath.

As they entered they looked around them and she could see their faces. The one at the front was John Marshal.

Relief flooded through her body as she stepped forward, ordering the men to stand down and re-bar the gate. She greeted him and made as if to speak further, but discretion prevailed and she ushered him and his companion towards the keep.

Once installed in her council chamber, she invited them both to sit, along with de Serland. John Marshal looked around. 'Your son?'

She would not permit herself the luxury of emotion. 'Dead.'

He looked as though he was about to say something, but thankfully he stopped and just nodded – she didn't think she would be able to stand any sympathy. She had a reputation to maintain and breaking down in public wouldn't do it much good, so she'd better move on swiftly. She outlined their desperate situation and the lack of time available to them. John Marshal listened intently, nodding and making sharp gestures if she began to explain in too much detail, grasping immediately the importance of what she had to say.

Once she had finished, she sat back to hear his news. After all this time, hearing finally of the presence of a relief column not ten miles away made her almost weak at the knees. Thank the Lord. She should have known that the regent wouldn't let such an important stronghold fall to the invaders and traitors. They would band together and drive the French out of the city for good.

But how was this to be achieved? She nodded to de Serland to join the discussion. As he entered into debate with John Marshal about the possibility or advisability of admitting more men through the postern in order to strengthen the garrison, she looked with some interest at the other man, Marshal's companion, who had not yet spoken a word. He was a nondescript kind of fellow – except for the reddish hair, she supposed, which wasn't overly common in these parts – the sort at whom she would normally barely glance. He sat on a stool in the shadows at the edge of the room, some way behind Marshal. She gazed more closely. Who was he? Not a soldier – he didn't have that aura about him – but not an idle cleric either, for he didn't have that soft look that one associated with men of inaction.

As if realising that he was being scrutinised, he looked up and his eyes met hers. She was surprised that he didn't immediately look away; instead he seemed to be studying her as closely as she was watching him. Insolent fellow! Although he didn't appear to mean any disrespect, he was merely watching her out of a genuine interest. She dragged her gaze away from him and concentrated on the discussion before her.

John Marshal was speaking. 'I don't like it.'

'I'm aware that it's far from perfect, my lord, but realistically I can't see any other way to proceed.'

Marshal made an impatient gesture. 'But the postern will only admit one or two men at a time. If we were to introduce as many men as we would need to make a difference, it would take us half a day at least. The French will realise what we're up to long before that, and will be able to pick us off at our leisure while we queue to be admitted. It's folly.'

Dame Nicola silently agreed, but she couldn't see any other way forward. The walls were about to come down and if that happened they would be overrun. The only way was to take the fight out of the castle and into the streets of the city or the open ground outside it. And the only way to do that would be to sally forth from the main gate and attack the enemy in greater numbers than they were expecting. Was there another tactic? A two-pronged attack perhaps, with some men issuing from the castle and others striking from outside?

John Marshal was a step ahead of her, already mentioning the possibility and then discounting it. 'It would split our forces too weakly and besides, they could bring their damned mangonels to bear on us as soon as we got within range to the south. No,' he sighed, 'there seems to be no other way than to use the postern.'

She hesitated to mention it, but times were desperate. She looked at de Serland. 'It's possible that there may be enough organised resistance in the town to help.'

Now Marshal looked more interested. She ran through the facts as she knew them: some sort of resistance had been organised in the city; a man of the garrison had somehow managed to contact his brother outside, and the brother had told him that he would bring more details the following night, but he had been killed before he could do so.

Marshal interrupted. 'Killed? You know this? He didn't just fail to turn up?'

She exchanged glances with de Serland, who answered for her, dryly. 'His head was catapulted over the wall the next day.'

A slight retching noise came from the man behind her, but she didn't turn. She continued. 'So, yes, we're fairly sure he was dead.'

There was silence as the jest fell as flat as it deserved. She hastened to continue. 'So all we know is what the fellow told his brother. He'll be able to tell you better than I.' She opened the door and spoke to the guard without. 'Have Stephen fetched here.' He nodded and hurried away.

Back in the room the air was thick and two of the ever-present flies buzzed around their heads. She offered Marshal wine and at his nod poured him a very small cup, for their stocks were low. She didn't offer him food, for there was none to spare, and he'd probably eaten more recently than they had anyway.

Eventually the guard ushered Stephen into the room. He clutched his hat in his hands, turning and twisting it, as they all looked at him.

'Well? Tell us of your brother, Alan.' She gestured at John Marshal. 'Tell him.'

The man's face became even more ashen. 'He didn't tell me much, my Lady, only that something was afoot in the city which was of importance, which would help. He had been told to go that night to the house of William the nephew of Warner, the mayor, and to knock in a particular fashion so they knew it was him. Then he would discover more, and he would come to tell me.' The tortured twisting of the hat intensified. 'I never saw him again – not until …'

He looked as though he would break down, which would not do, so she dismissed him with a wave of her hand, bidding him wait until she called him again, and he fled.

John Marshal turned immediately to the other man.

'Good. This is how we'll proceed, then: I'll go back to my lord regent now, telling him that we can wait three days at the most. We'll make ready to bring men forward in order to push them one by one through the postern. They'll be here a couple of hours after sunrise the day after tomorrow. In the meantime, you'll go into the town and see what you can discover of this resistance. You'll report back here before dawn in two days, and if you've found anything of use you'll come back out as quickly as you can and let us know. I'll leave some men to cover your retreat in case the French see you.'

No wonder he was such a useful man for the regent to have around, thought Dame Nicola. No delays, no qualms. All that pent-up energy. If she were thirty years younger …

The other man was nodding and rising, still without speaking, but he hesitated and turned to Marshal. 'If I may, my lord?' He received a nod of permission, and moved forward to murmur something that Dame Nicola didn't quite catch.

Marshal nodded once. 'A good thought. I'll see what I can do. Now, I bid you Godspeed, and hope we will meet again in the next two days.'

With that he was already striding out of the room. Dame Nicola followed to bid him farewell at the postern. Her curiosity was piqued. 'Who is he?'

Marshal paused in his advance. 'A spy, a man of Warenne's.'

Now she was taken aback. 'Warenne? Surrey? Has he re-joined us? I didn't know he would be with the host.'

He made a derisive noise. 'He isn't. He tried to join but others were wary. This is his way of attempting to curry favour with the lord regent. Apparently this man is one of the best, so if he can help us, Warenne will be welcomed back to the fold.'

She spoke sombrely. 'A heavy burden for the man to carry.'

Marshal nodded as a soldier began unbarring the postern. 'Aye. And we will see what results from it.' He moved out of the gate. 'Until two days hence, then.' He slipped into the darkness as the gate closed behind him.

Up in the council chamber Edwin's heart seemed to be running all over his body, and he looked uncertainly at the knight who remained with him. He didn't know what to say and wasn't sure he'd be able to get any words out anyway, but the knight assumed control and spoke briskly.

'Now, we must see about the best way of getting you into the city. Come.'

He led Edwin out of the room and across the ward, calling as he did so for a man to bring rope. Edwin was so frightened he barely heard anything, concentrating on putting one foot in front of the other without stumbling, but he was brought up short by that one word. Rope?

They ascended the wall at one edge of the ward, and once at the top the knight spoke again. 'There's not much time, but I'll give you as many details as I can. We can't let you out of the main gate, for the French are directly in front of it and you'll be seen for certain. This is the north-east tower of the castle – see how it's shaped like a horse-shoe, and remember it. Look down to both sides to see where you are.'

Edwin complied as the knight pointed to the left. 'Over there, the north wall. The alley down there should be fairly safe once you're in it. The French don't patrol there as it's too close to our walls, and nobody can come from the other side as the great west gate is blocked.' He moved around to Edwin's other side and pointed to the right. 'Over there, the east side of the castle. You'll see that they've razed the houses over there to create an open space. I'm sure they mean to besiege us from that quarter as well once they get the chance, but at the moment they can't, as their forces would be stretched too thinly. They patrol the area occasionally. If you can avoid them you should be able to get across to the remaining houses and that will give you cover.'

Edwin nodded, trying desperately to take in all the information without showing his fear.

The knight continued. 'You'll need to get to the house of William the nephew of Warner, the mayor, who lives in the shadow of the church of All Saints on Church Lane, north of the minster. Here's Stephen to tell you how to knock.'

As he was speaking the man who had been in the chamber earlier arrived with a length of rope. Edwin belatedly realised how he was going to get into the city and his heart quailed, his hands shaking as he tied it around his waist. The last man who had tried to act as a go-between for the castle and the city had ended up dead, his head hacked off and shot over the wall … he hoped he wasn't about to be sick.

He realised that the man was speaking to him. 'All I can tell you is what my brother said, God rest him. When you knock at the door, do it three times quickly, then wait, then three times again, and then wait, and then twice. Hopefully they will know it and let you in.'

The jagged thought of what might happen if they didn't let him in stabbed into Edwin's mind, but it had no chance to pierce deeply because the knight was speaking again.

'We'll keep watch for you here. Listen for the bells of the cathedral, which are still chiming at Matins and Lauds each night, thank the Lord. Tomorrow night and the night after as the bells chime we'll lower the rope and wait long enough to say three paternosters. After that we'll haul it back up, so you'll only have those four chances. Do you understand?'

Edwin nodded, preparing to swing out over the parapet as the men took the strain on the rope. The knight gripped his shoulder and wished him good luck. He straddled the wall with one leg, swung the other over and leaned precariously outwards. He held his breath as he was lowered over the parapet. Suddenly the ground seemed much further away than it had done before, dizzyingly distant. If the rope were to break he would plummet down to shatter his body on the ground below … don't think of that! He struggled to regain his composure as he swung slowly down. He was going to need his wits about him if he was to survive the night. Keep calm. Breathe slowly.

After what seemed like hours his feet finally touched solid earth. He fumbled at the knots around him, forcing his trembling fingers to work them loose. Eventually he was free, and he looked up to the top of the wall in the darkness. He could just make out the shape of the knight's head as he peered over the edge. A low voice floated down to him. 'Remember, tomorrow night and the night after, as the bells strike. Godspeed …'

And then he was alone.

———◦———

To start with, Edwin could do nothing but hover in the alley, pressing himself back against the comforting presence of the wall, but he knew that he would have to leave it. He strained his eyes out into the moonlit night to try and see across the blank space he would have to cross. Once past that he would be able to hide himself in the streets, or in the rubble of the destroyed houses. But first, he would have to cross the open space. Was there any other way around it? He thought not. There was nothing else for it. Better to get it over as quickly as possible. Taking a deep breath, he waited for another cloud to cross the moon and then pushed himself off from the wall and ran as fast as he could out into the open.

Surely the space hadn't been as wide as this when he'd seen it from above? He was exposed, expecting at any moment to hear shouts or the deadly hissing of an arrow being loosed. What did it feel like to be hit by one? An arrow or crossbow bolt would thump into his body, tearing into the flesh as it embedded itself deep inside him. He could virtually sense the searing pain … almost sobbing, he finally hit the ruined wall of a house, hard, and flung himself down in its shadow. His chest heaved as he sucked in huge breaths. He listened but he could hear nothing except for the beating of his own heart. He waited again. Still nothing.

He stayed in the shadow of the house until his breathing returned to normal – or, at least, as normal as he thought it was going to get – and he could marshal the thoughts properly in his head. He had survived the first stage, but now he had to continue, to the cathedral, then north to the church of All Saints. You need to do this for your lord, for your mother and for your friends.

Edwin stood up.

Chapter Four

Edwin arrived at the house. This must be it. What if it wasn't? What would he do? What if …? He raised his hand to knock, wavered, and then lowered it again. Then he lifted it once more. If he didn't knock, where would he go? There was no way back, so he had better hope that the way forward was safe. He knocked, three times, three times, then twice.

No sound came from inside. He knocked again, but dared not do it any louder lest he wake everyone else in the street. What if there was nobody there? That was a possibility he hadn't considered. But as he knocked yet a third time, he heard sounds of stirring in the house. He saw a glimmer of light behind the shutters and sensed someone on the other side of the door. That someone paused for a long, agonising moment, and then Edwin heard the sound of a heavy bar lifting. The door opened and Edwin felt a hand clutching his shoulder and pulling him inside. He staggered into the room and turned to see an elderly man dressed only in a shirt, who was already re-barring the door. He opened his mouth but didn't get the chance to explain himself.

'Who are you? What in the Lord's name are you doing here? Do you not know that you could get us all killed?' The old man's voice wavered.

Edwin shifted his weight, but before he could move the man held out a knife in front of him. 'Stay where you are! I will have out of you who you are and how you came to knock like that.'

The knife was a small kitchen thing and the hand holding it was trembling: Edwin felt a strange and unfamiliar confidence at the thought that here was someone he could probably over-power if he needed to. But he didn't move.

'I've come from the castle. The people there sent me, and I found out how to knock from Stephen who was the brother of Alan. Are you William the nephew of Warner?' Now was the time to find out whether his nocturnal mission had been all in vain.

Rather unexpectedly, the old man let the knife drop, sank onto a stool and assumed an attitude of despair. 'I am he. Alan was a brave man. I am afraid I am not so brave, and you are too late.'

———◆———

Alys was so tired that she couldn't keep the thoughts straight in her head. The last candle was burning low, and she stared at the increasingly waxy face of her father, the only part visible as he lay in his winding sheet. Tomorrow, even that would be covered as he went to his eternal rest. She would be in the dark soon, but it was nearly dawn so it wouldn't be for long. She had plenty of time to think, alone here with the silent dead, and she drew her shawl closer to her as she shifted position, her knees becoming uncomfortable and stiff after such a lengthy vigil. It didn't seem that long since she had watched over the body of her mother in the same bed, and she was drawn to reminisce as her head started to nod … Mama's face seemed so distant now, just a passing shade in her mind, but she could still remember her gentle laugh and the comforting scent as she held her daughter close and safe. Mama had died of the childbed fever after Randal was born, and Alys had wondered how she would ever survive the loss. She had been totally bereft, beside herself with grief. She had cried herself to sleep for weeks and months afterwards, roaming the house during the day and looking in every corner in case Mama should suddenly reappear and everything would be all right.

Back then she could hardly have imagined that seven years later she would be kneeling in the same room, with no tears left to shed, looking back to that time almost with fondness: at least then she'd had Papa to tell her that she would still be looked after, and other family surrounding her. Thomas had just gone off to his apprenticeship with Peter of the Bail, but he wasn't all that far away, and, of course, she and Nick had had each other to cling to as they tried to help look after the little ones. And yet now here she was alone. The children were still too young to fend for themselves, and she was the sole person who stood between them and the outside world, between them and starvation. How could she leave them, even for a while, to carry out her father's wishes? What would happen if …

The candle guttered and the sudden flickering of the light made her come to. First things first: she was supposed to be here praying for Papa's soul and imploring that his passage through purgatory would be short. Once he reached Heaven he would be together with Mama again, and Alys prayed with all her might that they might find each other; and that if Thomas and Nick had not survived, that they might all be together as they waited for her. It was so tempting to wish that she might be there too, reunited with them, resting, peaceful, and not having to struggle on, but she must put such thoughts out of her mind. She must. She would. It was ungodly and sinful to wish one's life over, and no matter how she suffered, the fight to live must go on.

Edwin looked across the room at the old man, still sitting with his head in his hands. 'When you say "too late", what exactly do you mean?' The relief of having reached his destination after being out in the streets was making his knees melt under him, and he eased himself down to sit on the floor.

William raised his head. 'In short, nobody trusts me any more. When the city first fell, I was all for fighting against the invader, but then I saw their terrible power, those awful machines, the way they were destroying my town, and I realised that we must make an accommodation with them.'

Edwin felt his stomach lurch. 'An accommodation?' He wanted to rise again, but found he couldn't.

William sighed. 'I am an old man and I have lived in Lincoln all my life. I am the mayor. I am supposed to look after the city and cherish her. Such a wonderful place, but look what they have done to her. If any more damage is done she will never recover. And so much bloodshed. My son is dead, and I must stop others from being killed also.' He sounded weary.

Edwin tried to speak, but the fear which had been building up over the last few hours had finally got the better of him, and his tongue simply wouldn't move. He stared dumbly at William.

The old man looked over at him. 'Oh, never fear, I will not denounce you to them. I am not a traitor, just a man who wants peace. But you must leave here, now, and you must not come back.' He started to haul himself up off the stool.

Something had to be done. He had to speak, to be eloquent, but nothing would come out. As William stood, putting one hand to his back and grimacing, Edwin was almost ready to let himself be shepherded out of the door, out into oblivion and despair. He must speak.

'No.'

Not exactly the best start, but it was all he could manage, and at least it had made William pause. He forced his throat to push out more words, to make his wooden tongue move. 'No. I've come to help you, and you must have hope. An army is on the way, coming to relieve the city. And Dame Nicola is holding out – you may have given up, but there is a woman who will not fold so easily.'

William stopped suddenly. 'Dame Nicola? She is still alive?'

'Yes.' The words came more easily now. 'And her ... she has also lost her son, but she won't let it deter her. She cares about this city as much as you do, and I am telling you that you must help!'

This seemed to sway him for a moment. 'Dame Nicola is … well, I have always held her in the highest regard, for she has been the castellan for many years, since we were both young. If she still believes that there is hope then there must be. Perhaps the Lord has not deserted us after all.' He paced up and down, his knees creaking. 'But how can I help? After I went to the French and said that there would be no trouble if only they would leave the town in peace, nobody trusts me. There may well be a secret resistance somewhere, but I do not know who. To start with I was in contact with Alan, as he had a way to talk to his brother in the castle, but after what happened to him …'

Edwin said nothing, partly as he was content to watch the ideas forming in the other's face, but mainly because he couldn't bear to bring up what had happened to the man Alan, in case it pushed him over the line between fear and madness.

William had reached a decision. 'We will try.' He drew himself up as straight as his frame would allow. 'For Dame Nicola, I will try.'

'Good. So I may stay?'

'You may stay. We will have to think of some plausible excuse, for it will look suspicious, you turning up out of nowhere like this. It will make people even less likely to trust me. And we will have to think of some plan – there is no point just going about the town and asking people if they are in league against the invaders: they would not say, for fear that we might be on the side of the French.'

'I'll think of something.' Edwin hoped he sounded more confident than he felt. 'But we must act quickly. I only have two days to find out all I can and to get back to the castle.'

'Then let us begin.' William moved to the shutters and peered out. 'It is still dark, but there is no point in going back to bed. Wait here while I dress, for the cold seeps into my bones more these days than it ever did. Then we will decide what to do.'

He shuffled off, taking the rushlight with him, and Edwin was left in darkness. He sat still, eyes closed, trying to rest his limbs and his aching mind. He hadn't had the chance to look about him properly since he came in, and he couldn't see anything, but now he realised that the room was scented with the exotic tang of spices. William must deal in them – of course, there would be many merchants in such a large town as this. The warm smell of cloves, cinnamon and powder douce, together with the sharp counterpoint of ginger and pepper comforted him, and he was transported back to the steward's office in the castle at Conisbrough, where he had spent many a long hour adding up accounts for his puzzled uncle. Life had been simpler then. He breathed deeply, inhaling the scent, and was calmer by the time he saw the flicker of light again and heard William tottering down the stairs with aching slowness.

William beckoned to him to come through to another room, and Edwin followed him towards the back of the house. He stumbled over something.

'Shh! You will wake the rest of the house. Stand still until I have made more light.'

Edwin stood while William moved about the room, fetching another rush and lighting it from the one in his hand. Then he stood it in a pricket on a table and Edwin could see that he was in a kitchen. He righted the stool that he had kicked over on his way in and sat on it, while William lowered himself into the chair at the head of the table.

'Now then. The best I can come up with at the moment is that we will tell everyone you are my nephew. Men who have known me some while will be aware that my sister married a man from the north, so that will explain your foreign accent.'

Edwin nodded. It was as plausible as anything else and he couldn't think of anything better right now.

'However, this does not explain why in the Lord's name you would be foolish enough to come to Lincoln at such a time. You could feasibly have entered the city, for the French are not actually preventing anyone from doing so, but as you can imagine, travellers are scarce at the moment.' William sighed. 'Still, it will have to do for now.' He shifted in his seat and then rose, stiffly. 'These days I cannot sit in one place for too long.' With one hand on his back he limped over to the shutter and peered out. 'Dawn is breaking. Here, help me with this and we will stoke up the fire before my daughter-in-law comes down. Better that she first sees you in the light.'

Edwin hefted the wooden shutter down from the window, allowing the sun's fingers to reach into the room. He sniffed the morning air, but it was not the clean fresh air of his home; here it was somehow thicker and greasier, and it smelled wrong. A pang of homesickness pierced him. What was he doing here in this alien place? He sighed as he stood the shutter neatly against the wall.

William had hobbled over to the hearth and was poking the fire to stir some life into it. The ashes smouldered and Edwin hastened to take a handful of dry kindling from the tiny stack next to the hearth. He knelt down and blew gently on the smouldering embers until a first small flame licked up over the sticks. Soon the room was filled with a warm glow, and he stood, brushing the soot off his knees.

Thumps sounded from over his head, followed by voices, and soon Edwin heard footsteps on the stairs. He cast a rapid glance at William and stood facing the door. A woman came through it with two children behind her. She stopped with a gasp and a stifled scream when she saw him, her hand flying to her mouth, but recovered when she saw William. She looked at him without speaking, without moving any further into the room. The children sheltered behind her skirts.

William cleared his throat. 'Daughter. This is my nephew …' His voice petered out and Edwin suddenly realised that he hadn't even told William his name. He leapt into the conversation, making a clumsy bow. 'Edwin. Edwin of … Retford. I am very pleased to meet you, mistress.'

William spoke again, a little too quickly. 'My son's widow, Juliana. You will recall, Juliana, that I have spoken of my sister Eleanor who married a wool merchant? Edwin is her son.'

Edwin held his breath, but Juliana said nothing, merely nodding her head and drifting into the room to set vessels and plates on the table. Her movements were emotionless, and now that he looked at her properly he could see the dead look in her eyes. The two children, a boy and a girl, crept silently to sit in the corner, heads downcast.

William gestured towards them. 'My grandchildren.' He spoke under his breath. 'You see now why I wish to avoid more bloodshed?'

Edwin slumped on to a stool, the weight of his duties suddenly lying heavy on his shoulders.

He felt better after some bread and ale; he hadn't realised how much he'd been flagging after his sleepless night, but there was no time to rest. After the brief repast, William instructed his daughter-in-law to take charge of the shop, with an aside to Edwin that there would not likely be many customers anyway, since people were not buying luxuries like spices these days. Then they left the house with the intention of walking about the town.

Everything about the city was big. Edwin had thought that he was accustomed to grandeur, living as he did in the shadow of the earl's castle in Conisbrough, but there the keep dominated a village of small single-storey dwellings, spread around the three sides of the green. Here there were streets and streets of houses all packed closely together, many of which seemed to have a second storey which jutted out above the first. And so many! How did such a large number of people live in such a confined space? How did they grow their food? The amount of space allocated to each person or household must be very small, *let me see, if each of these houses is about a perch wide …*

Such thoughts occupied him as he followed William through the maze. One other thing which struck him almost immediately was how filthy the place was. Even though the weather had been dry for at least the past couple of days, the streets were ankle-deep in mud and rutted with the marks of cartwheels, and he kept carefully to the edge of the roadway to avoid having to wade through the worst of it. He soon discovered that it wasn't merely mud; the place was oozing with ordure and sewage. What in the Lord's name were these people doing? Throwing their waste out of their doors and onto the streets directly in front of them? It was disgusting. And it stank. The village of Conisbrough might seem rustic compared to the great city, but at least people had the decency to dig middens in their yards. He cursed under his breath as he planted his foot squarely in something noisome – he didn't want to investigate it too closely for fear of finding out that it was something even worse than he imagined – and then realised with a wrench that this was something he would never have done had he been at home; if his mother had heard any kind of oath issuing from his lips she would have boxed his ears, no matter that he was nearly twenty and taller than her by a head. But as he followed the old man through the frightened streets, his mother and the life he had left behind seemed a very long way away, both in distance and in time. Was it really only a week ago he had been there? He could only visualise the peaceful village through a haze as the images faded.

He must concentrate. He looked about him at every person who passed. Which ones were helping the castle? Which ones might be traitors? Which were neither, but just hoping to come out of this alive? And how in the Lord's name would he tell? He would have to look out for the slightest hint. He felt jumpy, with a dizziness and nausea which he tried to ignore.

At first he thought it was some kind of illusion, but as they drew nearer to the cathedral he could see that it really was that big, and he could feel his jaw sag. He knew, of course, that a cathedral was like a church only larger, but he had not been prepared for the immensity of the structure. Had he not been aware of the urgency of his mission, he would have stood in front of it all day, content simply to drink in the sight of something so unbelievable. He had never been overly religious. He went to Mass in the village church, of course, but even though he was one of the few there who could understand Latin, the priest's dry and gabbled speech had never moved him and he felt no yearning, no vocation. But now, to think that men could build such a thing to the glory of the Lord … he wanted to drop to his knees in awe at God's power and pray for salvation. Despite the weight on his mind he stopped and simply gaped. It was so beautiful it took his breath away, soaring into the heavens. How had they made it so tall without the walls tumbling down? How had they fitted a roof so high above the ground? How …

But William was pulling him away. 'For God's sake, boy, stop gawking! You will draw attention to yourself!'

Edwin's mind returned to earth and he followed the older man towards a market which was being held in the open space to the side of the cathedral. To him it looked like a grand affair but William sniffed and muttered under his breath that things were not what they used to be.

They were hailed by two men who stood very close together at the corner of the market. William raised his hand and steered Edwin towards them.

'Ah, good day, William, good day. We were just speaking of the latest news.'

The men were both dressed in what looked to Edwin to be very showy clothes – although who knows what might be considered normal in a city like this – and they were both staring at him. He felt uncomfortable and knew he was beginning to flush.

William cleared his throat. 'Gentlemen, I do not think you have met my nephew, Edwin of Retford?

Each of the men nodded to Edwin, curiosity writ large on their faces, as William continued. 'Edwin brings me news of my dear sister Eleanor. Living that far away, he had not heard of the trouble here, and once he did, he thought he was so close that he may as well carry on and get here, to see what had happened to me and to bring tidings back to my sister and goodbrother ...' Perhaps realising that he was gabbling and that everyone was staring, he tailed off and gestured at the men. 'Edwin, this is Peter of the Bridge and Peter of the Bail, two of the most respected merchants in Lincoln.'

Edwin nodded at them, although he hadn't quite grasped which was which. Probably better to stay silent and let William do the talking.

But the old man was interrupted by the Peter on the left. 'Dear Eleanor. She was always so kind to me when I was a boy. I do hope she is well?'

Edwin tried to swallow the lump in his throat. 'Yes, good sir, very well.' Dear Lord, how typical that the first person he had run into should know William's sister. He had better make sure he found out as much as he could about her from William, lest someone else should ask him.

But the merchant was continuing. 'And that very handsome man she married, I can't remember his name now ...?'

Edwin opened his mouth but no words came out. The silence stretched on for what was probably no more than a moment, but it seemed an eternity. He was saved by the other Peter, who elbowed his companion. 'Never mind that now! We have yet to tell William the news.' He leaned closer. 'Nicholas Holland is dead.'

William gasped. 'When?'

'Just last evening, or so I hear.' Peter turned to Edwin. 'I'm sorry to involve you in this when you're so newly arrived, but you must know that Lincoln is not a safe place these days. Nicholas Holland was a respected merchant and he was struck down in the street some nights ago, the back of his head crushed in.' He leaned closer into Edwin. 'You must beware, young man.' The merchant smelled of some kind of scent which was slightly off-putting, and Edwin tried to back away from him without looking rude.

The other Peter took up the tale. 'And his son is still missing.'

William looked confused. 'Thomas? But I thought …'

The merchant waved his hand, revealing soft fat fingers and a number of gold rings. 'No, no. Thomas has been out of the town since before the trouble started – I sent him out to meet with one of my wool suppliers and he never came back. Hopefully he's safe somewhere and waiting outside the city until the trouble is over. He's a good apprentice and I shouldn't like to lose him, especially when he's so near the end of his indenture. No, it's young Nick who has still failed to return, so Peter has also lost an apprentice.'

The second Peter looked at Edwin. 'You look confused, young Edwin, the son of Eleanor.' He patted Edwin on the arm, which Edwin found mildly discomfiting. 'You will soon learn. We all live very close together here in Lincoln.'

William was muttering to himself and Edwin tried to catch it; '… did not say anything about Nick – but then again, she did not say much at all …' he looked up and spoke out loud again. 'But what of Nicholas? Where is he?'

The first Peter answered. 'At home. He was being looked after by that charming daughter of his, who will no doubt have to arrange the funeral. She had better hope one of her brothers comes back soon, or she'll stand no chance – a girl with all those other children to look after. The wolves will soon be sniffing around her. She's as pretty as a butterfly, but girls like that are not made for this sort of situation.'

The other Peter sniggered. 'Come, Peter, you sound as though you're about to say what pretty young girls *are* for, and that's not the sort of conversation for this time in the morning!'

His companion seemed to find this very funny and they laughed together, jowls shaking. Edwin felt sorry for this nameless girl, and tried to get straight in his head the information he had just heard. A man. His daughter. His son. No, two sons, both missing. And how had he been attacked? And by whom? Had Peter said that? He didn't think so. But maybe …

Peter was continuing. 'Well, if neither of those boys comes back, I suppose the shop and all the goods will go to the next lad, though he is but a child. So perhaps young Alys had better get herself married as soon as she can, in order to have a man to look after things. A shame my son is so young, but perhaps something could be arranged so that I could look after everything for her? It's a good business that Nicholas had there …'

A thunderous crashing noise suddenly sounded from not very far away, and Edwin was startled out of his wits. He leapt in fright and almost grabbed William's arm, before noticing that none of the others had so much as flinched. One of the Peters was still murmuring to himself about business and had taken no notice.

William looked at Edwin sadly. 'The siege machines at the castle. We are all so used to it that we hardly hear it. I am sure the walls cannot last much longer. It will all be over in a week or two.'

Sooner than that, thought Edwin. Both of the Peters shrugged at the same time, and one of them spoke in a peevish voice. 'Yes, yes, the walls. The garrison. But how soon will it be before we can recover proper trade again? These people simply have not considered the inconvenience to us and to our businesses. Who cares about the king and the war when there is money to be made?'

Edwin gaped, wondering if it were possible that he would ever hear such a selfish statement again, but he was saved from replying as the two Peters turned away and strolled towards the market, chattering and gesticulating.

As they walked, William whispered to him as many of the details of his supposed life as he could. Edwin tried to rehearse everything in his head. As if it wasn't bad enough being here and meeting all these new people, but he had to try and remember to be someone else at the same time. He went over and over again the names of his supposed mother, father and family, and the few facts he had learned about their business of cloth. It might be enough to get him past a general enquiry, but he prayed that nobody would have the opportunity to question him closely. And he begged the Lord to make sure that nobody would ask him anything about wool.

It was later in the morning, and after what had turned out to be a fairly uneventful walk around the town they were back at the cathedral again. He had been conscious of its looming presence throughout the morning, for there was no escaping it, but he wasn't sure whether he should feel protected or intimidated. Now they were on the other side of it from where they'd been earlier, and here there was some activity – masons working on large blocks of stone. William saw Edwin looking and explained that there had been a terrible accident there some twenty years ago, when the building was split from top to bottom, and that since then work had been on-going on building a new cathedral in the modern style. Edwin had no idea that cathedrals could have a modern style, or any other for that matter, but of course he'd never seen one before, so what did he know? He merely felt a huge reverence, both at the size of the building and its purpose. He was reminded that the Lord was watching and saw all.

He looked up, squinting, and realised that there were men right up at the top, balancing precariously on scaffolding. At floor level there were ropes and pulleys, and as he watched, a large carved piece of stone was hauled up. He marvelled at the way the men above seemed unconcerned at being so high. He was sure he could never manage it.

'It must be a very difficult task to make sure all the pieces go in the right places properly.'

William nodded, animated as he considered the huge building. 'Yes. But it is to the glory of the Lord, and of the Blessed Hugh, the old bishop who will be a saint before too long if miracles at his tomb continue. I have lived in the shadow of this building since the day I was born, and it comforts me to know that it will soon be whole again. We have one of the best master masons in the country in charge of the building works. There he is over there, but before you meet him I should tell you that I am almost sure that he is a French spy.'

Chapter Five

Edwin wasn't sure he'd heard properly. 'What did you say?'

'I said I am sure he is a French spy.'

Edwin spoke with great care. 'And why do you say that?'

William looked uncomfortable. 'Well … he is a foreigner. At least, he is not from around here, and I did hear him say once that before he came to Lincoln, he worked on a cathedral in France.' He folded his arms and looked satisfied.

Edwin thought that he probably needed a bit more information than that before he could condemn a man as a spy. But here was his first real piece of information. 'Do you have any evidence that he's been spying? Has anyone seen him trying to communicate with the French?'

William unfolded his arms and stroked his beard. 'Not as such, no. But he is always roving about here and there, and he has a good many men working for him who are not local, either. And … well, he has an air of suspicion about him. Look.'

Edwin followed the direction of the pointing finger and saw two men deep in conversation: one tall and gaunt-looking, the other small with hunched shoulders. 'Which?'

'The tall one. You see what I mean?'

Edwin conceded to himself that William did have a point – if the man had set out to look as suspicious as possible then he'd done a fine job, what with the skeletal frame and the black tunic and cloak.

William pulled his arm. 'Come, let us greet him, and you can talk to him and see what you think. I shall engage him in conversation on normal matters, to try and draw him in, and you can see what you can discover.'

As they drew near, Edwin could hear the master mason speaking.

'… and he didn't regain his wits at all?'

The other shook his head. 'No, or so she says. But …' He stopped as he became aware of the men approaching.

William greeted the mason. 'Master Michael, how good to see you being able to carry on with the work.' He threw a broad wink at Edwin.

The tall man bowed his head at William, casting barely a glance at Edwin. 'Greetings, Master Mayor. Yes, it will not be many more years before all the cathedral's wounds will be healed and she will be well again.'

William looked again at Edwin. 'If only the same could be said of our poor city.'

Master Michael stroked his chin. 'Of course. I have been here nearly fifteen years now and think of it as my home; I shall be sad to leave once the cathedral is complete. But perhaps the current situation will work in my favour in the end – there will be many repairs to be done to the city walls and the castle once this is all over.' He looked up, squinting high up towards the scaffolding. 'But now I must ascend to see that keystone safely installed, for the next arch will be completed once it is in place.' He turned and strode off without another word; his cloak swirling dramatically in a manner which Edwin felt almost sure was intentional. Edwin looked around him for the other man, but he had also disappeared – presumably he was one of the masons and had returned to his duties. He sighed. How in the Lord's name could he tell whether someone was a spy or not from such a short and banal conversation? And he'd met so many others this morning who might have all sorts of motives or none – how was he to find what happened to the dead messenger, and whether the city folk had any plans to help the castle? Time was passing – half a day, almost one quarter of his allotted time – and as yet he knew nothing. And to be forthright about it, the company of William wasn't really helping much.

He moved to a quiet corner, thinking to sit and consider things for a while, but then saw William speaking to three more people whom he hadn't met. This time it was a woman of maybe just more than middle years and a young man who bore a strong resemblance to her, together with a slight man wearing a jaunty red hat with a feather. William saw him looking and beckoned him over.

'Mistress, I do not think you know my nephew, Edwin of Retford? Edwin, this is Master Pinel, who imports dyes' – he gestured to the man in the red hat – 'and Mistress Guildersleeve, a widow who runs a haberdashery business down in the Drapery.'

This time Edwin was ready with his lines about his supposed family, but they were not needed. The woman nodded, introduced the young man as 'My son, Gervase' and barely stopped for breath as she chattered to William. Gervase looked sheepishly at Edwin and shrugged his shoulders, by which Edwin guessed that this was probably a regular occurrence. He occupied himself trying to work out what haberdashery might be.

From what the woman was saying, it sounded as though there would be a funeral that afternoon. Edwin caught the name 'Nicholas' and realised that it was probably the man that the two Peters had been talking about that morning. If that were the case then he had only been dead a few hours, which would have been a little too soon for a funeral in Edwin's home village, where they might have waited until the morrow, but perhaps here in the city they did things differently. With so many people around they probably didn't want to leave bodies lying around for too long, lest they spread disease.

He had lost track. He needed to concentrate more on the conversation, where William was speaking.

'… and such a shame about those boys being missing.'

On one side of Edwin, Gervase opened his mouth, but he couldn't speak before his mother cut in. Edwin felt trapped between them. 'Oh yes, such fine boys. But no doubt they will come home once all the trouble is over.'

Edwin thought to himself that everyone he had met today was talking about 'when the trouble would be over', but he wasn't sure whether this was just a common phrase in the city, much in the way of the villagers at home saying 'once the winter is over', or whether they really knew something about what was going on. He glanced furtively at the slight man – what had his name been again? Pinel? – and wished he could develop the ability to judge people just by looking at them. It would make his present situation much easier, that was for sure.

He had missed another part of the conversation. They had apparently stopped talking about boys and were speaking of a girl, William interrupting the flow from Mistress Guildersleeve. 'It must be such a comfort for her to have you nearby, for is she not betrothed to your son?'

To Edwin's left, Gervase started to put his hand out towards his mother, but dropped it again; to his right, Mistress Guildersleeve took in a sharp breath and looked as though she were about to launch into some kind of tirade. The words that came out of her mouth did not match, though, for they were platitudes about nothing being formal yet, things needing to be settled, and the inevitable aside to 'waiting until all this was over.' William didn't seem to have noticed anything strange, so Edwin thought it was of no great importance. After all, William knew these people much better than he did.

Gervase spoke for the first time, touching his mother on the arm and pointing out yet another citizen whom Edwin didn't know. He had no idea how he was going to keep track of them all. This latest was a youngish man who craned his neck forward and peered at them carefully before stepping over a pile of muck in the street to join them. Gervase greeted him, but infuriatingly he didn't say the man's name. Edwin listened as the newcomer was told all about the funeral that afternoon, and was firmly instructed by Mistress Guildersleeve to tidy himself up and be there.

The conversation turned to the late Nicholas Holland, with Pinel wondering aloud what he could have been doing when he was struck down. Mistress Guildersleeve seemed ready to gossip, but Edwin happened to be looking at the man whose name he didn't know, and he was interested to note that at the mention of Nicholas he looked immediately wary, almost backing away. Edwin tried desperately to think of some way to engage him in conversation to find out more about him, but the man made a quiet nod to the others and slipped away before he had the chance to think of something. Damn!

The rest of the party was breaking up now, with promises that they would see each other that afternoon. Pinel and the others nodded as they departed, and after they had all gone, William decided it was time to go home for something to eat. As they trudged back to the house, and as the silent Juliana put bread and ale down in front of them on the table, William quizzed Edwin about everything he had seen. What did he think of the town and its people? What did he think was going on? Did he have any ideas as to who might be in league with the castle?

Edwin said as little as he could. Firstly, he had scarcely had time to think things through himself, and wasn't really sure what he thought; and secondly, William seemed just a little over-eager to hear his impressions. It was like having an elderly puppy fawning round him, and it was a little disconcerting. Edwin was not quite sure that he wanted to share everything with his host – if the last couple of weeks had taught him anything, it was to trust absolutely nobody.

After they had eaten their frugal meal, and Edwin had thanked Juliana and received no reply, William rose stiffly and announced that it was time he went to Nicholas's funeral. Edwin decided not to accompany him – not only had he not known the man, but he could use the extra hour or two to wander round the city free of his host, to see if there was anything else he could pick up. So, as William shuffled off towards the southern end of town, Edwin walked the other way, towards the castle.

He couldn't get too near it of course, but he would get something of a closer look to see if anything was to be gained by observing the men besieging it. First he went round to the north-eastern edge, but as all the houses there had been razed, he would look suspicious loitering in the rubble, so he turned to walk towards the southern side. As he turned, he noticed a large dark stain on the floor which had a cloud of flies buzzing over it. He stooped and looked at it, realising it was dried blood. Someone had been struck down here, perhaps even the very man they were burying this afternoon. He looked up at the castle and saw that he was pretty much as close as he could get without moving right out on to the open ground. Nicholas, if it was he, had been attacked within shouting distance of the castle. Had he been trying to contact them? Or was he a spy for the French? Or could there have been another explanation? He needed to think. Over to one side was a stone, also smeared in blood. He picked it up. On examining it more closely he saw that there was hair stuck to it and what looked to be flesh – this was presumably what had been used to hit the man over the head. It was fairly weighty but he could lift it in one hand – probably why Nicholas had been knocked senseless but hadn't died straight away. He didn't want to take it with him but couldn't bear just to leave it there in the open. He put it in the rubble of wooden spars where a house had once stood, and stirred the debris with his foot to cover it.

Next he set off for the south side of the castle. Here the houses approaching the open ground were still intact, so he had more cover, although one or two people on the street were looking at him strangely. He tried to appear nonchalant as he looked over towards the besiegers, crouching to fiddle with his boot.

Along the flat ground, a number of machines were lined up, with men moving round them. They were strange contraptions made of wood, with ropes round them here and there. As he looked more closely he could see that they were of two different types. One or two had long arms balanced in the middle, with a sling at one end and a weight at the other. These did not appear in use at the moment, but he could see how they would work: if you put a stone in the sling, and then lifted and dropped the weight, it would cause the stone to be thrown at the walls. Fascinating. He wondered how someone had thought of such an idea, and what else such a machine might be used for … people were looking at him. He had better move on. He supposed that the engines had become a regular sight for the citizens, so by staring so openly he was marking himself out as a stranger. Fortunately none of the men at the machines appeared to have noticed him. He moved into a shaded alley and fumbled as though he were about to relieve himself. That was better – he would not be so obvious here. He kept to the shadow as he looked back at the machines.

Some men were working on one of the other type of engine. Again there was wood and rope, but the arm which would carry the stone was pivoted at one end instead of in the middle. That end was stuck in the middle of what looked like a pile of rope, but as he watched, the men started to winch the arm backwards, and he could see that the rope was tightly twisted, and that as they turned they were winding it ever tighter, so that it was exerting greater and greater force on the machine. Still they pulled, straining themselves and grunting with exertion, and the timbers of the engine started to groan and creak with the force. For no reason that Edwin could think of, John Marshal suddenly came to mind – all that tightly wound, pent-up energy just waiting to explode.

The men were putting a stone in a sort of cup attachment which was at the end of the arm. Then they all moved back to a safe distance, except for one who held the end of a line, which was joined to a pin holding all the wound-up rope in place. At the command of the man who seemed to be in charge, he pulled it and the pin flew out. All the force was released at once, and the arm of the machine shot round so quickly that

Edwin couldn't follow it with his eye. The great stone was flung out and flew towards the castle. Edwin felt a stone in his own throat, but was pleased when the missile appeared to miss the wall, sailed right over it and into the bailey. But his relief was short-lived as a terrible scream came from inside. Dear Lord. He closed his eyes and gulped, listening to the cheers of the men at the machine and the congratulations given to the man in charge. He prayed in silence for whoever had been hit by the stone, and swore revenge on those who were doing such evil things and enjoying it. His resolve hardened into a knot in his heart. He would find out how to help those people in the castle, and in the Lord's name he would help them to fight against that evil bombardment. He slipped out of the alley and away down the street.

———— ※ ————

It had been a very small and plain funeral. Her father had been a popular man in the city, but Alys wasn't surprised that so few people had attended the burial, for everyone was too frightened to come out of their homes unless they were forced to do so. Apart from her and the children there had only been her neighbours from both sides, plus William, the two Peters and Ralf – and, strangely, Master Michael – but none of her father's other acquaintances or fellow merchants. As she had been turning to leave the church she thought she'd also glimpsed a woman slipping out of the door, but she couldn't see who it was – possibly someone who wasn't even there for the funeral, but had just come in to pray. Still, at least Papa had been properly buried with the due sacrament, and she supposed she should feel grateful that Father Eustace was still willing to bury the dead, and that he had managed to find another man to help him shovel the earth back over the grave. It was done now, and her father had gone forward to everlasting peace – something which was in very short supply for the

rest of them. She walked with the neighbours back towards
the Drapery, her thoughts dwelling on her father and his love
for them all. The sight of Master Pinel in his red hat saddened
her, reminding her of those better times – the red had been a
new dye he'd been trying out, and he'd tested it on a piece of
wool only big enough for two hats, passing the other on to her
father as a gift for his birthday, once he was satisfied with it.
How they had all laughed at the garish colour and joked about
them being seen as popinjays in the town …

Suddenly they were approached by a group of soldiers,
and the children crowded around her in terror. She too felt
a wave of fear and tried to disguise it for their sake. How for-
tunate that she was also with the others: although Master
Pinel was small, and sought to hide behind his wife without
anyone noticing, Gervase stepped out boldly, and at the sight
of the strong young man escorting the women and children,
the soldiers backed down from a confrontation and contented
themselves with standing arrogantly by while they passed.
How she wished that Thomas and Nick were there, so that
she didn't have to rely on the pity of neighbours. Close as they
were, family was better. But they weren't here, and they might
never come home. She said yet another prayer for their safety
and took the children home.

Now it was the middle of the afternoon and Alys could put
off her task no longer. She couldn't bring herself to tell the
children that she was going out on such a potentially dangerous errand, so she contented herself with saying that she
was going out to try and find some food – the Lord knew
they needed that as well – and slipped out of the street door.
Immediately she felt suspicious, as though she was marked in
some way with a sign saying that she was up to something.
She had an urge to try and creep quietly up the street. This was
ridiculous. She must calm herself down. Although there were
not many people on the streets, she was perfectly entitled to
be out there on a quest for food, as were others, and to act

differently would only arouse suspicion. She must try to quell her racing heartbeat and act normally. She hitched her basket higher on to her arm and walked on.

Their home was on the eastern side of the Drapery, so once out of the door she turned right and walked – calmly, she hoped – up towards the top of the street and then rounded the corner to start up the steep hill which led up towards the higher part of town. She was struck again by just how strange and alien the city looked. Normally there would be people everywhere, noise and traffic: carts and porters bearing goods which had been delivered at the staithe by the river; traders and apprentices bellowing about their wares; children and animals milling round and getting under everyone's feet. Now the place was almost deserted – not even a chicken pecking round in the gutter. All the edible animals had disappeared, and she even had a feeling that there were fewer stray dogs than before.

She looked around her again, in case anyone was follow-ing, trying to tell herself that there was no reason why anyone should be. Her path was the way to the castle, to be sure, where nobody who was in control of their wits would be going, but it was also the right direction for the great cathedral, and it was there in the open space of the minster yard that the remnants of the market could be found, so it was an entirely sensible place for a respectable woman to be going. So far so good; nobody seemed to be giving her a second glance. The few people who were on the streets were busy hurrying about their own errands, keeping their heads down and eager to reach the safety of their own houses again. The danger in the city was ever-present, and as Alys reached the top of Steep Hill she heard a deafen-ing crash coming from the direction of the castle: the French were unleashing their fearsome siege machines again, in another attempt to batter down the curtain wall. It was alarming from out here; it must be terrifying for those on the inside. Hastily she crossed herself and muttered a brief prayer for those who were trapped, before realising that she should perhaps also be praying for herself. As she reached the junction with Michaelgate, her courage failed her and she turned right towards the cathedral instead of left towards the castle.

Once in the open space of the minster yard she forced herself to calm down. Here there was a scattering of people, visiting the sparse stalls which still remained of the market, in search of food or other necessities. Alys took a short while to walk around, looking at the scanty wares on display, and was appalled to hear the prices. She would need to spend some of the stock of pennies on provisions, but should she do it now? By the time she got back after her errand, everything might be gone and the children would be hungry again. She drifted towards one of the stalls as the man behind it looked at her in hope, calling out what he had to offer. But then she became aware of the dangers of purchasing now: she would have to walk through the town on her own, past the homes and hiding places of hungry people, with a basket of food. That was no good – she would have virtually no chance of getting home with it unmolested. She would carry out her errand first and then return to buy whatever she could before hurrying home as quickly and unobtrusively as possible.

It was only a short distance from the cathedral, but as she reached the area near the castle it was a different world. Almost immediately she began to pass houses which had been badly damaged when the city had been taken, and further on there was nothing but charred ruins and a foul smell. She shuddered at the thought that some of the destroyed buildings might hide corpses under the debris, and crossed herself once again.

The French had cleared an area near to the castle which she would have to pass. There were no people here: she was alone. What was she going to use as an excuse if somebody should ask her what she was doing? She moved back into the partial shelter provided by the rubble of a destroyed house to think, and it was then that she heard the sound.

She froze. Silently she listened, straining her ears, but it didn't come again. Perhaps it had just been a rat or something, but she was sure that the noise must have been made by something bigger. Was somebody following her? Who could it be? What would she do if ...? Her throat was constricting. With terror she realised that she was more or less in the same place as her father had been when he had been attacked – murdered, she should say now that he was dead, for the man who had struck him had surely caused his death, albeit three days later. Dear Lord, protect me from harm, I am trying to do what is right for the city and for my family. She dared not move.

She continued to crouch in fright, but for long agonising moments she heard nothing. Perhaps she had imagined it. But it was certain that there must be evil-doers in the city somewhere, for who else would have struck her father down? Somebody must have followed him into this very street and lain in wait for him, raising a weapon to crush the back of his head and take him away from his family. The thought of him lying there in the dark, alone and mortally injured, made her want to weep. But mixed together with the sadness she felt the first stirrings of – what? An indignation, an anger that one of his fellow citizens should have done such a thing; for surely it was a townsman – had it been the French forces themselves, they wouldn't have left him there in the street, they would have dragged him off to their area of the city to try and get information out of him. She had heard of it happening. But the French were one thing; they were invaders, and one must expect them to be enemies. The people of the beleaguered city, on the other hand, should be working together to rid themselves of the invaders, not joining with them to do their dirty work. The anger became more pronounced and she felt a determination to do whatever she could to help the city's cause. She would deliver her message no matter what the cost.

She peered cautiously out of her hiding place and looked over at the castle wall. Perhaps there might be some possibility of signalling to them, but there was nobody there. Even if there had been, it was too far to be able to hold any meaningful conversation: she could wave her arms perhaps, but the distance across the deserted open space was too wide to shout anything. If she tried she would merely alert the whole city, and soldiers would come running. No, she would have to come back once it was dark, and try to get closer. If she could only get to the north side of the castle, close to the walls and away from the French forces, she might be able to communicate with those inside. She would return later to carry out her task. Her mind made up, she stood, only to be seized by a pair of hands.

She screamed.

Chapter Six

Alys felt a hand over her mouth, suffocating her. In a panic, she struggled.

A voice spoke urgently. 'Miss Alys, Miss Alys, stop. Stop, I beg you, or you'll get us both killed!'

She recognised that voice. Feeling the hands slackening, she released herself and turned to face Aldred. He watched her warily, but somehow she got the feeling that he was pleased he'd frightened her. He stood between her and the way out to the street, and she doubted she could get past him without a struggle.

She was angry, but some sense of caution remained and she spoke in a furious whisper rather than a shout.

'What in the Lord's name are you doing here? You frightened me half to death!' A suspicion arose. 'Have you been following me?'

He stepped nearer and she could smell the rank odour of sweat. 'I saw you at the market, Miss Alys, and wondered what might bring you this way. It's dangerous out here, you know, for a woman on her own. I thought you might need some … protection.' He leered.

'Protection! The only protection I need is from you, skulking around in ruined buildings.'

'Ruined buildings, miss? Seems that's what you were doing as well. A strange thing to do on your own – or were you perhaps waiting to meet someone? I'm shocked – taking a lover with your father barely in his grave …'

He was cut off as she slapped him hard about his leering face. She couldn't help herself, but immediately realised that this had been a mistake. His eyes narrowed and he hissed at her.

'Be aware, miss, that only my respect for your father stops me from striking you back. Otherwise I would punish you for that.' He looked at her. 'But know that I shall not forget it.'

She could say nothing. They stood in a furious silence for a moment. Alys couldn't work out how she might extricate herself from the situation, for he still stood between her and the street.

The problem was taken out of her hands as he stood aside. 'Might I *suggest* that you go back home where you belong. I will escort you to make sure you don't fall into any trouble.'

There was nothing to be done. Casting one last glance at the castle, she moved out on to the street and started to walk back towards the cathedral, unwillingly bearing his presence at her side.

———•◦•———

It was evening; perhaps an hour before the curfew, and Edwin was taking a last walk around the town with William. He was so tired he could barely put one foot in front of the other, but he needed to keep going. As they passed through the last remains of the day's market, traders packing up around them, he saw a face he recognised from earlier. It was the small man who had been speaking with Master Michael, and who had disappeared. He was walking with a woman, although Edwin could only see her back as she looked at something on one of the stalls. Then she turned, and Edwin jerked out of his stupor, feeling as though someone had thumped him in the stomach, hard. She was very young, certainly several years younger than he, and she was – well, perhaps she wasn't actually the most beautiful thing he'd ever seen, but it was definitely close. There was something about her which held his attention, and he couldn't keep his eyes off her. He realised he was holding his breath and slowly let it out. The mason, or whoever he was, had certainly made a catch there. He was hovering very close around her, so presumably she was his betrothed or his wife, although she seemed less keen to be close to him – as he watched she shied away and put an arm's length between them. She looked melancholy. Perhaps they weren't betrothed. He should stop staring. He must.

William saw him looking and expelled a long breath of his own. 'She is a brave girl, to be out so soon after her father's death, but I suppose she has a family to feed.'

Edwin didn't quite make the connection, but he couldn't speak anyway. He hoped his look would ask the question for him.

William nodded. 'It is Alys, the daughter of Nicholas. We buried her father this afternoon.'

The words bit so deeply, so personally, that Edwin felt tears coming unbidden to his eyes. He looked at the girl and felt the first crack appearing in his heart. He stood unmoving as it widened, rending itself in two, and his life's blood poured out. It would never be entirely his again, a piece of it lost forever. As he watched, she lifted her head to speak with the stall-holder, and Edwin observed her pale, fragile cheeks. How he wanted to care for her. How he wanted to protect her. For the second time that day, he made a vow, more solemn than the last. He would find who had killed her father, and he would keep her safe.

William was looking at him quizzically. He should say something. What should he say? 'Who's the man?'

'One of Nicholas's weavers. Aldred, I think his name is. Not nearly as good as Ralf the son of Lefwine, whom you met this afternoon – he does the fine patterns while Aldred turns out the cheaper stuff. I suppose he is accompanying her as she has no man to look after her now – the older brothers are still missing and the younger ones are children.'

Oh, you're wrong, thought Edwin, for she does have someone to look after her, someone who would do anything for her. But his attention was dragged away from her face by something else. 'A weaver?'

'Yes. Why, should he not be?'

'No, no, it's just – oh, never mind.' He gripped William's arm.

'They're coming over.' He could feel himself becoming hot and red. What would he say to her?

William greeted her, speaking kindly. 'Alys. Should you be out this evening, so soon after your father's funeral? Could you not stay in and rest?'

Now that she was closer, Edwin could see that she was not perhaps as fragile as she might have appeared at first. There was something in her eyes. This only made him admire her more.

She spoke with composure. 'Thank you for your concern, Master Mayor, but I have the children to feed. I thought it better to try and find something this evening to bring home for them to eat tomorrow, in case there was nothing in the morning.'

The man with her interrupted. 'And of course she has me to protect her.' He laid one hand on her arm. William was smiling at him paternally, so Edwin thought that he alone could have seen the look which Alys gave her companion; not quite hatred, but something akin to it. If her eyes could have burned a hole in that hand which had dared to touch her, they would. There was something wrong here, and Edwin wanted to find out what it was, longed to strike away that touch which was so obnoxious to her. He looked directly at her, and found her staring back.

William spoke again. 'Forgive me. Alys, this is my nephew Edwin, who is visiting from the north.'

The ghost of a smile played across her face as she curtseyed. 'I am pleased to meet you, sir, but I must say that your timing is very bad.'

He nodded, not willing to risk saying anything in case he fell over his words.

William spoke again. 'And still no word of your brothers, I fear?'

Edwin could almost feel the waves of pain emanating from her, but her voice remained level. 'No, Master William. But we must live in hope. Now, if you will forgive me, I must get home to my little ones.'

'Of course, of course. And would you like us to accompany you? We could just about make it there and back before the curfew, even with my aged gait.'

Good Lord, thought Edwin, even the ancient William is stirred to gallantry. But yes, he wanted to go with her, to keep her safe on her way back home.

As she opened her mouth to reply, he saw the man increase the pressure on her arm, and she declined. Damn fellow! Who did he think he was? She was obviously not welcoming his attentions, so what was he doing? Edwin felt indignant. But there was nothing he could do as the two of them marched off, and William turned in the opposite direction to head back to his house. 'Come, you must tell me what else you have learned this day.' Edwin cast one final glance over his shoulder and then followed him, past the towering cathedral, seeming even taller in the dusk, and into the maze of streets.

He was hungry. His insides groaned and cried out for food so that he couldn't concentrate on anything else. He hadn't dared to go home for three days, since the night he'd been followed. He and his father had parted ways, and he didn't know what had happened after that, only that he had to run and hide. During the long dark night he'd doubled back and forth through the streets of the town, using every alley and yard he knew, and finally he thought he'd shaken off the shadowy figure who was following him. There were traitors in Lincoln, this he knew, fellow citizens who had sold themselves to the French invaders rather than trying to defend their city. He despised them. All true men should be helping those who resisted the enemy; but someone, somewhere, was trying to find out what they had been doing, and they wouldn't stop until they knew. He would have to move again, even though the light hadn't yet gone completely; he'd been in this hiding place for nearly a day and he couldn't risk being found. Besides, if he didn't get something to eat soon he felt he might die anyway.

As he slipped out of the ruins of the house, something was thrown over his head, blinding him. A cloth, a sack, something. He struggled hard and tried to cry out, but a hard punch to the stomach sucked the breath out of him and left him gasping, winded, unable to speak. The sacking was tied around his neck and he could see nothing as arms encircled him like a band and forced him to walk. Then he was thrown on to something hard, which started to move. Blinded, breath-less and in pain, he couldn't keep track of where they were going, and he simply lay, trying to collect his wits for the questioning which he knew would follow.

Eventually the movement stopped, and he was being grabbed, pulled out of the cart. He felt that he was inside a building, and was shoved forward into a space. He stood, and then the sack was taken off his face. He blinked and looked around him. He could tell nothing of his location save that he was in a bare room, which he took to be an undercroft. The only door was shut, presumably locked. He could see one other person in the room in front of him, and he looked full into the face. He gasped.

And then he knew fear, and pain.

———•◦•———

It was dark. Edwin lay wrapped in a blanket on the floor of William's shop, staring upwards and breathing in the aroma of spices. As his chest rose and fell, he tried to order the thoughts in his mind, but they wouldn't stay still – they skittered and scattered, refusing to do as he wished. Someone, somewhere, had been organising resistance against the French invaders, and someone, somewhere, must know something about it that he could tell those inside the castle and the regent's host. Had he only been here a day? The people of the city were much clearer in his mind than those outside. Those in the castle were hazy, the regent's host further away still, and any thoughts of a life before that were just a fading memory. One face kept appearing before the others in his mind, but he tried to push it firmly away to concentrate on the huge task which threatened to overwhelm him, to send him mad. Think again. Think straight. The man Alan had been in communication with someone in the city. Initially William had been involved, but then he'd been shut out – no wonder, if he'd been behaving like he had today – and Alan had been talking to someone else. It could be anyone. No. It would be someone with at least some influence on others or on events. Who had he met today? Peter of the Bail and Peter of the Bridge, the merchants, although he still didn't know which was which. Master Michael of the cathedral works, who William thought was a spy, though with little justification from what he could see. Aldred, the man he had taken for a mason but who was a weaver. Pinel, who was Alys's neighbour. Gervase, the younger man; there was also a priest called Father Eustace and a dead man by the name of Nicholas Holland, whose two sons were missing. Any of them were likely candidates. And how did Nicholas's death fit into this? A murder. Had he been the organiser of the resistance, struck down by a traitor? Or had he himself been a spy for the French who had been stopped by the loyal men? Or had he simply been killed for the purse at his belt? That was something he could find out tomorrow. Now he had to keep thinking, despite the sleep which was trying to overwhelm him. He had been awake all last night and the exhaustion was creeping into his bones, but he had to fight it off.

With a start he heard the cathedral bell sounding for Matins in the distance. Had he fallen asleep? Or had he simply been staring into the darkness that long? The men inside the castle would be letting a rope down for him, unaware of how little progress he had made in his quest. The threads were as tangled as ever and he didn't know if he had the wits to make sense of them. The perfume of spices was very relaxing, and brought to mind the face of a girl, a girl who wouldn't leave his thoughts …

By the time the bell sounded for Lauds, he was fast asleep.

———•———

As Alys walked through the market alone the following morning and spoke to some of the stallholders, she heard that the price of food had gone up even since yesterday. She hadn't had a pleasant journey home that afternoon, in the company of the odious Aldred, but she had at least persuaded him to walk home via the market so that she could buy something to eat. She hated to admit it, but his presence had probably been the main reason why she'd managed to reach her home without being molested: carrying a basket of food through the beleaguered city was becoming a more and more dangerous exercise, as starving people watched with hollow faces and empty eyes. She'd paid for it, though: he'd made her give some of the provisions to him, still claiming that he was starving, although he looked strong enough. She contented herself with despising the sort of man who would steal bread from the mouths of children. And so here she was again. The business of being solely responsible for the little ones was exhausting, but it had to be done, and if not by her, then by whom?

She saw Peter of the Bridge and Peter of the Bail looking at some of the stalls, their heads close together, probably discussing some spiteful gossip, as usual. She would try to get past them without being noticed. As she drew near and passed them with her head turned aside, she overheard a part of their conversation.

'Well, it's no secret that she entertains men there, you know.'

'I know, I know, for how else is a widow to make a living? She's very young and attractive, probably makes quite a tidy sum out of it.'

'It's not decent, I tell you. She should marry again.'

'Yes, but that would deprive many of our good merchants of agreeable company. Haven't you ever…?'

'How dare … Oh Miss Alys, how nice to see you!'

They had seen her. Quickly, she tried to look unconcerned and hoped they hadn't realised they'd been overheard. She wanted to walk on, but now they'd greeted her she would have to stop or it would be taken as a gross incivility.

As she turned, they both hurried over. She tried to look pleasant as they oozed compassion, but it was hard going. Irritated, she decided to strike back, and asked them innocently what they had been speaking of. She was rewarded by a look of some guilt from Peter of the Bridge, but Peter of the Bail merely smiled and said they had been discussing the sudden appearance from nowhere of William's nephew.

Peter of the Bridge took the opportunity of the change of subject and waded straight in. 'And do you not fancy, Miss Alys, that there is something strange about that?'

She ventured no opinion, feeling sorry for the young man who had made her heart beat a little faster the previous day. But it didn't stop the diatribe. They seemed really riled – perhaps she shouldn't have goaded them in such a way, for the poor stranger was sure to suffer if they took against him.

'Can he really be William's nephew? He doesn't look like a wool merchant's son to me – did you see the state of that tunic?'

Peter of the Bail threw up his hands in horror. 'The fabric! I can scarcely credit that anyone would sell that. It almost looks homespun.'

Peter of the Bridge sniggered. 'But perhaps they make their own clothes out of what nobody will buy?'

Alys pitied the young man even more. 'Is it not possible that he simply put on such a tunic for travelling, so that he should not be too conspicuous on the road?'

They were silent for a moment. Then Peter of the Bridge continued. 'Well, in any case, I intend to test him. If he is a merchant's son then he will have knowledge of different fabrics and their names, qualities and costs. If that young man has ever worked in a shop I shall – I shall eat my hood!'

They giggled, and then Peter of the Bail nudged his companion. 'But look – here they come. Let us go over to the stall there and intercept them.'

Both men started scurrying, and Alys trailed along behind them, hoping to be able to limit the damage, and drawn to the man who was about to be tested.

As they reached the stall she examined the contents of it. Poor stuff, certainly – nothing like what her father traded in. Or what she traded in, she supposed she should say now, at least until either Thomas or Nick came back, or until such time as she married. Married? Why had that thought leaped into her head all of a sudden? It wasn't surprising that it should be at the back of her mind, of course, as with anyone her age, but it certainly hadn't been to the fore for a good number of weeks. She felt herself blushing and examined the fabrics more closely as William and his nephew approached.

The stallholder, facing hardship but now presumably thinking that his luck was in, expounded on the number and quality of wares he had available even in these difficult times.

As the two newcomers were greeted, Peter of the Bridge began to speak in an unnecessarily loud voice. 'So, fellow, how much is that sarsenet there?'

'Sevenpence the yard, sir, and a finer you will not find …'

Peter of the Bail cut him off with a wave. 'Yes, yes, but look, Peter, at the cambric. Would that not do for some new hangings in your chamber?'

Alys looked under her eyelashes at the young man – Edwin – as Peter haggled the man down to one shilling the yard for the cambric, and started another discussion about needing some cheaper burel to make new clothing for his servants. He wasn't looking at her, but she got the feeling that he might have been a moment ago.

The Peters were finally coming to the point. 'So, let me see, I have perhaps a mark of silver available, and I may want eight yards of the burel at fourpence the yard, four yards of the sarsenet at sevenpence, and – now, if the cambric is for hangings I will want five ells, but at a shilling the yard …' they were giggling together like a couple of apprentices, but as they turned smugly towards their victim, he interjected before they could draw breath.

His voice was amiable. 'Eleven shillings and threepence, Master Peter, so you would have two shillings and a penny left from your mark.'

Alys had to put her hand over her mouth to stifle a smile. She didn't think she'd ever seen anyone deflate so quickly. Both Peters were completely speechless, a sight she certainly hadn't seen before. William, unaware of the undercurrents in the conversation, was congratulating his nephew.

'Well done, Edwin. My sister and goodbrother have taught you well – I have never known anyone reckon so quickly. A real merchant's son.'

Peter of the Bail was looking spitefully at Edwin, and Alys realised he hadn't finished the test yet.

'Yes, a fine calculation, young man. Perhaps you would be kind enough to pass me the bolt of cambric so that I may inspect it more closely?'

Edwin agreed, but Alys saw the slightest hesitation as he looked over the stall. She was not going to let the Peters win their nasty game.

'Here, let me help you, you won't be able to reach across me from there.' Smoothly she picked up the fine white linen and passed it over to him. Their eyes met, and she caught a glimpse of his relief before he dropped his gaze.

The Peters didn't look too happy at being bested, but they hadn't seen what she had seen, and were content to take Edwin at face value. The stallholder was looking hopefully at Peter of the Bridge, perhaps unable to believe that nearly a whole mark of silver was about to come his way. He was right, it wasn't: Peter turned on his heel and strode off, followed shortly by his companion, leaving the man staring after them. He spat disgustedly on the ground and looked pointedly at the rest of them until they moved on. William was asking her if they could assist her in any way, but before she could reply, the gaunt figure of Master Michael stalked up to them.

He took her hand. 'Alys. My dear girl. I wanted to speak to you yesterday after your poor father's funeral but didn't have the leisure as I had to return here straight away. I haven't asked you about his final moments – was he shriven? Was he in the Lord's grace?'

She assured him that this was the case, hoping he would drop the subject, but he seemed particularly keen to continue it, probing further.

'And did he never recover consciousness before he died? You weren't able to speak with him?'

She was on her guard immediately. What business of his was it whether he had regained his wits? And why did everyone seem so interested? Of course, there was one obvious answer to that question, but it didn't mean that she was about to go telling the whole marketplace. How could she know whom to trust?

Aid came to her in the form of the young man she now knew was not a wool merchant's son. 'Mistress, you look so pale all of a sudden. Are you quite all right?' He stepped forward in concern.

She took the hint, raising one arm wearily to her head and agreeing that yes, everything had taken a toll on her, and she would like to go home and rest.

Master Michael looked as though he might press the point, or even offer to walk with her, but again Edwin forestalled him, encouraging William to take her arm and lead her off. There was no arguing with that – if the mayor wanted to walk her home then she could not be in better hands. She would be glad to escape.

Edwin hoped he'd done the right thing. People just wouldn't leave her alone, and she needed some peace. But he was forestalled in his efforts, for the man whose name he hadn't learned had appeared again, and he looked agitated. As he approached he took off his cap, and he stood screwing it in his hands. He opened his mouth but seemed unable to speak.

Everyone stopped and looked at him as he stammered. It was Alys who finally broke the silence. 'Yes, Ralf, what is it?'

Ralf – aha, finally – blushed a deep red. 'I – mistress, there's something I have to tell you.' He looked around him. 'Perhaps we could speak privately?'

Alys seemed about to answer, but one of the Peters stepped forward with a smirk on his face. Edwin wanted to hit him. No doubt he wanted to hear whatever gossip it was, hoping it would be hurtful to someone. 'For shame, man, do you think we will let you walk off with an unescorted young woman? If you have something to say, say it to all of us.'

Ralf was in an agony of awkwardness, almost hopping up and down. He addressed Alys alone, pleading with her. 'Please, miss, please. It's about your father. I need to tell you what he was doing the night he was struck down.'

Alys had turned as white as an altar cloth. Edwin was in a dilemma: he desperately wanted to spare her any pain, wanted to whisk her away so she could speak to the man in peace, but he needed to hear what was going to come next.

Once Ralf had spoken the words in public, though, it seemed there was no turning back. All the men were crowding round him, demanding that he say more.

He screwed his cap even more between his hands and spoke to Alys again. 'You see miss – I'm worried about his soul. He was a good master, the best I've ever had, and yet he was sinning, and I'm not sure he will be allowed into heaven.

And I need to tell you what I've done – I can't keep quiet any longer!'

There was a deep silence. Ralf took a gasping breath and plunged in further. 'I would see him, often, leaving the house. As I was locking up the weaving shed. I knew it was none of my business, but I wondered where he was going. So one night, as it was getting dark, I saw him slipping out of the alley between the houses and up the street, and I couldn't help myself – I followed him.'

Edwin realised he was holding his breath. He looked around him to see that every eye, Alys's included, was riveted on the weaver. She was holding one hand out as though she really did want to guide him to a quiet corner now to speak privately, but it was too late.

Ralf was continuing. 'I followed him all the way up through town – I couldn't think where he might be going. He went right past the place where all those houses had been knocked down, and kept going up to the northern part of the town. I saw him knock on a door and go in.'

He stopped, looking straight at Alys. Peter of the Bridge couldn't contain himself, and burst out. 'But whose house? Damn it, man, tell us more!'

Ralf's eyes never left Alys. 'It was the widow Gunnilda's house.'

Edwin had absolutely no idea who this woman was, or why the mention of the name should have such an effect on everyone round him. He looked at them in turn. Both Peters had a look of cruel triumph, though one of them was gloating more than the other. Master Michael was unreadable. William merely looked sad, a little disappointed. And Alys – well, there were so many emotions on her face that he couldn't hope to read them all. There was definitely surprise, and a huge anger.

Everyone now looked at her, William offering his arm as a support. But she wasn't weak – she was furious.

'How dare you! How *dare* you say such things about my father, with him hardly cold in his grave!'

The words tumbled out of Ralf as he backed away from such anger. 'Mistress, I – I didn't mean to cause trouble, I've been so sorry since I found out, I didn't know how to tell you, or whether to say anything to him ...'

She was almost spitting. 'Lies! My father would never go out to see another woman at night. Never! He loved my mother.'

William tried to placate her, laying a hand on her arm. 'My dear, you know, your mother has been dead a very long time, and men do need ... female company.' He cleared his throat.

Alys rounded on him. 'So now you know my father better than me? I'm telling you, he wouldn't go to see another woman, and that is *not* what he was doing.' Her voice broke and she started to sob. Belatedly all the men became more gallant, but Edwin managed to get himself between them and her, so that only William was offering support. He kept the others at bay until William and Alys had walked off. Ralf began to slink off in the other direction, and Edwin left Master Michael and the Peters to themselves. He didn't care what they spoke of – he just needed some time to think.

Of course, in such a large city there was not likely to be a quiet place anywhere, not like at home, and he found himself surrounded by people on all sides. He became agitated, bumping into the people who crowded him, and receiving evil looks and a few shoves in reply. This was no good; he needed some space and some peace. He needed to calm down. Eventually he took his eyes off the hurly-burly around him and looked up. Of course! There would be quiet and somewhere to think in there. He made his way into the cathedral.

As he entered the great stone building he felt the cool air and the space, the high vaults soaring to the heavens. Footsteps echoed on the tiled floor, but there were fewer people in here, and the sound was not intrusive. He stopped and inhaled the aroma of the incense which remained from a previous service. He forced himself to remain, breathing, until his heart had stilled a little, and then he looked around him. Finding a corner, he moved to it and knelt in prayer – firstly, for the souls of those dear to him whom he had lost, and secondly, for some divine guidance as to what he should do next. He was clueless. He'd been so sure that Nicholas had been the key, that he'd been trying to find his way to the castle when he was attacked, and now it seemed that this wasn't the case. He'd wasted his precious time on a thread which turned out not to be part of the weaving, and if he didn't come up with something else within the next few hours, all would be lost. If he had ever needed to pray, it was now.

As he knelt and offered up his desperate supplications to the Lord the cathedral emptied, and stillness reigned. There were a few others here and there, perhaps praying for the safety of loved ones, but they were as silent as he, and he was able to shut them out as he drew closer into his own thoughts. He stayed on his knees as he tried to empty his mind. If the Lord wanted him to find out the truth, he would help him in some way. Here in this holy place He would guide the thoughts of His humble servant. Edwin clasped his hands and prayed for salvation.

Alys fidgeted as she watched the children eat. How could Ralf say such things about Papa? They couldn't possibly be true, for she knew what he'd been doing on the night he was attacked. Or did she? Perhaps ... no, he wouldn't have lied on his deathbed. But maybe there had been other nights, other times where he had slipped off in the dark to visit the woman – after all, hadn't she said in the street the other day that she knew Papa? Surely not; it was unthinkable. He wouldn't have forgotten Mama that way. But …

She needed to stop thinking about that. There would be time enough in the future to try and unravel the threads of what had happened, but for now she needed to concentrate on the task ahead. First she needed to get the children fed and in bed, for she couldn't leave them otherwise. They'd grown to depend upon her so much that they gathered close around her all the time, as though she were a rock and they adrift in the river. Even now, small hands clutched at her skirts. She would put them to bed first and then go out, although she chafed at the delay. Forcing herself to be patient, she shepherded them upstairs and into her father's bedroom. It seemed eerie and somehow wrong for them all to be in there, but he no longer needed the large bed – Lord rest his soul – and they may as well sleep in it rather than on the straw mattresses on the floor in the other room. She settled them in the bed and drew the covers around them. Margery and Edric looked wan and Randal was crying again, so she sat by the side of the bed holding his hand, seeking to give comfort where there was little to be had, and waited for them all to fall asleep.

She awoke a little later, having fallen into a light doze. She felt exhausted, drained. And yet she must try again.

What was that?

A noise had sounded from outside, from the yard which was shared by the four houses. Her heart thumping as though it would force itself from her body, she crept down the stairs into the kitchen and peered out between the cracks of the shuttered window. It was night, but the moon was nearly full, and as the clouds came and went across it in the stiff breeze the garden was illuminated in stark black and white. She could see nothing untoward as her eyes swept the yard; perhaps her fear had made her imagine things. She was preparing to move away from the window when something caught her eye to one side of her: something had been left by the door. She couldn't make out what it was: a large, shapeless object.

She looked again out into the garden, more suspiciously, but could see nothing, no movement. She ached with the dilemma facing her, but eventually curiosity won out. Cautiously she unbarred the door and began to open it.

Chapter Seven

Edwin knelt in the cool silence of the cathedral, thoughts scattering like sheep in his mind as he tried to order them. Start from the beginning. There was some sort of resistance in the town which was meant to help the castle. But what exactly is it I'm supposed to be looking for? Is it a cache of weapons? Some kind of information that would stop the siege engines or that would help a relieving force? There was no way of knowing. But someone in the city knew what it was, and he'd failed in his task of finding out who. Try as he might, he kept coming back to Nicholas Holland. Had he really been going out that night in search of his mistress? Ralf seemed to think so, and the others had all been ready to believe him. No, not all – Alys had been certain that that wasn't it. But was she just a naïve girl who wouldn't believe any ill of her father? He tried to summon up an image of her face. It wasn't difficult. He saw her as he'd seen her this afternoon, tried to analyse her expression again as it had been when she heard Ralf's tale. There had been anger, surprise, and something else. What was it? He screwed his eyes up even tighter as he tried to look more closely at the picture in his head. Surprise, anger, and … yes – that was it. A look of relief. But what did that mean? He sighed, shifted his position and started all over again. Someone had tried to help the castle …

As the afternoon drew on into evening, and the cold of the hard stone floor seeped into his knees, he tried one last prayer. Please Lord, help me. Help me not for myself, but for all the people here who will suffer and perhaps die if I don't succeed. It's growing dark and I need to be back at the castle tonight, yet I have nothing to say. What is the missing clue? This is probably blasphemous, but Father, if you are up there among the saints and the blessed, please ask one of them to intercede for me. I need your help.

He felt a touch on his arm and saw an aged, wrinkled hand. His breath stopped. But the hand belonged not to a spirit. It was William.

'Edwin – there you are. I have been looking for you everywhere. Master Michael said he had seen you enter earlier, but I had not thought you would still be here.'

Edwin tried to rise, but his knees were stiff. William put out a hand to help him, but his balance wasn't good, and the two of them were nearly bowled over by a slight man in a dark cloak and red hat, who stopped to offer an apology and help them up. Edwin recognised him as being the neighbour of Alys. Not the young man Gervase, but the other one, the one who lived on the other side. Pinel, that was it. As the man assured himself that they were both all right and turned to move away, the Lord finally whispered in Edwin's ear. He gripped William's arm.

'Nicholas Holland. Was he shorter than most men? Perhaps a little smaller and slighter than me?'

'Why yes, if you must know. But what has that got to do with –'

'I have to go.'

'Now?'

'Yes, now. I have only a short time left and there is someone I must speak to.' He reached out and gripped the old man's hand. 'Thank you, William, for what you've done for me, and may the Lord keep you safe in the days to come.'

He turned and ran out of the cathedral into the darkened streets.

———

Alys gulped as she unbarred the door and started to open it. She was cautious, pulling it softly, but all of a sudden the weight of the object shoved the door inwards and opened it fully. A corpse collapsed into the room, thumping on to the floor in front of her, and before she could help herself she screamed and screamed and screamed.

She knew she was doing it, and knew she had to stop, but somehow she had lost control of her voice, and she had to gather up her apron and stuff it into her mouth to control her frenzied outburst. Eventually she managed to quieten herself and stood, huge shudders running through her body.

Sounds of alarm came from upstairs. She'd woken the children. They must be terrified up there, thinking someone had got in the house. She must go to reassure them. She was halfway up the stairs before she wondered what in the Lord's name she was going to tell them. She couldn't reveal the truth. She reached the top and just stood as they gathered round her. But merely seeing her alive and unharmed seemed to quell their fear a little, and they allowed her to calm them with soothing words which came unbidden to her lips. They became content enough to be put back in bed, so she tucked them in and went back down. As she stood at the bottom of the stairs, a vague hope stirred in her that she'd been imagining things and that a normal kitchen scene would await her. She closed her eyes as she entered, praying before she opened them.

The corpse lay spread on the floor, face down, the door behind it gaping into the night. She stood, unmoving. She knew who it was, knew who it must be, but somehow, if she didn't touch it, didn't turn it over to see the face, it wouldn't be real.

Time passed.

She knew she had to face it. Standing here would do no good. She moved forward towards the body, then stopped. She stoked the small fire to get as much light as possible, and knelt down.

She took a deep breath and reached out gently to touch the boy's shoulder. For boy it was: there was no doubt of his identity. He was wearing the familiar tunic of best scarlet which was slightly too small, which he had been wearing when he went missing. Oh Nick, what has happened to you since that day? Her hand lingered tenderly on his shoulder for a moment before she turned him over.

He rolled on to his back, and she scrabbled away in horror. His dear face was almost unrecognisable, bloody, lacerated and swollen. More blood crusted the front of his tunic, and both of his hands were covered in it. What had he been through? Fourteen years old and beaten to death in the town that was his home. She gathered her brother to her, his head in her lap, and embraced him as she rocked back and forth, weeping.

Once the storm inside her mind had subsided a little, Alys was able to realise that sitting on the kitchen floor with the back door wide open might not be the safest place for her to be. Especially given that somebody had already been in the yard once that night to leave Nick's body on the threshold. She laid his head down carefully, unwilling to cause any further damage, and forced her shaking legs to straighten and carry her to the door. She shut it, checking several unnecessary times that the latch was firmly in its place, and then barred it and wedged a stool under it as well. Then she turned back to Nick's body. There was no way she would be able to carry it upstairs on her own, and anyway she was determined not to wake the children again. Let them sleep if they could, giving them a few more hours before they needed to return to their waking nightmare to find that another loved one had died – had been murdered.

With some difficulty she lifted him into a sitting position and put her arms around him, clasping her hands in front of his chest. Then she heaved him backwards out of the kitchen and into the shop, his feet dragging in the rushes on the floor. Once inside the front room she laid him down again and considered how best to proceed. The shop counter was too high, and besides, that would be somehow unseemly. The small part of her mind which had retained its wits wondered how on earth she could consider something unseemly when here she was in the middle of a war, dragging a dead body through the house in the dark on her own, but there it was. And he was too young to be laid out in such a formal way. He was barely a year younger than her; of all the family they had been the closest in age, and the memories of their childhood came rushing at her, the cold body making way in her mind for the imp with the roguish smile, the tricks he'd played and the scrapes he'd dragged her into.

She knew what she would do. Heedless of the value of the cloth, she dragged a bolt of linen down from its shelf and unrolled yards and yards of it, making it into a soft bed in front of the hearth. Then she hauled him over to it and laid him down, rising again to position two thick rolls of broadcloth between him and the rest of the room. There. Now he had his own cosy little den next to the fire, like the ones he used to make as a little boy, whenever he could get away with it. Then she knelt by him and prayed for his safe passage into God's grace, another soul who had passed over and left her alone.

———

The hill was getting steeper, and Edwin slipped down the final few feet as he neared the bottom. As he regained his balance he thought he heard a noise. He paused. There it was again. Footsteps and a jingling sound – a group of men heading this way; armed. He peered about him for somewhere to hide. In the darkness he made out a narrow alley between two houses and ducked into it, just in time. He stood as still as his heart would let him, trying not to breathe too heavily, as a group of soldiers tramped by. They were French; their accent was difficult to make out, but he understood enough to learn that they weren't searching for anyone in particular – it was a routine patrol, and they were bored. They passed very close to the opening of the alley, and he held his breath until they moved on, but just at that moment his stomach made a loud growling noise and he clutched it in a panic, screwing up his eyes with fear. He waited. They hadn't heard it. They were continuing on their way, and the sound of their feet gradually receded. Edwin became conscious of the fact that all his muscles were clenched and he tried to make himself relax. He hadn't realised how hungry he was, but now he came to think about it, it was a fair while since he'd had anything to eat and he was starving. This was hardly the time to go looking for a meal, so the quicker he completed his mission, the quicker he might be able to fill the void in his stomach. Cautiously he peered out from the alley, nervous in case the men should have left one of their number watching silently, but he couldn't see anyone. He stepped out on to the main street to continue on his way.

At the foot of the steep hill the road split into two, and he followed the left-hand route which led him down a shallower incline with more houses close on either side. Here there were fewer marks of destruction; presumably the fighting had passed by this part of town. The only damage he could see were a couple of shutters which were hanging crooked from one or two of the buildings.

When he judged that he was about halfway down the street he stopped. He looked at the buildings on the left. How was he to tell which was the right one? They all looked the same with the shutters closed. He hadn't thought of this. As he considered what to do next, he sheltered in the lee of one of the houses, leaning against the door as he looked up and down the street. As he stood there it opened, and he fell.

Alys looked down at the body. The prayers had dried up and she had been kneeling in silence for some while now. She knew what she must do; it was just that she could not summon the will or the energy to do it. She must complete the task. She must finish the work that her father and brother had died for, so that their deaths might not be in vain. It was possible that she held the key which would save the city. And yet she couldn't move from the floor. She knew that she ought to be afraid for herself and for the others asleep upstairs – if she too were to die then who would take care of them? But somehow she wasn't frightened, she could feel no emotion. If she didn't do something then they would all die anyway, so what was the difference?

She needed to shrug off this inertia. Had Papa's and Nick's deaths been for nothing? They had tried and tried, and was she now to be the member of the family who would let them down? She would not. The task must be completed. If she were to be killed then the children must try to survive as best they could until Thomas returned; the neighbours or the priest would help to look after them. She gathered up her skirts and her courage and rose, stretching her aching muscles. She would just have to risk making her way through the town during the dead of night. It meant that there would be fewer people about who might see her, but that anybody who was out and about was probably up to no good. Still, the message must be delivered. She crept towards the front door and gathered her shawl around her. She couldn't really believe that she was about to do this, but then, it was also beyond belief that the city which had been her home for all of her life should be crawling with French soldiers, that she should have been left to assume the role of head of the family, with no father or brothers to support her, and that Nick's murdered corpse should be lying by the hearth. The whole world was going mad, so she might as well accept it and step out into the fast-flowing river of the times. Steeling herself, she opened the door.

A man fell into the room, and she screamed.

It was so like what had happened earlier that in her initial panic she thought it might be another body, but this one was definitely alive. She was immediately aware that she hadn't picked up anything to carry with her which she might use to defend herself – how naïve and foolish! – and she looked around in a panic for anything she might use as a weapon. Unfortunately the shop was full only of the bolts of cloth, which wouldn't be much use. The man started to rise, and she kicked him hard in the ribs, still terrified. There was nothing else she could do. Almost out of her senses with fright, she kicked him again and again, trying to push him out of the door so that she could bar it.

He was saying something, but she couldn't hear it at first. Then it broke through her consciousness. 'Stop, stop, please! I haven't come to hurt you.'

Startled by the lack of hostility in his voice, she ceased her kicking and stood back warily, still searching the room for something to use as a weapon. Then he looked up: it was Edwin. She backed away.

He raised himself to a kneeling position, holding his ribs as though in some pain, and spoke with care. 'I haven't come to hurt you – I just want to talk.' He repeated himself. 'I won't hurt you. See?' Slowly he moved his hands and held them out to either side of himself, away from his body. He held nothing in them, although she could see that there was a dagger hanging from his belt. He had clearly made no attempt to draw it.

She took a deep breath and stood, shuddering. 'What do you want?'

'Well, for a start I'd like you to stop kicking me.'

The tone surprised her. The voice didn't contain any malice. She waited. He shifted position and she was immediately on the defensive again. 'If you move I can scream loudly enough to wake my family and the neighbours before you can get to me.'

He froze. 'Please don't. See, I'm not moving.' He kept his hands away from his body.

'All right. But tell me why you're here. We have nothing to steal, there's no money or food.'

For some reason he seemed tongue-tied. This was not her idea of a violent housebreaker or soldier intent on looting, nor yet a murdering spy, but she remained on edge. She had been drawn to him earlier, but when all was said and done he wasn't a local man and she had no reason to trust him. She looked more closely at him. He was definitely not from anywhere around here or from anywhere they traded: the weave of his tunic was not one she had seen before.

Finally he replied, looking if anything slightly abashed. 'I suppose I may as well tell you, as I can't think of anything else to say. I know what your father was really doing the night he was killed, and I need to talk to you about it.'

Her surprise was total, and she was speechless. She couldn't order her thoughts. How best to react? Was this some kind of trap? Or could it be that this man was one of her father's co-conspirators?

The silence grew longer as they stared at each other; he still kneeling, she backed against the shop's counter. She felt breathless, unable to speak a word. Why was he looking at her like that? Why could he possibly be here? Who was he? The decision she was about to make might have catastrophic consequences either way: if she let him in and he was an enemy, she could be dead within moments; if he was a friend and she sent him away, she might miss her best chance of helping to save the city. She considered him again. Her eyes had grown accustomed to the darkness, and the moon gave some illumination through the open door. He looked young and his eyes were friendly. He still showed no sign of violence, but this could all be a deception. He certainly wasn't the merchant he'd claimed to be, and probably wasn't even William's nephew. So what if he was lying now? But then again, why had William trusted him? Had he been taken in by the stranger, or did he know something which she didn't? She was torn by the agony of indecision. Still Edwin waited for her reply, saying nothing. What was she to do?

As the moments passed her resolve grew stronger. This might be the most hopelessly foolish thing she had ever done, but if the city was to be saved then chances would have to be taken.

And, all said and done, if she was going to die then she would rather do it here in her home than out on the cold streets, where her father and brother had met their ends.

She moved around him and shut the door. 'You'd better come in.'

They sat in the kitchen, facing each other across the table, where she had placed a burning rushlight. It wasn't as good as a candle, for it spluttered and spat flickering shadows across the room, but it was better than sitting in the dark with a strange man, and besides, she had used the last candles during the vigil over her father's body so there was no other choice. Also on the table was his dagger in its ornate scabbard, which he had placed there as a sign of good faith. She glanced down at it, knowing nothing of such weapons but aware that it looked to be a fine thing, much finer than the man in front of her, judging by his clothes. The fabric was some kind of tabby weave, and not of the highest quality either, as Peter had been so quick to point out – probably homespun and certainly not of the standard which her father would sell. But the dagger drew her attention; it was definitely a weapon, not an everyday knife – a blade whose purpose was to maim and kill, and the sight of it made her shiver.

As she'd ushered him into the back of the house she'd paused at the bottom of the stairs, listening carefully for any sign of movement, but thank the Lord it seemed the children hadn't wakened again. Their fear had led to exhaustion and they hadn't stirred. Nor had there been any sign of life from Mistress Guildersleeve's house next door or from Master Pinel on the other side; perhaps her scream hadn't been as loud as it had seemed to her, or perhaps they had heard it and were too frightened to come and investigate.

Edwin, too, had paused ahead of her at the foot of the stairs, and again she felt the danger they were in – if he wanted to go up the stairs, she wouldn't be able to stop him. Ice-cold blood ran through her at the thought, but as she was wavering about her decision he moved on into the kitchen. Now they sat, and all around them was silence.

It was she who broke the deadlock. 'How do you know what he was doing?'

'Well, he was out in the night during a dangerous time, so there were only three possibilities.' He ticked off the numbers on his fingers as he spoke. 'One, he was a spy for the French and was going to talk to them. Two, he was going to visit the widow Gunnilda, as Ralf said. Or three, he was working for those inside the castle and was trying to contact them.'

'And?'

'If he'd been a spy for the French, he would probably have been near their encampment, not in the area of the town where he was found. I know that was where he was when he was hit, because there was a stone there with blood all over it … Oh. Sorry.'

The nausea passed, but bitterness came behind it. 'This afternoon everyone seemed very eager to believe it was the second of your choices.'

He leaned forward. 'But not you. You were adamant that that wasn't what he was doing. You were so sure that I knew you weren't just speaking up for him, for the way he loved your mother. You *knew*. And you could only have known that he was not going to the widow Gunnilda if you *did* know where he was going.'

She nodded.

'And besides, I think I know what Ralf saw. One or two nights, he may well have seen your father, as he was about the town looking for ways to fight the invaders. But Ralf's eyesight is poor, and on the night when he followed someone all the way to the widow's house, it wasn't your father. It was your neighbour Pinel.'

'Pinel! No, he wouldn't. He's a married man …' She tailed off. Actually, when she thought about it, it wasn't all that unbelievable. And that red hat …

She looked at him in silence. He shrugged.

Now she wanted to question him. 'Fine. So you know what Papa was doing on the night he was killed. But who are you? And what have you got to do with all of this?'

He replied cautiously. 'I can't tell you.'

She folded her arms. 'Then I won't tell you what I know.'

He seized on her response. 'So you do know something?'

She was flustered at giving herself away so easily. 'Well, I …' She must get a hold on her mind. Her thoughts were still too jumbled, and this wouldn't do. There was no point in denying it now, so she must work from here. 'Yes. But I won't tell you unless you explain who you are.'

'I told you, I can't say.'

She clenched her folded arms tighter around herself. Could he tell how frightened she was? Probably he could, but now she had started she may as well plough on. 'Then you may leave, for it is the only way you will get your information.' As soon as the words had left her mouth she realised that there were plenty of other, less pleasant ways in which he could get his information and that by sitting in a darkened room in the middle of the night with a strange man, she had left herself open to many of them. She squeezed her arms even tighter, gripping her sides, trying to stop herself from shivering.

He gazed at her steadily and she quailed. But then, for reasons she could not fathom, a look of horror developed on his face. For a moment she thought he was going to be sick, but he collected his wits and spoke. 'All right. I've come from the castle to find out about what's been going on in the town. Those inside believe there may be information available which will help them.'

Briefly, a tide of relief swept over her. He'd come from the castle! He could take the message back so that she wouldn't have to venture out into the streets! But just as quickly she was assailed by suspicion. What if this was all a trick? Again she wrestled with indecision. She looked at him carefully again, inspecting him closely to see if she could gain any awareness of his motives. His face was open and honest, and for some reason she wanted to trust him. Of course, if the enemy was sending spies out to gain information, they too would look open and trustworthy. But she had taken a chance thus far, so why not continue? He had made no move to harm her and besides, if he was a spy, why would he have blurted out straight away what he was looking for?

If she was honest, it came down purely to instinct – she didn't believe he was a traitor.

She sighed.

'As you know, my father is dead.'

Now she'd started, there was no sense in holding anything back. She sent up a small prayer for what she was about to say.

'But he did have information, important information, and before he died he passed it on to me. When I opened the door a few moments ago I was on my way to the castle myself to try and deliver the message. Now you are here you can take it for me – that is, if I'm right about you and you aren't a French spy who will kill me once you know everything.'

For the first time he smiled. 'I suppose you have no reason to trust me, but for what it's worth, I'm not a French spy.' He leaned forward. 'Tell me what you know.'

And so she told him. Not just about what her father and others had been doing these past weeks, but also about his death and what had happened since then, the funeral and the danger on the way home, and the terrible events of that evening. Once she started talking she couldn't stop herself and it all poured out – things she couldn't have told family and neighbours, but things which it suddenly seemed quite natural to divulge to a complete stranger in the middle of the night. The loneliness, the responsibility for the children, the difficulty of providing for them, the fear at being the holder of such valuable information, the sadness of the funeral, the fright in the street on the way back, the determination to rid the city of the invaders, and the absolute, bone-melting terror of what had happened to her father and Nick. It all rushed out in a reckless flood, words she would surely regret in the cold light of day. But she would never see him again, so what did it matter?

Through it all he listened, never saying a word, never interrupting or asking her to come to the point, never belittling her feelings. Instead he sat attentively, waiting for the most important part. And finally she told him; she relayed the information which might be the saving of them all. It was a very short message, but its significance was colossal. And when he heard it, his smile widened until it illuminated the entire room.

Chapter Eight

Edwin listened carefully to Alys, but at the same time he ran over the events of the past half an hour or so. He was glad that the light in the kitchen didn't show his face properly, or she might see how red it was; how humiliating to have been caught off guard without any kind of story to explain his presence. How many other agents of the earl or spies would have been so tongue-tied, so ready to blurt out the real reason for their mission to a complete stranger? And he didn't even want to think of the mortification of having been bested by a girl … he'd been taken by surprise when he fell through the door and he'd had no time to draw his weapon before being attacked. Of course, with hindsight, he was glad that he hadn't, but next time he might not be so lucky – and he certainly didn't intend to tell anyone the exact details of the encounter.

His emotions had ebbed and flowed once they were in the kitchen. He had been wary of removing Sir Reginald's dagger from his belt, but had realised that this might be the quickest way to gain her confidence. Strangely – for he hadn't been used to carrying weapons – he felt naked and exposed without it, although he was reasonably certain that she wouldn't attack him. His thoughts had initially been for his own safety, but once he became aware of the undercurrent of feeling in the room a slow horror came over him at the idea that she might be afraid of him, might consider him capable of violence against her. He was appalled – what must she think of him? He supposed that he shouldn't really care what some strange girl thought of him – he had his task to accomplish and he would never see her again anyway – but deep down he knew that he did care what she … what anyone might think of him. It made him feel sick to imagine that anyone might suppose him a violent ruffian.

And so he had foundered once again. As there was no question of attempting to beat the answer out of her – something he suspected that John Marshal might advocate – he realised he would have to tell her the truth if there was any chance of getting the information he needed. Surely this couldn't be too much of a gamble, as the citizens of Lincoln must be eager to end the siege? He risked it. It was a test, and the Lord was with him; he wasn't punished for his naivety and clumsy tactics. Still, he was embarrassed at his lack of anything resembling a talent for this kind of task, and evidently he wasn't ruthless enough for the work. If by some miracle he should live through this night, he would summon up the courage to tell the earl so. He would. He really would.

But for now he listened carefully. Sympathy pierced him to the heart as he heard the details of the death of her father, his own emotions still raw. As her tale continued, any pity he might have felt turned to admiration at the way she appeared to have handled everything. She wasn't the fragile creature he had imagined when he'd first seen her at the market, but his heart bled nonetheless. Would he have coped so well in a similar situation? She'd managed to feed her family and keep them safe, despite the dangers, and had even taken on the burden of her father's knowledge.

Ah, the information! At last he was about to hear it. Would it be any use? Would he be able to bring glad tidings back to the castle? He listened, and his heart leapt.

Once the news had been given, the weight of responsibility shifted, she fell silent. He looked at her in the flickering half-light, somehow aware, despite not knowing her, that she was happier. He must return to the castle urgently, but he felt himself reluctant to rise. Perhaps it was just tiredness and hunger. He had been on the move for more hours than he cared to remember and was exhausted, and the effect of warmth and rest had induced a feeling of drowsiness and comfort. Yes, that must be it. It couldn't be anything else.

Something else she had said jerked him awake again. In his excitement over the message he hadn't taken it in properly the first time.

'Did you say that your brother has been killed this very night, and that he's here, in the house?'

She nodded, tears coming to her eyes.

'Can I – ' that wasn't going to sound right. 'I mean, would you allow me to look at his body?'

She seemed not to think that this was an odd request, and led him back through to the shop. She pointed over towards the hearth, and by the light of the rush in her hand he saw what he hadn't noticed earlier while he was trying to protect himself against the barrage of kicks – the body of a young boy lying in a nest of cloth. Gingerly he knelt down next to it, as did she. He noticed that her hands went almost instinctively to straighten his clothing and hair, and that her eyes were glassy. She seemed to look through him.

He couldn't put a name to the emotion, but he recognised it, having felt it himself just a few days ago. He had seen too many bodies recently.

He stretched out a hand and then stopped, unsure what her reaction would be. 'Do you mind if I touch him? I might be able to …' he didn't know how he would end the remark, for he wasn't sure what he'd be able to do, but something within him was urging him to look at the body to see if he could discover anything.

Again she nodded, so he moved the light nearer and started to examine the boy.

He was very young, perhaps about the age of Adam, the earl's new squire. He had certainly been the victim of a considerable amount of violence; he had been beaten viciously, and there was blood all over him. A particularly large amount of it seemed to be concentrated over his left hand and arm, and Edwin gently lifted it to get a better look. When he saw the damage he felt queasy: the smallest finger had been hacked off and it had bled profusely. He tried to hide the damage from her, not wanting her to see how much her brother must have suffered. Poor lad, what could have happened to him? But of course he knew the reason: the boy had been aware of the information which he himself now carried, and he had paid the price for it. But had he kept the secret or had the extremes of pain and fear forced him to give it up? That was the question. If the enemy were aware of the information then all might yet be lost. He could say nothing, but looked in silence at Alys. She gazed back at him without speaking.

He continued to stare at her as the silence grew longer and more awkward, aware that he ought to break it and say something. He opened his mouth, but before any words could be said, the tolling of the cathedral bell sounded from afar. The bell! The rope! The importance of his mission flooded back over him. He must get back to the castle now. What was he thinking? He scrambled to his feet, almost falling again in his haste.

She rose, too, and hurried back into the kitchen. He thought at first that she'd become afraid of him again, but she returned almost immediately with his dagger. As she handed it to him their hands touched briefly, and a jolt of feeling ran through him. He tried to disguise it by busying himself attaching it back to his belt. He fumbled and hoped she didn't notice. Once the dagger was safely fastened he stood facing her. Time to say something. He opened his mouth and was again thwarted by a sound, but this time it was the rather more embarrassing one of his stomach giving a loud rumble. It broke the awkwardness, though, and the blank, dazed expression left her face.

'What am I thinking of? You're here to help us and I haven't even offered you anything to eat.' She looked around and seemed to become slightly less confident. 'We have ... some bread and a scraping of pottage left – please, take some before you leave.'

His first instinct was to accept with alacrity, but then he looked at her again, noting even in the dim light that she was tired and wan, dark circles under her eyes. How difficult it must be to care for her brothers and sister in these dangerous times, and how much she'd had to cope with this very evening.

He reached one arm out towards her, but stopped before he touched her. 'No, please, you must keep it for the children.' He paused, unsure of how much to say. 'There will be fighting in the city soon – you must keep yourself safe. May the Lord watch over you.' And with that he turned and walked purposefully back out of the shop and into the street.

———

Honestly, they were like children, the bloody lot of them.

John Marshal stalked up and down inside the tent, sick of all the squabbling between the nobles. Two nights ago he had been able to pick his way back across the open fields unnoticed by the French, had reached his companions, and had made all speed back to the regent's camp to inform his uncle of the news, but since then all they'd done was argue about what they should do and who should be in charge of the attack on the city. For God's sake, why couldn't they just shut up and get *on* with it? Chester in particular was becoming more and more belligerent, and some of the others weren't taking it very well. Honestly, who *cared* about who would lead which part of the host? There was a city to be attacked, and all this bickering over rank served them naught. Of course, he was in the minority when it came to caring nothing for rank – as a bastard son he would never rise to an elevated station. He made his living by using his wits and his right arm to serve his uncle, and that fitted him perfectly well. But these others …

He tried to close his mind to the social machinations in the tent and concentrate on the task in hand. He still didn't like this business of being able to slip only a few men in at a time via the postern, but it was the best that they could do, so why did the earls not just accept it and move on? Action was needed. But no, they continued to wrangle incessantly, and he grew more and more frustrated. He thought of Dame Nicola, an elderly woman, deprived of her son, holding the castle fast while those bloody engineers and their bloody machines went about their business. And yet she was unyielding: she had more steel inside her than all the men in the tent – the regent being the exception, obviously – put together. She knew that action was needed, and if they didn't get on with it soon then she would be the one to take the consequences. He didn't want that on his conscience, not after all her efforts.

His one hope was that the man Weaver might come back with news which would aid them in their task, but the chances of that would grow slimmer as the hours passed. Meanwhile all he could do was kill time. His agitation grew as he waited, and his pacing became increasingly urgent, until his uncle was forced to tell him to sit down lest he wear a furrow in the floor of the tent. He threw himself on to a stool and tapped his foot impatiently, unaware that he was doing so. What in God's name could be happening in Lincoln?

The night was chill after the warm comfort of the house, and Edwin shivered as he paused outside the door. The past hour had seemed somehow unreal, a combination of the horror of looking at the boy's body and the contrasting haven of almost familial warmth he had felt as he sat and talked with Alys in the cosy kitchen. But now he was back in the real world and he needed to concentrate on returning to the castle unharmed, so that he could deliver the all-important tidings. He shivered as he remembered the fate of the boy he'd just seen, and of the father who was already buried. His heart ached for Alys, left alone and fatherless, and he vowed once again that he would find out who had committed such foul deeds. It could not possibly have been a coincidence: somebody out there knew they'd tried to pass a message on to the castle, and they had paid the ultimate price. Either one of the French invaders had found out about it, or there were traitors in the city, ready to give their fellow citizens up to death.

He must stop thinking about this. The thing to concentrate on now was trying to stay alive long enough to pass the message on. He would be no help to Alys if he was dead.

He stayed in the shadow of the doorway for a few more moments, scanning the street before deciding that it was empty. He slipped out and began to pick his way up the hill, keeping to the edge as much as possible. The silence in the city was eerie. He reached the top of the Drapery without incident and paused before starting his ascent up the steep hill. Had he heard something? Was there another patrol of French soldiers in the vicinity? He strained his ears, wishing simultaneously that the moonlight was brighter so that he could see better and that it was darker so that he could hide himself more effectively. The sound, if there had really been one, had gone. He was imagining things. Just concentrate. Breathe. It's not that far and soon you'll be back behind the stout walls of the castle. All will be well.

The hill beckoned, lined with houses on either side, each with an alley that might serve as a hiding place if he needed one, but which also might harbour enemies. As he passed each dwelling he looked into the dark gap, his mind imagining every kind of horror emerging from them. Occasionally he heard a small sound emanating from one of them, but in each case it was just an animal. Or so he sought to convince himself.

No, this time it was definitely a patrol. As he reached the top of the hill he ducked into the final alley, his heart racing, as a group of soldiers passed. Perhaps they weren't on watch: it was clear they'd been drinking, and some of them were staggering, being supported by their colleagues. He felt relief that they didn't seem to be searching for him, but he still waited until the last trace of sound from them had disappeared before emerging from his bolt-hole. He was concentrating so much on that particular group of soldiers that he never noticed the figure which appeared from another alley and followed him as he continued on his way.

Dame Nicola strode up and down, knowing she should attempt to appear more calm, but she was unable to help herself. She looked up as de Serland entered the room. 'Anything?'

'Not yet, my lady. But we will try again at Lauds.'

She nodded as he left, before resuming her pacing. More men had died that evening, and the ones who were left were so weak and exhausted that they wouldn't be much use in the forthcoming fight. What they needed was some tactical advantage, something which would offset the fact that the French and their allies had superior numbers and that their men were in better condition. But for that they would need to hope both that the townsfolk – not exactly hardened warriors – had been able to do something useful, and that they could find out about it.

No. It was time to assume that the man wouldn't return; that she would need to come up with another stratagem. It would be more difficult, but that couldn't be helped. She would not surrender. She hadn't given up twenty-six years ago when they'd been besieged and she wasn't about to do so now, by God. She might have lost her husband and son since that time, but she could stand without them. She would rather die and see every last man of the garrison lying in his own blood than hand over her birthright. The shame of it would be unbearable. Despite the fact that she had spent decades succeeding, despite the fact that others might have surrendered in the past, she, as a woman, would be held up to ridicule as the female who could not keep her castle safe, the example of how the weaker sex could not be left in charge of anything as they were unsuited to it. Damn it, that would not happen. Would. Not.

She stopped her pacing and picked up a knife from the table. She might never have learned how to use a sword properly, but she swore that the first man who dared to come over those walls would be met with sharp steel. She imagined the satisfaction of spilling the blood of the enemy and, better still, that accursed chief engineer who laughed every time he heard screams of agony from inside the castle. But if the walls fell, he would certainly be nowhere near them, the common coward. If the walls fell …

She hurled the knife across the room and lashed out at a stool which got in her way. If the walls fell they were all dead, and she would be remembered as a failure. But the regent's host was on the way, and she supposed there was still hope of other news.

Her frustration grew. Where was the man? What had happened to him? And how in the Lord's name were they all going to get out of this with their lives intact?

Edwin had passed the cathedral and was inching his way into the part of town where the houses had been destroyed. As he came nearer to his goal, the tension within him increased, his head feeling stretched to breaking point. Was it really possible that he was going to succeed in his quest? That he could deliver the message to the castle and survive the night? Earlier he hadn't thought it achievable, but as the moments and the yards passed in an agony of slowness, hope resurfaced. He was going to do it. He was actually going to do it!

It was the tiny sound behind him which saved his life, giving him a moment's warning. He whirled faster than he would have thought possible, drawing his dagger as the figure leapt at him in the darkness. He saw the pale outline of the blade streaking towards him and managed to swerve out of the way just in time, the knife slicing through his tunic but not his flesh. His assailant seemed bigger than he was, and was no doubt more experienced, but he had lost the advantage of surprise, and may have been taken aback by the speed with which Edwin drew his own weapon. The two of them grappled desperately in the darkness, each seeking to stop the blade of the other. Edwin was starting to panic – just as he had been so close to his goal! – and he fought to keep his head. He strained against the force of the other man, feeling the blade draw closer to him. The struggle continued for a few moments in a strange silence, each unwilling to risk alerting potential allies of the other, but Edwin knew he would eventually lose out to the stronger man. He started to kick out frantically with his feet, and more by luck than by judgement was rewarded when the other backed against a pile of rubble and was momentarily distracted. Edwin managed to jerk his arm free and lashed out with his dagger. He heard a cry – whether of pain or of surprise he couldn't tell – and used the moment to shove his attacker away and run, unsure of how much he might have disabled the other man. The sound of footsteps behind him told him that he hadn't caused as much damage as he might have hoped.

He fled through the darkness, sobbing, his breath coming in harsh gasps. He'd been so close! But was there yet still hope? How long had it been since he had last heard the bell of the cathedral? Had it rung again yet? Could it be that the rope might be waiting for him when he reached the castle? In his headlong rush he tripped on a loose stone and stumbled before regaining his balance and sprinting on. His shoes were slippery, he wasn't used to running. His breath came in laboured gasps. He could hear the other man and tried not to look behind. He was nearly at the castle. The open space beckoned. He would have to dash across it. Was he close enough to shout for help, or would he merely be giving his position away to other attackers lurking in the darkness? He was almost there. He opened his mouth, and it was then that he heard the blessed, blessed sound of the cathedral bell.

Hope giving him new strength, desperation making him careless, he flew across the open space with no regard for stealth, shrieking out to those inside the castle as he did so. As he hit the wall he heard voices above him, and he clutched frantically in search of the rope. His attacker had followed him close behind and was even now grasping at him. Edwin flailed around again with the dagger which was still in his right hand, seeking the rope with his left as he did so. Shouts came from above, but no arrows came hissing down. His attacker seized him by the belt and tried to pull him away from the wall, away from the safety of the rope. He was succeeding, and Edwin felt himself starting to move even as he dug his heels into the ground.

And then the miracle happened. Edwin wasn't quite sure that he wasn't imagining things, but a third figure appeared out of the darkness, threw his arms around Edwin's assailant and dragged him bodily away. The brief respite allowed Edwin's questing left hand to find the rope, and he wrapped it once around his wrist, grasped with his hand, and shouted with all his might to those above to pull. His arm was nearly jerked out of its socket as he felt his feet leave the ground. The figure in the darkness made one last attempt but was held back by the third man long enough for Edwin to get too high for him. Then the third man escaped back into the shadows, and the assailant finally gave up and retreated, fleeing back across the open space. Edwin shoved the dagger into his belt and gripped the rope with both hands as he was hauled upwards to safety.

———◆———

Dame Nicola heard the shouts as she was walking in the ward, and ran towards the tower as quickly as age and dignity would allow. When she reached the top of the steps she was rewarded by the sight of the spy, dishevelled but apparently unharmed, being untangled from a rope by two men. De Serland and an archer were both leaning out over the wall to look into the darkness, the archer loosing a hopeful arrow, although he could surely have no visible target at which to aim. She helped the spy – what was his name again? It didn't matter – to his feet and let him draw breath before assailing him with questions. What had happened? Had he met the contact? Was there any news? As he recovered himself he gasped that he had an important message; urged on by her questioning he seemed about to spill the words there and then, but she gathered her wits and told him crisply to wait until they had reached her council chamber. Jerking her head at de Serland to indicate that he should follow, she led the spy down the steps.

Once in the chamber, with the door safely closed, she could contain herself no longer and demanded the news even as she shoved him towards a stool. The man raised his face to her and her heart began to lift – was there a chance that they were all going to get out of this alive?

He spoke. His message was very simple, but the import was profound.

For a moment she couldn't take it in. How ...? But then the realisation flooded over her, and she heard the intake of breath from de Serland, which indicated that he too had understood. She worked her way through the implications, and breathed again. There was hope. For the first time in weeks, there was hope. Thank you Lord.

She turned to the man. 'There is no time to waste – you must get back to the lord regent as soon as you can.'

He nodded wordlessly and dragged himself up and towards the door. As he was leaving she stopped him for a moment to speak again, reaching out her arm.

'We are grateful to you, and I thank you from the bottom of my heart. It is just possible that you have saved all our lives.'

Again he said nothing, but his face held much emotion. He bowed his head briefly to her and left the room.

Edwin tried to marshal his thoughts as he was led towards the postern, but he couldn't think straight. He had delivered his message, but what now? It would be of no use unless the regent was to hear of it, so he must concentrate on getting back. They couldn't spare a man to go with him and besides, as the knight was saying, one man alone was less in danger of being seen than two. It sounded sensible as the words washed over him, but he didn't quite grasp what this actually meant until the knight gripped his shoulder, wished him Godspeed and then pushed him outside the castle, alone.

He took a moment to orient himself, trying to identify the group of trees where the other men should hopefully be waiting with his horse. Horse. He winced at the thought of getting back on the animal yet again, but it wasn't so terrifying: riding had become not an obstacle in itself, but merely a means to an end – he would be able to get back to the camp all the sooner. What on earth was he thinking about? Who cared about the horse? He had to get himself across all these fields first.

The moon was still bright, so he could make out the edge of the forest in the distance. How wide the open ground seemed! It was fields, or at least it had been – there wasn't much growing there now. The French must have taken it all and cleared the ground so that they could see anyone who approached, giving themselves due warning. That wasn't going to help him, of course, as he had to cross it now. He had no doubt that the man who had attacked him had been one of the enemy forces, rather than some common thief, for it was too much of a coincidence that he should be assailed so near the castle. Therefore he'd probably gone back to his friends to warn them that something was afoot, so others might be watching from the city walls. He had no choice, though – he would have to risk it. He waited a few moments more until a cloud moved and partially obscured the moon, and then he set out.

It was slow going, as he thought he would be better off crawling along the ground in order to minimise his chances of being seen. He made his way through the scrubby, stubbly ground, scraping his hands and knees, and pausing in any dip or behind any small patch of undergrowth. This was going to take ages, and he wasn't even sure that he was still heading in the right direction. He would have to stand up and look. Shoulders twitching, as though he could already feel an arrow fizzing towards him, he stood and peered into the darkness.

It was at that moment that the moon burst forth from behind the cloud, illuminating the whole plain, and the first shouts came from behind him.

He began to run.

Chapter Nine

Sir Reginald had been sitting on his horse and scanning the open ground. He'd barely dismounted since John Marshal had returned two nights ago, although the others did so. They were lounging around in the cover of the trees, but he couldn't bring himself to stop watching. He wasn't very good at waiting. He was worried about his young companion, following Edwin's admission that he didn't know how to fight. What would he do if he was attacked? He needed someone to look out for him.

As he heard distant shouts issuing from the direction of the city he urged his horse forward out of the cover of the trees so that he could see more clearly. The moon was bright, flooding the plain, and his eye caught the movement in the middle of the open ground. Edwin. He was running. Sir Reginald looked behind the hurrying figure to see a number of men on horseback moving swiftly towards him. His heart leapt. There was no time to waste. Roaring to his companions to catch up, he shoved on his helmet, spurred his horse forward and galloped out on to the plain.

The tactics came to him without thought as he rode. If he were to stop and try to pick Edwin up, the attackers would be upon them before they could return to the woods, and it would be difficult to defend against them while there were two of them on the horse – no, better to try and delay the attackers while his companions caught up and rescued Edwin. All this went through his mind in less than a moment as he couched his lance, bracing it under his arm so that he would have the full weight of the horse to add to his own as he crashed into the enemy. There were a dozen of them, and he would have to take out as many as possible to stop them reaching Edwin. This was what life was all about! He barely gave Edwin a glance as he swept past, intent on his enemy, a wild exhilaration building within him.

―――

If Edwin had thought about it, he would probably have said that his greatest fear was archers aiming at him. But the sound of hoofbeats drumming behind him as he raced across the open ground instilled a terror so profound that he could hardly force his legs to keep moving. He was tiring, slowing down as they approached him. He would have no chance of reaching the woods before they caught him. He was going to die. Sharp steel would thrust into his body … and then, dear Lord, the sound of a cry from the tree line. They were still there. They were waiting for him. There was hope.

The darkness of the woods erupted as a figure burst forth, and Edwin gaped as the awe-inspiring figure of a fully armoured mounted knight thundered past him, lance lowered. He was so close that he was splattered by earth thrown up by the galloping hooves. He tried to keep running, breath labouring, but the combination of fear, hope and exhaustion united to prevent him. His legs gave way and he fell to his hands and knees. He was drawn to look behind him.

The lone man continued his charge, and Edwin watched in a kind of fascination as he smashed into the party of pursuers. They were lightly armed, dressed for speed, and individually they were no match for the knight. The lead man, at whom the lance was aimed, stood no chance, and the sharpened steel head plunged straight through his body. The knight made no attempt to retrieve it but instead drew his sword and lashed about him, killing and maiming his opponents. Edwin had never seen a knight in real action before, and the sight was awesome, the violence sickening. Men scattered before his blade as he wreaked havoc.

But there were too many of them, even Edwin could see that. Gradually the knight's momentum slowed, he became mired in the encounter, and four of the men left their companions to deal with him while they spurred past in search of their original target. Him. Edwin tried to scramble to his feet, running before he was standing, slipping in his haste as he tried to flee. The sound of hoofbeats seemed to be coming from everywhere.

As he regained his balance and forced his screaming limbs to move, he became aware that the sound really was coming from all around him. A further party of knights was issuing from the woods. He crouched and covered his head as they thundered past barely an arm's length from him, turning to watch as some hurtled into the unfortunate pursuers and others surged forward to aid the lone knight who was still frenziedly fighting off his opponents. One horse pulled up next to him and Edwin looked up. The rider's voice was muffled and dull inside the helmet, and Edwin couldn't make out what he was saying, but he didn't care. The knight reached his arm down and hauled him up behind him onto the horse before wheeling and making for the safety of the trees.

Once they were there, Sir Gilbert – for it was he – removed his helmet and turned his horse so they could see the progress of the rest of the party. He looked anxiously towards the furthermost encounter, where it seemed that the knight, with the help of his friends, had succeeded in fighting off his opponents. Bodies lay sprawled on the ground around them, as they did at the site of the second encounter. From what Edwin could see, his companions had killed all the attackers without losing a man of their own.

Sir Gilbert seemed to read his mind. 'We had surprise on our side, and they were but lightly armed. Still, it was damned foolish of Reginald to set off on his own like that. He could have got himself killed.'

Edwin's eyes opened wide as he realised who the lone knight was. 'You mean … Sir Reginald attacked all those men, on his own, in order to save me?'

The knight snorted. 'Reginald would attack a party of French for far less reason than that, I can tell you.' He softened slightly. 'But yes, he did, and we are glad to see you safe. Do you have news?' Edwin nodded. 'Good. The others can catch us up on the way, but we must get you back to the lord regent.' He pulled the reins around and set his heels to the horse's flank. 'Hold on.'

———◦———

John Marshal stabbed his finger at the plan of the city which was laid out on the table. The smoking torches didn't make reading easy, but the thick black lines which represented the castle and the city walls and gates could still be seen in the uneven light. 'The French have their main concentration of forces *here*. Their siege machinery is *here*, to the south side of the castle, and they also have troops in the north-eastern corner of the city, north of the cathedral. This area *here* to the east of the castle has been razed, so there is some open ground, as there is in the minster yard. But the rest of the city, south-wards towards the river, is still standing and is inhabited, so we will have to prepare ourselves to fight in narrow streets.'

He turned to the nobles around him, amazed that they had managed to stop arguing long enough to listen to him.

His uncle nodded. 'This is perhaps not the way we would have chosen to fight, but there is no choice.' Briskly he turned to the other nobles surrounding him. 'We will deploy in four battalions. I will lead one – '

He was interrupted by the Earl of Derby. 'But my lord – surely you don't intend to ride into battle yourself? I mean, at your age … oh.' He tailed off into silence, realising his mistake. The other nobles watched like crows circling over carrion as the regent pivoted to face him, enunciating his words very slowly.

'Old I may be. But even if I were over eighty I should still be leading my men into battle. I am the leader of this force, William, and you would do well to remember it.'

Derby stepped back in silence, cowed, glaring at those who were casting him gloating looks. The group looked more fractured than ever. The regent made as if to continue, but the Earl of Chester forestalled him.

'You are the leader, my lord, and none of us doubt it. But your men are not the greatest in number – mine are. So the honour of leading the first battalion should fall to me. It is my right, and I demand it.'

John looked on as the regent raised one eyebrow. 'Demand, Ranulf? You make demands of me?'

The withering look would have intimidated many a lesser man, but Chester was made of sterner stuff. He met the regent glare for glare. 'Aye. I demand my rights. For if I do not lead the first battalion, I will take my men and leave. You have already dismissed Warenne of Surrey – do you dare do the same to me?'

A collective gasp was quickly suppressed by the other lords, but Chester stood still, his jaw thrust forward pugnaciously.

John Marshal watched his uncle with interest. Knowing him better than most of the other men in the tent, he could glimpse the rapid calculations being carried out behind the flat stare. William Marshal was no fool, and he would know that he couldn't take the city without Chester and his men. Was the realm about to be riven further? But if the regent backed down, would he lose face before his men? Would they doubt his authority? But not for the first time, John had underestimated both the tactical intelligence of his uncle and his extraordinary personal charm. The future seemed to be hanging by a thread, but he overcame the difficult situation with ease.

'I did not say *which* battalion I would lead, Ranulf. Of course you will lead the first.' His tone held exactly the right amount of dismissiveness to avoid any suggestion of a *volte face*. Before anyone could think about it, he moved swiftly on to a self-deprecating humour. 'I will stir my ancient bones in order to lead the second –' his wry glance swept them all and lingered a moment on the Earl of Derby, who heartened, 'William of Salisbury will take the third, and my lord the bishop of Winchester the fourth.'

There was a slight stir at these last words, but John grasped immediately how clever the regent had been. Peter des Roches, the bishop, was a warlike man with a shrewd mind; his leading one battalion would lend the right gravitas to the occasion, convincing the host that God was on their side. Meanwhile the other three sections of the host would be led by the two most powerful men in the kingdom, and a third who, although not supplying as many troops, was the young king's uncle and so ranked above the others. Thus the order of precedence was set and none of the other earls and lords had been elevated into a potentially resentment-inducing higher place than the others. Everybody was satisfied, and all this with a few simple words and gestures. He marvelled.

The regent continued. 'Now, as to the order of the march; we will have all the crossbowmen, under Falkes de Breauté, a mile ahead of the main host,' – John nodded to himself at the sense of this – 'and the baggage train a mile behind, to keep it out of the way.'

Mention of the baggage train had put John in mind of something else and he drew breath, but then stopped again, unsure as to whether he should bring it up. The regent noticed the sharp movement and bade him speak.

John decided that it was better to declare his thoughts. 'My lord, our sources inside the castle indicate that the enemy forces outnumber us: they estimate six hundred knights and about a thousand foot. As we approach they're bound to see us, and they'll know that we're small in number. We need to make sure that they don't sally forth and attack us on open ground, where we would be at a great disadvantage. Might we devise some strategy to make them think that we are more numerous than we are?'

The regent looked interested. 'What would you suggest?'

'Well, my lord, it might not be strictly according to the rules of war, but some ruse might be employed. Most of the knights in your host will have two banners: instead of each displaying one and keeping the other stored, why don't we fly all the extra ones in the baggage train, to make it look like another force of knights? To be sure, it might not fool the enemy for long, but if it stops them attacking long enough for us to approach the castle and enter via the postern, it will help.'

The Earl of Chester seemed about to say something, but the regent cut him off, speaking with authority. 'I do not think we need to dwell too much on the niceties of chivalry. Anything which gives us an advantage will be needed. We will do this.' Others nodded as the regent continued. 'A good strategy, John, you have done well.'

John Marshal basked briefly in the appreciation, but was too scrupulous to take all the credit. 'Thank you, my lord, but although the idea of the banners was mine, the original plan to make the host look bigger was devised by the man Weaver who was with me in the castle.'

The Earl of Chester grunted. 'Well, let us hope that he isn't still there. We must prepare to leave soon, regardless of whether he returns or not.'

The regent acknowledged this. 'Within the hour. It will take about three hours to march the host to Lincoln from here, so we will need to leave as soon as dawn breaks. That way we should get there round about Prime.' He slapped one hand into the other. 'Damn it! I am still not happy with this entering through the postern – it will take too long and they will be able to assail us while we wait to be admitted.'

The Earl of Salisbury spoke. 'But my lord, we have no time to build siege machinery, and short of battering down the city walls, there is no other choice. Your nephew has already told us that the castle and its garrison are near to breaking point.'

John Marshal stepped back from the table and resumed his pacing. There must be another way. There must! But he was damned if he could think of one. Again he berated himself for leaving the man Weaver to enter the city alone. He should have gone himself. His sense tried to speak to him – it would have been much worse if he hadn't been able to bring back what news they already had, and Weaver was by far the better of the two of them to go into the city. He spoke English, for a start, which he himself couldn't do. But his heart overruled him. If something needed to be done he should make sure he did it himself. No good ever came of relying on others.

His thoughts were interrupted by cries from outside the tent and he strode out to see what they signified, hoping rather than expecting that there might be more news. He was greeted by the sight of Gilbert de l'Aigle riding straight through the middle of the camp, ploughing through the surprised men right up to the regent's tent. He reined in his horse.

'I am sorry to disturb you thus, my lord, but I thought you might like us to be as swift as possible.' He turned in his saddle and John Marshal could see another man behind him on the horse. The other man tried to dismount and fell in a heap on the ground, to be assisted to his feet by one of the guards outside the tent. The man stood and faced him. Marshal's heart jumped several times. It was Weaver. He looked exhausted, breathing heavily, and he was dirty, covered in mud splatters. But as he stepped forward, his smile lit up the night sky.

Alys had stared into the fire until long after it had gone out, the flames dying into glowing embers which in turn had become cold grey ashes. What had she been thinking about? In truth, she couldn't say. Everything. Nothing. She had simply gazed into the middle distance while the room cooled and the sun came up. As the first rays slanted in through the ill-fitting shutter of the kitchen window, she finally awoke from her trance and shook herself. She was cold. She pulled her shawl more tightly around her shoulders as she rose and began to prepare the room for the day. The familiar tasks increased the sense of unreality at what had happened during the night. She would like to think that Nick's death had just been a nightmare, but she knew it was true, did not dare go into the shop to see him there again. But she supposed she must; there was always the chance that one of the children would go in there, and she couldn't bear it if they saw him. And as to the rest of the night's events, had she really welcomed a stranger into the house, a spy who would help to relieve the suffering of the city? Or had she dreamt it all? And what had happened to him once he left? Had he reached the castle in safety, or would he turn out to be another corpse discovered in an oozing gutter?

She shivered at the thought. As dreamlike as the overnight events had become in her mind, one thing still seemed real: Edwin himself. His honesty, his openness, the feeling that one could trust him; how nice it would be to have a man like that around during these times. She ached for someone to take the responsibility away from her. She wanted to be looked after. But there was nobody. After all the death, she doubted even that Thomas would ever come back. What were the chances that he had somehow survived the ravaging of the countryside around the city? No, it would be up to her to look after the remains of her family. But how could she care for them if the current situation continued? She had a little wood left, so she relit the fire in the hearth to warm the leftover pottage. There would be food for the morning, for the day if she eked it out carefully, but what then? There was nothing in the house, very little in the city, and every day it became more dangerous to venture out of the four walls of the building. If something didn't happen soon they would all starve.

The first sounds of movement came from upstairs. She went up to fetch the children and brought them down to the kitchen, now warming again, for their meagre meal. She sighed as she thought of the long day ahead. What would she do? How could she keep them occupied and out of trouble?

A knock sounded at the kitchen door and immediately they all stiffened, Randal almost falling off his stool in fright as he looked around for somewhere to hide. Alys stood, unsure whether she should open it, but she was reassured by the voice of Master Pinel calling out that it was only him and that he'd come to see if they were all right. Relieved, she opened the door to him. His ruddy face emanated sense, solidity, something to hold onto. And yet, Alys knew he had been visiting another woman and leaving his wife alone. What else might he be capable of? But she needed to appear normal. As she greeted him, a movement in the back yard caught her eye, and she moved her head just in time to see Aldred slipping away through the back gate. What was he doing here? Had he been hanging around the house all night? He had clearly been doing something since she last saw him, for he had a stained bandage tied around his head, covering one eye. He saw her looking at him and quickly turned his face away as he went through the gate.

Master Pinel turned to follow her gaze. 'What is it?' He seemed as jumpy as she was, but then, it would be strange if he wasn't.

She recollected herself. 'Nothing. Do come in.' She moved back to allow him entry, and he stepped inside, wincing as he did so.

Alys was concerned. 'Are you hurt?' She put out a hand to steady him.

He grimaced. 'No more than I am due for a man of my age. Recently I've been getting pains in my back, but it's not serious.'

She apologised that she had no food to offer him, but he waved away her concern, saying he was fine, and besides, the children needed it more. She made an effort to try and dredge up some small talk, but he spoke first and she was immediately wrong-footed by his first question – he thought he had heard screaming coming from the house in the night, had something happened? Hence his concern for them all this morning. He looked at her pleasantly.

Alys floundered, not wanting to mention Nick, not now, not to him, not in front of the children. She came up with a weak excuse about nightmares – although it was probably less feeble than it would normally have been, given what had been happening recently – but was saved from further embarrassment by the arrival of Mistress Guildersleeve and Gervase, who called out from the yard seeking entry and saying they had brought some bread.

Relieved, Alys went to the door to greet them and asked them in, seeking to cover her confusion in a fuss over the new arrivals, thanking them for their gift and dividing the bread up among the children, who fell upon it without a word.

She bade everyone be seated, but there weren't enough stools, so Randal moved to stand close to her, one hand clutching her sleeve, and Edric clambered happily up on to Gervase's knee. He ruffled the boy's hair as he asked if anyone had heard any further news about the siege.

Alys was spared from speaking by Master Pinel, who immediately launched into a report of a conversation he'd had yesterday with a friend who had told him that he'd heard from someone he knew that the castle couldn't possibly hold out for much longer. He was interrupted from time to time by Mistress Guildersleeve, who peppered his monologue with remarks on how dreadful everything was and how difficult it was getting to find anything to buy. Between the two of them there was no pause for anyone else to add anything, for which Alys was profoundly glad. As the conversation went on, she slipped into the shop at the front of the house. She stood for a short moment looking down at the beloved face, now more peaceful in everlasting sleep, and covered the body in a swathe of cambric. Then she unbarred the front door in order to peek out into the street. Normally it would be bustling by now, with shops and stalls trading and all the goodwives out to make their purchases. But the street was deathly silent. She guessed that everyone was about the same sort of activity as they were: staying indoors, gathering in small groups, desperately worried about their fates, talking and trying to predict what might happen next, attempting to stay hopeful but knowing that time was running out. She took one more look at the street before moving back inside and barring the door. It was not just the absence of people; the emptiness was suffocating. The city was holding its breath.

———

They were on the march. Their plans had been remade and now they were on their way to do battle. Edwin could hardly believe it. Things had been such a blur since he'd arrived back in the camp.

He had been exhausted, falling off Sir Gilbert's horse – he really must stop doing that, especially in front of noblemen – and virtually into the arms of John Marshal, who had dragged him inside the tent to tell his story. He had left out most of it, of course, such as the details of his conversation with Alys and the fact that he'd been attacked on the way back to the castle, but he'd conveyed the essentials. When all was said and done, the message had been only six words, but they might hold the key to the whole siege, even the future of the kingdom: *the western gate is not blocked*.

Even with his lack of military experience, Edwin could see that this was hugely important. John Marshal had been concerned at only being able to send a few men in at a time through the postern, meaning that precious hours would be wasted and the French might have time to attack; now they would be able to flood the city with troops very quickly. It turned out that the townsfolk, in whom the nobles in the castle had so little confidence, had organised a resistance and had spent many nights painstakingly moving the rubble while still making it *appear* that the gate was blocked. This must have been an incredibly dangerous thing to do – well, of course it was; he knew of at least three people involved who had been murdered – but the citizens had been willing to risk their lives to help save their town.

He'd had no need to explain all of this to the leaders of the host; the mere knowledge of the gate being unblocked had stirred them into immediate action. He'd been rewarded by a thump on the back from John Marshal which made him wince, and something he could never have dreamt, not in his most fevered imaginings – courteous thanks from the regent of all England. Then he'd been permitted to remain at the back of the tent while the plans were laid, listening in numb exhaustion as it all washed past him.

He was surprised now to find how much of it he recalled: his mind must have been less deadened than he'd thought. They were to leave Torksey at dawn, to march towards Lincoln. Apparently a strategy for the host to be split had already been made, and this plan was to remain intact: they would be divided into four battles, or some similar word, plus the crossbowmen and the baggage train. When they reached Lincoln, the host would divide into three parts. One group, led by the Earl of Chester, would move to the north gate and would strike the first blow, hoping that most of the French would run up that way to defend it. The crossbowmen and some foot soldiers under someone with the strange name of Falkes somebody would be sent in via the postern, in order to sally forth from the castle and cause a further diversion, while a few men, Edwin among them, would slip out to open the all-important west gate. The remaining three battalions – yes, that was the word – would enter via the opened gate, and then they would all join forces, sweep the French down through the streets and out of the southern end of the city, over the river. At least that was the theory. Edwin had thought that it all sounded clear and easy when it was being confidently explained by the regent, but he had no doubt that things would be much more difficult in real life.

Finally he'd been dismissed so that he could catch an hour's rest and eat a huge meal before he was to start the march back to Lincoln again. He'd been glad of Sir Gilbert, who had instructed his own men to feed him, otherwise he would be hungry still.

Now he rode again with the host on its way back to the city. It was strange: had he ever thought of himself in an army, he would have imagined trudging with the footsoldiers, as was his place in life, but now his position seemed to have changed. In some ways he was glad of it – riding might be somewhat painful but it was better than walking – but in other ways it was disturbing. He'd been fairly sure that he'd be dismissed once he'd given his message, but John Marshal had said he needed him to come back. He was the only one who'd been in the city, and there must be no delay or mistake in finding the all-important west gate. So here he was. He had too much time to think about what was to come, and now he was wishing that he hadn't eaten quite so much breakfast.

His companions noticed his grim silence and sought to distract him. Sir Gilbert chaffed Sir Reginald amiably about his single-handed attack on the men who had pursued Edwin, but the younger knight sought to play down his deeds, asking instead about Edwin's experiences in the city. He grinned knowingly when Edwin told him of his meeting with Alys, and Edwin was uncomfortably aware that his heart beat faster at the thought, and that his face was becoming hot and red while the knight teased him. He thought of her again. How would she fare once fighting took place in the city? Would she be safe? Would the fighting pass near to her home?

He couldn't bear to think of her being frightened, and trying to protect the little ones against armed men. Perhaps he might have the chance to warn her once he was in the city? But that would mean that he would have to bypass the fighting in order to get to her. Perhaps once the gate was open there might be the possibility of slipping away through the streets to reach her house. He wasn't going to be much use in the battle, after all, and she would need protecting. Plus she would be facing other dangers. Someone, somewhere in the city, had murdered her father and brother, presumably in order to get the very information which she had passed to him. Her life was now in danger because of that, as well as the siege. But how could he help? He must try and think through everything she'd told him, to try and work out who had done such a foul thing. Then if he could only manage to reach her once he was in the city, he might be able to help. He concentrated, closing his eyes against the world, looking inside himself as he tried to remember every word she'd said, every place and time and person she'd mentioned, but somehow he was distracted by the remembrance of her face in the firelight ...

His thoughts were interrupted by Sir Gilbert asking about his return to the castle. How had he managed it? He was interested, having had no time to question Edwin on the way a few hours ago as they made all speed back to the camp. Edwin told them of his journey through the darkened city, and was gratified when they both drew breath sharply at the mention of his attacker. Their motives were different, though: Sir Reginald wanted a blow-by-blow description of the fight, which Edwin was not sure he was qualified to give (unless the knight wanted to hear that he'd been frightened out of his wits and then lucky), but Sir Gilbert had a deeper purpose.

'If someone attacked you as you made your way back to the castle, it's possible that this person knew that you carried a message and sought to stop you delivering it.' Edwin agreed, thinking of the body and particularly the beaten face and missing finger: what had the boy given away under such pain?

The knight continued. 'But what if this person didn't simply know that you carried a message, but also knew the content of it? If that's the case, then it's possible that he's already informed the French of it and they might be aware of our plans.' Edwin hadn't considered this and felt a jolt to his heart as he looked at the knight, grim-faced now. 'This is important – I must warn the lords. If we're attacked out on the open ground then all will be lost.' Sir Gilbert nudged his horse and cantered forward to where John Marshal rode at the head of their section of the host. Sir Reginald returned to his pastime of baiting Edwin about 'his girl', and Edwin's face grew red once more.

———※———

It was the hour of Prime, and the knight Robert Fitzwalter was standing on the walls of the city, looking out over the countryside to the west. Behind him, the mangonels and petraries under the command of the chief engineer were continuing their deadly work, sending huge stones hurtling into the castle. He was so used to it by now that he barely noticed when another huge crash sounded – at least this one hadn't been followed by a shriek of agony. There was something almost cowardly about standing around here letting the common engineers break down the castle walls bit by bit. There were noblemen in there who deserved better than being crushed to death by rock. He had come here to fight, damn it, and he chafed at the inaction. Still, it didn't look as if the walls would be able to hold much longer, and once a breach had been made he would be one of the first into it; then there would be fighting aplenty, proper man-to-man combat with sword or lance.

He sighed as he scanned the countryside again, wondering how he'd ended up here, an Englishman in England, under the command of a French noble. It all went back to King John, and his refusal to … but what was that? Over there on the ridge to the north-west?

He looked again more carefully and realised that his first instinct had been correct: it was indeed a column of armed men advancing towards the city. They were nowhere near within bowshot range yet, but he shouted for a party of archers to come up anyway, while he ran for his superior.

Saer de Quincy, the Earl of Winchester, didn't particularly appreciate being hauled away from his breakfast, but as soon as he heard the news he jumped up and shouted for a man to saddle his horse. Then he and Fitzwalter rode with all haste out of the city on to the plain to reconnoitre the new force.

'Who are they, my lord?' Fitzwalter was sure he knew the answer, but he had to ask just to break the silence as they cantered over the ground. He felt very exposed being outside the walls, but the approaching men were still some distance away, so there was no danger.

'It can only be a relief force,' replied the earl, 'for we aren't expecting any of our French allies to arrive from the south.'

Fitzwalter winced again at hearing the words 'French' and 'allies' in the same sentence, but he had made his bed and now he must lie on it.

The earl continued. 'I can't see properly, for the sunlight is glinting off their armour. Your eyes are younger than mine – can you make out the banners?'

Fitzwalter strained his eyes. The banners were hanging limply at the moment, but as he watched a slight breeze came upon them and they floated out so that he could see the devices. His blood ran cold. He had known who it must be, but the stark sight of the emblems reminded him of how deep his trouble might turn out to be. Arrayed against him were the forces of the regent and the king.

De Quincy took the news calmly, saying only that it was to be expected, and bidding Fitzwalter ride back to summon their overall commander, the comte de Perche. 'It doesn't look as though they are overly large in number. We'll probably be able to attack them out on the open ground and cut them to pieces before they get anywhere near the city. But the comte will no doubt want to see for himself. Go now.' Fitzwalter urged his horse into action.

Chapter Ten

Edwin tried in vain to calm himself. The attack on the city was about to go ahead. He had seen two men ride out from inside and examine the host, before being joined by a third man, and there had been much pointing and waving of arms. Had the ruse worked? Had they been deceived as to the size of the host, enough to put them off attacking over the open ground? The tension grew and grew within him. If they were going to be assailed, when would it happen? Now? In a few heartbeats' time? He couldn't stand the waiting, the apprehension. He needed to scream and run, but he couldn't. He had to stay, for those were his orders; he couldn't run home and hide until all this was over. How would he face his lord?

He had dismounted, and watched as the Earl of Chester and his men peeled off from the rest of the host, ready to go around to the north side of the city in order to assail the gate there. The sound of combat emanating from that quarter would be their signal for a mixed group of men to move forward and enter the castle via the postern. Then some of them would sally out into the streets to create a diversion, aided by the crossbowmen who would stay inside the castle and shoot down from the walls, while a small group comprising Edwin himself and a few others would slip around to the city's western gate and open it. Yes, that is what will happen.

And still they had not been attacked.

His stomach cramped as he stood, and he thought he would embarrass himself, but his thoughts were distracted by the sound of shouts and the clash of steel issuing from the north. The signal. The Earl of Chester's men had struck the first blow, and now it was his turn. He ran forward with the others, expecting at any moment to hear a deadly rain of arrows hissing down, but none came. The men inside the city obviously had other things to worry about. *Lord, protect me this day.*

As they neared the castle, the postern opened and the first of the crossbowmen entered. Edwin waited his turn and then passed through the small gate for the second time in several hours. Then he was inside the castle, wincing and ducking his head as a thunderous crack signalled another stone hitting its target. His heart beat faster with the terror. How had the garrison survived such an onslaught for so long? Surely they must have been driven mad by the fear. He kept his head down as he moved forward quickly into the courtyard, even though he knew deep down that this would do him precious little good if he were to be hit by one of the gigantic missiles. He would be crushed like an ant, the rock shattering his bones. Desperate to take his mind off that image, he followed the man in front as the rest of the party formed up. Those with crossbows ran up the steps to the curtain wall and took up position, while Falkes de Breauté and his men waited by the main eastern gate of the castle. Once everyone was ready the bar was lifted, and with a great shout the knights and men began to pour through into the city, weapons at the ready. Edwin drew his dagger and followed.

———◦•◦———

They were still sitting in the kitchen when the first sounds of battle erupted. It was Margery who heard it first, recognising that the noise was different from the horrible reverberations of the stones crashing into the castle, but not knowing what it meant. But the two men seemed to understand: they both leapt to their feet.

'Combat!' Master Pinel opened the back door to hear better. 'The men from the castle must have come out to fight.'

Gervase was beside him. 'Either that or a relief force has arrived.'

Alys felt her heart soar. He'd done it! He must have returned to the castle in safety and passed the message on. The king had sent an army and they would be saved.

But there were more immediate concerns. It was Mistress Guildersleeve who voiced them first. 'There will be fighting in the streets of the city. We must protect our homes.'

Gervase took charge. 'Mother, come home with me now. Alys, is your front door barred?' She nodded. 'Good. Now take anything else you can find and pile it up behind the door, in case anyone tries to break it down.'

Master Pinel took up the theme. 'I'll do the same in my home, although Appylton's place must, I fear, be left to fend for itself. Is there any way of defending the yard?'

Gervase thought for a moment. 'We'll see. Come.' As they all hustled out of the door, he turned and cast a parting remark to Alys. 'Once the doors are barred, take the children upstairs and hide. If anyone does get in, they might only loot the shop. God protect you.' And then they were gone.

Alys was terrified, hardly able to move, but as she looked at the stunned faces of the children she realised again that she would have to be the strong one. She tried to sound decisive. 'Margery, Edric, take Papa's chair and put it behind the shop door. Then take these stools and try to wedge them in to keep everything fast.' Used to the voice of authority, they obeyed without speaking, starting to drag the heavy chair through to the shop. Dear Lord, she hoped they wouldn't look too closely at the mess of fabric near the fire. She turned to Randal, who was shaking. She could barely get him to understand her. 'Randal, help me.' He didn't move. She knew how frightened he was, but this wouldn't help him. 'Randal!' Still he stood, quivering and rooted to the spot. Hating herself, she drew back her arm and slapped him across the face, hard. In shock he brought up his hand, looked at her and burst into tears. She could have wept herself, could have curled up on the floor, sobbing until her heart broke, but there was no time. At least she'd roused him.

'Come now. Help me move things across to block this door.' The kitchen door, opening as it did on to the private yard, only had a fairly light bar which wouldn't withstand much of an attack. She did as best she could by heaving the flour barrel over to it and packing around it every other movable thing she could find.

Once they had barricaded themselves in as best they could, she took them all upstairs, where they huddled together in terror, praying that they might survive the day.

———————

Sir Gilbert's horse pawed the ground as he waited with the rest of the regent's part of the host. They were on the ridge to the north-west of the city, waiting for the gate to open. He'd heard the clash of weapons from the north gate, where the Earl of Chester's men were attacking, and had seen Falkes de Breauté's party entering the castle's postern. Reginald and Edwin were both there, and he prayed for their safety while he waited.

And waited.

He shouldn't let himself become too nervous. Think about what you're going to do. Now was the time to find out whether Edwin had risked his life in vain, whether the information was true, whether they were going to get into the city unopposed or whether they would end up being sitting targets for a forewarned and forearmed enemy force. What would happen to his estates? What would …

That wasn't the right thing to think about. He needed distraction and fortunately it was provided, for the regent rode up in front of his men, removed his helmet and began to address them. His oration was spirited, and men straightened in their saddles as they listened to him declaring that they were fighting for a just cause, to drive the French out of their realm on behalf of the true king, and crying out that God was on their side. As a roar went up from the host, Sir Gilbert had a momentary heretical thought that the enemy were probably also claiming that God was on their side, and that presumably He couldn't be supporting both factions at once, but despite this, he still found himself stirred by the words of the old man. He was a knight, it was his calling to fight for a just cause, and today he would do it, by God. He felt his heart lift and the cares about family and estate melt away. He was here, he would engage in battle, and the Lord would decide the outcome.

The regent ended his speech amid rousing cheers and turned to face the city. He seemed about to ride off, but one of his men ran forward with his helmet, which he was evidently about to forget to don, and stopped him. Then he too was encased in faceless steel, a killing machine ready to cut his way mercilessly through the enemy forces. He took his position as the papal legate − ah, that settled it, of course: if the Pope supported them then God must really be on their side − blessed the host. All eyes were on the city gate, and as Sir Gilbert looked at it he thought he saw the tiniest crack appearing in the opening. Or was he imagining it? No, it was definitely opening, but only the Lord knew who would be behind it. He readied himself for the charge.

———

Sir Reginald watched as the crossbowmen rained their deadly bolts down on the besiegers. The order had been given that they should concentrate on killing the horses of the enemy, rather than the men, for which he was glad. For one thing, it still felt slightly odd to be fighting against fellow countrymen, even if they had allied themselves with the French, and for another, there would be the possibility of capturing other knights for ransom. Besides, men of rank should be fought by other knights in proper hand-to-hand combat, not merely mown down from a cowardly distance by commoners.

While these thoughts ran through his head, he was preparing with other mounted men to sally forth into the city. This was it – his chance had come. Falkes de Breauté gave the order and as the gate was opened he watched John Marshal and the men on foot run through, and then he rode out, ready for battle.

The first thing he noticed was that city streets weren't made for fighting on horseback. The space immediately outside the castle gate had been cobbled, and his horse slipped and slithered as he tried to control it. After that it was slightly easier, the stones giving way to earthen roads, but the fight would be along a narrow front, made worse as the hooves churned up the ground into a mire. Still, he would make the best of it. Combat was his reason for living, and he felt the elation building up within him and the smile growing on his face; he whooped as he spurred towards the foe.

But immediately in front of him was an enemy knight on horseback. There was no time to set his horse into a proper charge, but he barrelled into the man, shoving his mount sideways. He couldn't get his long lance into position, so he simply threw it at the man's face to distract him momentarily while he drew his sword. That was better – he was able to move his right arm more freely now, ignoring the stabbing pain from his broken hand, which was still sore after the night's exertions. He struck a sound blow at his opponent's helmet: the knight was obviously stunned as he let slip his own weapon and slid off his horse. This would be a good opportunity for a capture, but unfortunately the press around him was too thick and he had to leave the man where he was lying in order to focus on further enemies.

Now he was surrounded by knights on foot, their dead and wounded horses lying still on the ground or thrashing their legs, crossbow bolts protruding from bleeding wounds. One knight reached up to try and seize his reins, intent on stealing his own steed, but he lashed down with his sword and saw the other fall away. More foot soldiers came towards him, commoners this time, defended only by light gambesons, and he laid about him mightily until he was surrounded by a pile of the dead.

Around him his compatriots were doing the same, but they had slowed. The impetus of their very short initial charge had worn off and they were becoming mired in the small confines, surrounded by more and more enemies. Ahead of him he saw Falkes de Breauté being pulled from his horse down into the press, and he pushed his own mount forward, lashing about him with his sword and using his shield as a battering ram, until he was over his fallen leader. He held off the enemies long enough for Falkes to stand and recover himself, but his horse had gone. Shouting to Falkes to pull himself up on to his steed, he tried to stay still long enough for the man to haul himself on to the beast's back, but it was difficult with so many assailants. A few more of his companions thrust their way forwards so that Falkes had the time and space to grab his saddle and try to heave himself up, but they were becoming hard pressed. A glancing blow caught him on the leg and he winced, but the damage wasn't serious, thanks to his mail chausses. More and more enemies came at him. The sortie was being repulsed, and he was stuck. Was he going to die here?

As he ran through the gateway, Edwin had nothing in his mind other than the thought of imminent death. To his surprise, this failed to materialise, and he followed John Marshal and six other men around to the north side of the castle.

There they were confronted with the sight of the massive western gate to the city. Edwin heard John Marshal swear, and at first he thought that there had been a terrible misunderstanding, for the gate seemed blocked behind tons of fallen masonry and debris. As they picked their way forward, however, it became clear that, apart from the bar across the gate itself and one or two pieces which had been left to disguise the rest, all the remaining rubble had been artfully placed to make it look as though the gate was blocked, when in fact it would be the work of moments to open it. He gave thanks for the souls of the brave men who had dared to defy their oppressors to clear the way, some giving their lives to do so.

Urged on by John Marshal, the men started to heave at the rubble and hurl it aside. Edwin tucked his dagger back in his belt and worked as fast as he could, tearing the skin of his hands on the rough stone and still in great fear, but the crossbowmen in the castle were doing their job well, and not a single enemy soldier appeared to distract them from their task. Finally all eight of them set their hands to the great bar and heaved it out of its metal sockets to throw it aside. They seized hold of the gate and began to drag it, protesting, open. As soon as the first chink appeared, a great shout came from outside and some of the regent's men ran forward and pushed it from the outside, until finally it lay wide open, offering access to the city for the hundreds of knights standing ready.

The men on foot quickly stepped back to allow them entry, and Edwin had to jam himself back against the wall to avoid being crushed by flying hooves. First through the gate was the regent himself, charging through the gap and roaring his men forward, armour shining and bright surcoat streaming; a sight which was to remain burned in Edwin's mind until the end of his days – the greatest hero of the age storming into battle in the cause of righteousness. Then he was gone from sight, followed by a torrent of steeds and men, forcing their way in and hurtling into the narrow streets. After them came the footsoldiers, taking advantage of their lighter bodily protection to leap over the fallen debris.

And then they were gone, except for the men on foot who had opened the gate and the remainder of John Marshal's mounted sergeants, who had come through it with the regent's men. They stood looking at each other in silence. Sounds of battle came from all around, but Edwin was standing in an island of calm. He began to heave a sigh of relief.

He was only halfway through it when John Marshal began shouting again that their task was not yet done, and that they needed to help with the fight. One of his men was leading an extra horse, and Marshal strode towards it. As he did so, he grabbed a fistful of Edwin's tunic and swung him round, surprisingly powerful for such a slight man. 'Not you. You get inside that castle and protect yourself. You are valuable and I don't want to explain to the lord regent that I got you killed. Go!'

He gave Edwin a rough shove and then he was gone, onto his horse in one swift movement and urging the mount past the castle walls, his men following. With cries and with the exhilaration of battle upon them, they were gone.

Sir Reginald was surrounded by enemies and handicapped by trying to pull his fallen leader up onto his horse behind him. There were too many of them … but then he heard a welcome sound. Shouts came from behind him as more mounted men crashed into the press around him. The footsoldiers assailing him screamed and fell back, as a knight whose device he recognised as John Marshal's drove past him, hacking down at them. Falkes de Breauté had the space to grab the reins of a spare horse and haul himself into the saddle.

The momentum of the new charge got them all moving again and they pushed further forward. The men ahead of them started to fall back, and they pressed their advantage. Ahead of them was the open ground where the French had their siege engines, which were still being manned, still hurling huge missiles at the damaged castle walls. If only they could stop that bombardment! Sir Reginald forced himself forwards to John Marshal and pointed, knowing he wouldn't be heard above the din. Marshal gestured to show he had understood, and the two of them made themselves into a wedge, thrusting their way through the enemy knights with their own compatriots fanning out behind them, as they sought to reach the machines.

Sir Reginald was stopped in his drive by another dismounted knight reaching for his reins, but as he paused to crack his sword down on the man's wrist he saw John Marshal continuing on. He had broken through the press of knights and was hurtling, alone, towards the siege machinery. The engineers manning the devices weren't properly armed or defended, and they stood no chance against the knight who sent blood and gore flying as he hacked his way through them, even as they tried to flee before the onslaught. Finally he reached the first mangonel, on top of which stood the chief engineer, still bellowing orders to his men. Without pause John Marshal rode straight at him, bringing his arm back in a wide arc, and the man's head flew off his shoulders in between the space of two words. The Royalist forces cheered and surged further forwards, and soon all the engines had been seized, the bombardment stopped at last.

Dame Nicola paused on her way across the courtyard and listened to the cheers coming from the south side of the castle. She stood still for a moment, listening. What was different? One of her men ran down from the south wall.

'My lady, my lady!' He skidded to a halt in front of her and she nodded for him to speak. 'My lady, they have captured the siege engines!'

Of course – that was it. She had become so used to the regular sound of the missiles that she had barely noticed when they stopped. For once heedless of dignity, she picked up her skirts and ran faster than she had in twenty years up to the parapet, a place which had been too dangerous to visit until a few moments ago. She looked out over the ground and saw a scene of carnage: blood and bodies and limbs everywhere, those of the damned engineers – served them right – and what were obviously the regent's men starting to break the wretched machines to pieces. Standing atop one of the mangonels was an armoured knight – John Marshal, might the Lord bless him for the rest of his days. As she watched, he saw her on the parapet and somewhat foolhardily removed his helmet in order to bow to her with a flourish. Then he was gone, back into the press of men, back onto his horse, the enemy not yet defeated. But the bombardment had stopped! After enduring it for so long, she could scarcely credit it. They were going to win. They were going to drive those blasted French out of her city, and she would be able to start the process of rebuilding.

She stopped herself from becoming too optimistic. Things were not over yet. For a few moments more she watched as Falkes de Breauté's crossbowmen shot at the remaining enemy within range, cheering inwardly as each bolt found its mark in an adversary's body. The weapons weren't much use against the knights, of course, for their mail protected them against every shot but those at close range, but it was thinning the ranks of the bastards, and she gave thanks. After watching one final shot which lodged in the spine of a screaming footsoldier and left him writhing on the ground, she grunted in satisfaction and descended from the parapet.

In the courtyard things were busy, as the wounded Royalists were being brought in. Now that the French were away from the immediate environs of the castle, it was safe to open the gate, so it made sense for the wounded to be tended here. She gave orders for her remaining garrison to help as best they could, while still keeping a sharp lookout on the walls for any stragglers among the French. As she surveyed the groaning men lying around her, she noticed Warenne's spy helping one of the wounded. Warenne would do well out of this, despite his absence, for the man had done good work and the credit must go to the earl for putting him forward. The regent might even let him back into the Royalist camp, if he was lucky.

She watched the man for a few moments, doing his best to stop a sergeant with a stomach wound bleeding to death; she had seen such injuries before and the man had no hope. She considered the spy again. No doubt Marshal had sent him back inside the safety of the walls, for he would be valuable, and he didn't look like he would be much good in a fight anyway. But her supposition was obviously wrong, for as she watched, the man laid down the dead soldier and ran out of the gate and into the city. Foolhardy – no armour and only a dagger with which to defend himself – but that was his concern, not hers. She had plenty of other things to worry about.

She sent a man for de Serland, who was at the north wall of the castle. She was feeling hopeful, but his news was not of the best. Chester's men had been embroiled in some brutal fighting there and the result was still in doubt. The battle wasn't over yet.

———

Once more, Sir Gilbert raised his weary arm, bloody to the elbow, and brought it down on the head of the man who was trying to stab his horse's belly. Since their charge through the west gate they had been involved in some vicious combat in the north-western corner of the city. The layout of the narrow streets had made it exceedingly difficult to fight properly, for they could only ride four abreast between the overhanging houses, and sometimes not even that. The French and rebels were in front of them at every step, and sometimes behind or above them as well, for they had seized the houses in that quarter, killing the citizens within or throwing them out into the street. There had been a number of fatalities which in Gilbert's mind were regrettable. Just a moment ago he had stopped his horse and made it walk around the body of a small child – he couldn't bring himself to step on it even though the mite was clearly dead already. But such things happened, and any deaths here would be a sacrifice towards the greater good of freeing the kingdom from the invaders.

He flinched as the man next to him was struck by an arrow, but fortunately it rebounded off his helmet with a loud clang, and after shaking his head the knight appeared to be all right. Gilbert was now not in the front rank of the advancing force, having taken his turn as one of the leading four in the street, but having been replaced there by another. He looked sharply around him as they inched their way forwards, looking for any soldiers in the houses, so that he might send his troop of foot inside to flush them out. It was bloody and messy work, not his idea of a battle at all, but it was working. The French were slowly giving ground along the high part of the city towards the cathedral, as the regent's men spread out through all of the streets and cut their way forwards.

Screaming sounded from a house to his right, and he immediately sent some men in. There was the sound of a struggle and they came out again to dump the body of an enemy soldier in the street. The screaming went on – it sounded like a woman, so there had probably been some violence in there. He couldn't stop to find out. He wondered for a brief moment about the girl Edwin had told him about, and hoped that she was safe. He didn't think that she would be in this quarter of the city – hadn't Edwin said that she lived further south, down the hill? Anyway, he hoped for his sake that she might escape unscathed. He hoped also that Edwin, and Reginald for that matter, were still alive. He had little fear for his fellow knight, but Edwin was hardly able to defend himself, never mind take part in a battle, and it would be a shame if anything were to happen to him. Gilbert had grown quite fond of him over the last few days.

Suddenly a patch of space appeared before him – the minster yard. The French had been pushed back so far that they were now in the north-eastern corner of the city. Gilbert could see their commander, the comte de Perche, trying desperately to rally his men in a group. There was a brief pause as the regent's men also broke off the engagement to regroup, and then both sides faced each other across the open ground. There was a stillness. The air could have been sliced with a knife. Somebody would have to make a move.

Perche rode round haranguing his men, trying to whip them up for a further fight. Then perhaps he realised that the best way was to lead by example, for he couched his lance and moved forward. There would be many men in the host who would love to have the glory of facing him, but before any of them could move, the regent himself burst forth from their ranks. Gilbert froze. The man was over seventy! What was he doing taking on such a young man in single combat? If he were to be killed, the blow to morale would be crippling.

But it was too late. The regent lowered his lance and charged, as he had no doubt been doing on the fields of battle and tournament since long before Gilbert had been born. He thundered forward, aiming at the body of his opponent in a clear attempt to unhorse and capture him, rather than kill him, and Gilbert remembered suddenly that Perche was the regent's cousin. So close were the factions that nearly everyone had some kind of relative on the other side.

Was Perche surprised? If he was then he didn't falter in his charge, but perhaps his concentration was broken. William Marshal was a legend, but he was still an old man, and there should have been no excuse for failing to unseat him. But Perche missed with his thrust, and the regent's lance struck hard and true into the centre of Perche's shield and shattered into flying pieces. The comte rocked back in the saddle and screamed – Gilbert couldn't make out why, until he noticed the huge splinter of the broken lance which had flown up and pierced the eye slit of his visor. He reared up on his horse, unable to control it, spinning, shrieking, blood spurting from the wound. Yet miraculously he drew his sword and managed to strike a blow at the stupefied regent, still screeching and bleeding. The regent parried it easily, but didn't make another strike himself. He didn't need to; Perche's sword dropped from his hand and he slid off the rearing horse to crash onto the ground, dead.

There was a moment of stunned silence, and then the French began to run.

———

Edwin tried desperately to staunch the flow of blood coming from the man's stomach, but in his heart he knew it was useless. He had retreated back inside the castle, as ordered, and had been followed by the first of what would probably be many wounded men. Some staggered in by themselves; others were dragged in by comrades who left them lying and ran back to the battle. One had landed virtually at his feet, and as Edwin tried to pick him up he realised it was the man Stephen, who had told Edwin about his brother on the night he'd arrived at the castle. Edwin sought to offer what help he could, but it wasn't much. He tried to press his hands over the gaping wound, to stuff some of the man's own padded garment into it, but the bright red blood soaked through with a frightening speed. Edwin gave up and knelt, taking Stephen's hand and looking into his contorted face.

He wasn't old, not really, but some years older than Edwin, and he looked as though he'd seen many an encounter. But now he was frightened, knowing that death was near. He spoke in a rasping voice. 'My wife – I don't know what happened to my wife. She was in the town when it fell …'

Edwin didn't know what to say, only gripped the hand harder.

The man spoke again, locking his eyes on Edwin's. He sucked in a huge breath and screwed up his face in agony. 'I'm going to die, like my brother …' Edwin tried to calm him, to shush him into saving his strength, but the man was desperate to talk, to spend his last moments on earth communicating with the stranger who held his hand. 'But I will pass into the Lord's grace.'

There was no point in trying to contradict him. Edwin nodded, and realised that he might be able to give some comfort after all. 'You will see the gates of heaven, and your brother.'

The man seemed to become more agitated. 'But his head … will the Lord let him into heaven without his head? How will I know?' His face became panicked and he writhed, as though he would try to move from his prone position. He fell back, gasping, more bright blood flowing over his body.

Edwin put his other hand out to hold him down. 'He will be there. He died in a just cause and the Lord wouldn't deny him entry. You too will be forgiven your sins and the saints will welcome you.' He prayed that it wasn't a great sin to say so, for he didn't know the man or what he'd done in his life, but he must at all costs give him comfort in his last agony.

It seemed to have worked, for Stephen calmed, lying flat again and seeming to lose his remaining energy. His face already had the pallor of death. He spoke once more, voice weakening. 'Yes. I will own up to my sins and not try to hide them. I shall go as I am. Alan will be there with his head intact, and I will recognise him when I see him …'

Edwin actually saw the life light go out of the man's eyes, and he sat for a moment before releasing his hand. He stared into the distance, words echoing in his head. He had been reminded of something, and now it was all becoming clear. He remembered exactly what Alys had said to him during their long conversation in the candlelight, and wondered why he hadn't worked it out before.

He knew what he had to do. Pausing to close the dead man's eyes, he stood, took a deep breath, and ran out of the gate and into the city.

As he ran he realised how incredibly foolish he was being. What in the Lord's name was he doing, venturing out into a city which had become a battlefield, with only a dagger to protect him, and even that was not much use as he didn't know how to use it properly. He must hope that the sight of the weapon would deter any casual attackers. If he were to be set upon by a real soldier then he would be dead anyway, so it didn't matter. It also crossed his mind that he was disobeying a direct order from a member of the nobility, something he could never have imagined himself doing even a couple of days ago, but there were some things which just had to be done. He was in danger, he would be in some kind of disgrace, but he was in the right, and he held that sentiment firm as he ran through the streets, seeking to avoid the bodies and the blood where he could. He must protect her. Them. Her. His feelings were confused. Two things were for certain, though: firstly, there were soldiers everywhere who were crazed with blood; and secondly, he knew who had already mercilessly cut down two members of her family, and who might seek to strike again. She was in terrible danger.

There was blood everywhere. Corpses lay grotesquely at every corner, not only fighting men but citizens, and some women and children also, those that hadn't managed to escape the carnage. The fear grew inside him of what he might find when he reached the house, but he only increased his pace.

As he neared the cathedral the sounds of battle intensified, and suddenly there was a flood of men roaring past him, some dropping weapons as they fled. Others were still seeking to fight their pursuers, and turned to strike at those behind them. The streets were impossibly crowded, and Edwin was caught up in the maelstrom, carried along by the press of men. He gripped his dagger hard, but none of those around him sought to strike him, concerned as they were with the armed men behind them and the constricted way ahead. He had no idea who was who, but in the whirl he managed to catch a glimpse of a banner being held by one of the pursuers: the regent's. They were winning. It was the enemy who were fleeing. Thank the Lord. That would increase all their chances of survival.

The tide swept him down the steep hill. At the bottom they were joined by another group of fleeing men and horses, and Edwin sought in vain to avoid being flung into the crowd. It was to no avail, though, as the panic of those around him was too strong. He was surrounded by men paying no attention to what they were doing with the sharp steel in their hands, and by the flying hooves of horses that were equally panicked. He was kicked, punched, and felt a sharp pain across his upper arm as a flashing blade hit him. Finally he fell.

As he hit the floor he felt the crowd start to move over him. Feet were all around him, on him, trampling him into the ground. He was going to die here, crushed. A small space cleared and he sought to roll into a kneeling position, but over him loomed the terrifying figure of a man on horseback, sword raised. With a terrible irony he noticed that the man wore the emblem of John Marshal, and realised that he himself bore no colours, the consequence of his secret mission. He was going to be killed by one of his own side. Dear Lord, forgive my sins and protect my mother.

The sword never fell. A second figure on horseback barged into the first, giving him such an almighty shove that he lost balance and fell away. The new man was an armoured knight, faceless in his helmet. But wait, the colours – he could have wept as Sir Reginald seized the shoulder of his tunic and dragged him bodily out of the press.

The knight heaved them both into a corner away from the worst of the eddying crowd. Against the background of screams he pulled off his helmet and shouted. 'What in God's name are you doing? You could have been killed!'

Edwin tried to explain, but there was too much noise, there was no time. He simply yelled that he had to go, that he was sorry, and then wrenched himself out of the other's grasp and dived back into the crowd.

Sir Reginald swore. What was the man about? Had he gone mad? He watched the crowd move further down the hill, the retreating figure lost among the other men. Damn it, he would have to follow. So much for his chances of taking prisoners for ransom, but some things were more important than money. He set his spurs to his horse and thrust his way forward, cutting down any in his path as he sought in vain to catch sight of his departing friend.

Eventually he was rewarded with a glimpse of Edwin's back, further down the hill, disappearing into an alley between two houses. He started to follow but was attacked by a knot of French footsoldiers. Too distracted to care, he simply rode them down as he continued. Others fled before him as he started down the hill. But which house had it been? Which alley? Was it this one or the one further down? He stopped, letting the tide of men run past him, thinner now as many of them had already passed.

He turned his mount again and again in indecision, but then heard a piercing scream coming from the house to his left. And another. A woman. Raised male voices. One of them was Edwin's. He threw himself off his horse and started to hammer on the door.

Chapter Eleven

Alys and the children had been hiding upstairs in their father's bedroom since they had finished barricading the doors. They huddled together on the bed, listening to the cries and clashing of weapons coming from all parts of the city. Alys hoped and prayed and begged that the fighting would remain elsewhere, that their street would be spared, but little by little the noise came nearer. She risked moving away from the bed and peering out of the shutter towards the street. She could see nothing with the narrow view afforded her, but she didn't dare open it.

Suddenly there was a hammering at the kitchen door.

They all froze. Margery instinctively reached out for the dazed Randal and drew him nearer to her. Alys was frightened out of her wits, heart in her throat, but then she heard the voice. It was Mistress Guildersleeve, calling from the yard.

'Alys! Alys! For the love of God, child, let me in!'

Alys bade the others stay where they were. Edric stood up and moved to stand at the foot of the bed, drawing himself up. 'Don't worry. I'll look after them.' He was shaking, but his piping voice was firm. She looked at him, so proud. Eight years old and prepared to be the man of the family. He had even drawn his little eating knife, bless him, and was poised with it ready. She burst into tears. A father and brother already dead, another missing; the world was collapsing around them – were they all going to die here?

The knocks and shouting from downstairs intensified. She moved swiftly to Edric and gave him a fierce kiss. 'I know you will. Stand here and whatever happens, *whatever happens*, don't come downstairs. If anyone except me tries to come up, you defend yourselves as best you can, do you understand?'

Tears were in his eyes now, but he nodded bravely and held his knife in front of him. She cast one final glance at the three of them and descended to the kitchen.

Once she had reached the blocked door, she shouted to Mistress Guildersleeve. 'What is it? What do you want?'

The voice came again, desperate. 'Alys, there's going to be trouble. You must come. Open the door!'

Gervase's voice was added to his mother's. 'Quickly! We think we've found a way to safety. You can open up, we're alone.'

It was against her better judgement, but the prospect of safety was too much. She moved the barricades aside and opened the door. After the last few hours it was a strange relief to have them in the house, to not be alone. Gervase was obviously ready for an incursion, for he had an axe in his hand, as well as a knife at his belt.

Mistress Guildersleeve was already pulling at her arm. 'Alys, come! The fighting is heading this way. I and some other women are going to take to the river, they won't reach us out on the water. We'll leave the men to defend our homes.'

Alys did not see the connection. Her mind was full of confused questions. The river? What sort of safety is that? Surely it would be more dangerous out there?

But Mistress Guildersleeve was adamant, half dragging her towards the door. 'You don't understand. Once one side or the other has won, there will be looting, and no woman will be safe. All those soldiers, crazed with blood and ale and lust, do you understand?'

Alys belatedly realised what she was talking about. Violation was a relatively commonplace event in the town; women and girls out on their own in strange places, especially after dark, were never safe, and since the town had been full of soldiers it had been worse. A victorious host full of drunken soldiers didn't bear thinking about. But the river?

She tried to use reason. 'But Mistress, we have no idea how to get a boat, or how to control one. And surely we're safer in here than out in the open? How will we reach the river? And the regent's forces are here to rescue us, surely they won't let the city come to any harm if they win?'

But her neighbour was beyond reason. 'Come, you must come!'

Gervase's face had changed at her last words. Perhaps he had seen sense and would be more level-headed. He spoke. 'Mother, you go now, with whatever belongings you can carry. I'll stay here and try to help Alys and the children.'

She seemed torn, but in the end the thought of her own personal safety was obviously too much. She kissed her son and was gone.

Once she had left, Gervase swiftly shut the back door and moved a bench across it.

She looked at him. He would help. He would see them safe. She opened her mouth to speak of her relief.

Before she could utter a word, he spoke calmly. 'So, you know it is the regent who is here.'

She gasped at her own stupidity. She had discovered that from Edwin. But surely it was a reasonable guess for anyone to have made? Could she cover up? And besides, Gervase was a townsman too … oh dear Lord. She looked at him closely.

He spoke again, still calm. 'It was you. After all this time, all this effort, I find that it was you who told them.'

In a huge surge, everything became clear to her, and she staggered from the shock. She whispered. 'It was you.'

Amazingly, he still seemed composed. 'Oh yes, it was me. For weeks I've been paid to see what the townsmen were up to, to find out what their pathetic little plans were. We followed your father but could find out nothing – after his head was crushed he couldn't say a word. I took your snivelling brother and beat him to a pulp, but he wouldn't say anything. Dear God, we cut one of his fingers off but the brat fainted from the pain, and there was no time to wait for him to come round. I couldn't find out, and they were growing more anxious for an answer!' He strode across the room, agitated now, almost talking to himself. 'I couldn't let him go in case he told anyone, so we had to kill him. I left him here as a warning, but I thought it was for Aldred, not for you. If I'd only known it was *you* …'

He moved towards her, hardly recognisable as the man she thought she had known, and she backed away, trying not to be sick. Behind him, the door started to inch open, the bench being pushed forward. She tried not to look in case it distracted him, but he was too wrapped up in his own diatribe to notice.

He continued. 'And now, and now – ' suddenly he snapped and spewed forth a searing rage. 'And now I find it was *you*! You betrayed me and told that spy about the gate! All the time it was you, you snivelling little girl! Pretending to care only for your miserable children while you were working for the castle!'

He raised his axe and leapt at her, but in the space of a heartbeat the door was flung open and a figure lunged through to throw itself at Gervase. The two men fell to the floor and rolled, snarling, each stabbing and gouging at the other.

It was Aldred. What in the Lord's name was he doing here? She didn't understand. Neither would she ever get the chance to find out, for as she watched, Gervase managed to free his arm and strike Aldred on the side of the head with his axe. Alys screamed. Aldred fell limp, and Gervase got to his feet and stood over him. With composed brutality, he raised the axe once more and brought it thumping down into the other's neck. Blood fountained everywhere and Alys hid behind her hands, trying to shut out the horror.

He turned to her, splattered in gore, and smiled like a demon from hell. With cold fear she knew she was going to die, and sought to prepare herself. But another figure had appeared in the doorway, and with huge disbelief she recognised it as Edwin. He'd come back!

She had no time to speak, for Gervase had whirled to face the new adversary. 'You! I should have finished you off last night while I had the chance!'

Alys looked at Edwin. He was battered, filthy, and covered in blood. She hoped it wasn't his. As his glance swept the room and took in Gervase, her, and the body on the floor, she didn't think she had ever seen anyone look so angry. He couldn't contain his rage. He cried out incomprehensibly and moved to attack Gervase, dagger drawn.

Dear Lord, he had come back to save her and he was going to be killed. He slashed his dagger wildly, missing Gervase by a long way but managing to avoid the other's swinging axe.

It was then that the first sounds of splintering came from the front of the house.

She ran through to the shop in time to see the door shivering under the weight of blows. Someone else was trying to get in. How could she stop him? The barricades wouldn't last for long under such an assault. But then she heard his voice, shouting Edwin's name over and over, and some instinct inside of her told her that this was a friend. Hands trembling, she tried to drag the things aside as he continued to hammer at the door. Behind her, the fight had spilled in to the shop as the two men swayed together in a grotesque kind of dance. The door finally opened and the man outside shouldered it open far enough to force himself through the gap. It was a knight, fully armoured, sword drawn, drenched in blood and bits of things she didn't want to think about.

She stopped for the briefest of moments, and so did Edwin, but their pause was almost fatal, as Gervase grabbed her arm, swung her around and sent her crashing into Edwin. He stepped forward with his axe; she was off balance but Edwin had his arm round her, trying to push her behind him and keep his own body between her and the weapon.

The knight roared with rage, kicked the rest of the broken furniture aside and strode forward. He grabbed Gervase and threw him aside in one movement, crying out in a great voice. 'If you want to fight, fight me!'

Edwin was as surprised as anyone to see Sir Reginald burst into the room, but he would thank God for the rest of his days for the knight's arrival. He knew he would never have been able to fight off his opponent. But now they were saved; Gervase stood no chance against him. The relief was overwhelming. Firmly he pushed Alys into the corner and placed himself in front of her, dagger at the ready, as he waited for the fight. And fight there would be. Sir Reginald could easily have struck Gervase down from behind with his sword instead of throwing him aside, but of course he would never do such a thing, true knight that he was.

Sir Reginald was angry, there was no doubt about that, but he didn't let his rage overcome him. Edwin couldn't see his face properly in the helmet, but he knew the knight was watching both his opponent and the weapon carefully as he circled. He was at a disadvantage, for there would barely be space in the room for him to wield his great sword, but surely, surely he must triumph. He was an armoured warrior. Edwin watched as he struck over and over again, Gervase parrying desperately but managing to deflect most of the blows, which were not at full strength, hampered as the knight was by the lack of space. But he was becoming ever more trapped.

And then it happened. By some means – ever after, Edwin was not sure how – Gervase managed a lucky blow. He brought his axe down hard on the back of Sir Reginald's broken right hand. The knight gasped. Armoured as he was, he didn't drop his sword, but the pain which he must have been feeling caused him to pause for that fatal blink of an eye. Gervase grasped his axe in both hands and brought it round in a swingeing arc to hack into Sir Reginald's chest. Even the best-made mail couldn't stop such a blow at close quarters, and it sheared through the hauberk, sending links flying, and through the gambeson and flesh, tearing a huge rent in the knight's body.

Behind him Edwin heard Alys scream, but it was muted, and it seemed to come from far away. He was in a world of his own, unable to hear anything outside his own head. He was barely in control of his limbs. And so he wasn't really even sure if it was he who struck the blow. In a fog, the air about him thickening, he stepped forward, drew back his dagger, and plunged it into Gervase's unprotected back.

Everything stopped. The world was ending. He felt the sensation of the blade entering the body, propelled by him, by his hand. He was killing somebody. The blade bit deeper and the man screamed. The steel grated on bone. He was deliberately pushing a weapon into the body of another person. This is what it felt like. The blade could go no deeper. He ripped it out, feeling the flesh tear beneath his hand, and the body fell to the floor.

———◦◦———

The world started again. The man was dead. He didn't know how he'd managed to strike so true, but it had happened. Numb, he dropped the dagger and stared.

He was brought to himself by a movement across the room. Miraculously, Sir Reginald was still alive, lying spread-eagled on the floor and twitching. Edwin staggered over to him and fell to his knees. With shaking hands he unfastened the strap which held on the helmet, and removed it gently from the knight's head. He wouldn't live long, that was for certain. The huge wound had torn his body almost in half, and his lifeblood was pouring out on to the floor. Blood ran freely from his mouth, but his eyes still sought to focus.

Edwin was blinded by his tears. He pushed the long hair gently back from the sweating face. 'Three times. Three times today you've saved my life.'

Sir Reginald tried to lift his arm, as though he would thump Edwin on the shoulder, but he couldn't raise it. He spoke. 'Brave …'

Edwin tried to reassure him. 'Yes, you are.'

The knight made a huge effort and spoke through the blood.

'No … you. Brave and stupid, can't defend yourself, but you tried. To save …'

Edwin shook his head. 'No, Sir Reginald. You are. To risk your life for me, for this.'

Sir Reginald coughed, sending more blood spewing from his mouth. 'A knight … to die in battle – an honour. And in the service of –' he choked again, breathless, bubbling, life slipping away, 'a lady. And … a friend.'

There was blood, blood everywhere, Edwin was covered in it, but he was oblivious as he cradled the dying man's head in his hands. He watched as the light died from the eyes and the hand touching his arm fell away. The cursed broken hand which had caused his death. Edwin lowered his head and wept.

———

Sir Gilbert felt the exhilaration building in him as he gained new strength. They were winning! They were going to be victorious! The French were suffering a crushing defeat and surely this would have repercussions far beyond the walls of Lincoln.

He was urging his bloodied horse on, down through the streets as the enemy fled southwards through the city towards the Stonebow gate and the bridge over the river. As they neared the space there his progress was slowed, as the press of men became thicker. The rebels were seeking to regroup, to make a last stand before the gate. He raised his sword once more, having long discarded his lance, and rode into the fight.

It was tougher than he had expected; the French and the English rebels had reached the stage of utter desperation, and they were risking their lives recklessly, knowing there was nothing else to fight for. Somehow some of the regent's men had disappeared, and there were fewer of them to attack the foe. He was becoming mired. The rebels were defending valiantly.

But suddenly, men wearing the livery of the Earl of Chester erupted from a side street. They stormed forward into the fight, and after that there was no doubting the outcome. Many of the rebels dropped their weapons and tried to flee out of the gate, but it was not large enough for such a huge number, being of a strange design which only let one or two men through at a time. There was also, of all things, a cow stuck in the opening, and Gilbert watched in some disbelief as the terrified animal thrashed about, impeding and injuring those who tried to pass. Many were crushed in the press, and those that did get through were too many to cross the bridge, shoving each other into the water where they drowned, dragged down by the weight of the armour they hadn't had time to discard.

Others were still fighting valiantly for their lost cause, and he drew himself back in order to charge into a knight at the edge of the press. His attack caught the other by surprise, and his sword stroke sent the man flying from his saddle and crashing into the ground. At last, a chance for some ransom money! He threw himself from his horse and levelled his sword at the other's throat before he could rise. He shouted, his voice hoarse. 'Yield!'

The other knight paused for a moment, and then dropped his own sword as a gesture of surrender. He struggled into a sitting position and removed his helmet, casting it aside. He stood, stiffly. No bones broken.

The victor spoke. 'Sir Gilbert de l'Aigle. You are not injured?'

The captive replied. 'Sir Robert Fitzwalter at your service.' He picked up his sword and passed it, hilt-first, to Gilbert.

Gilbert passed it over to the group of his men who were behind him and bade them take him away and keep him secure. One of them caught the reins of the loose horse and they led away man and beast.

Gilbert mounted his own horse again and looked around. Most of the fighting had stopped. Knights and lords were surrendering all around him, while their foot troops fled as best they could, knowing that only death awaited them. He didn't think they stood much of a chance: there were many miles between them and their nearest allies, miles which were filled with the local peasantry who had had their homes and livelihoods destroyed, their families killed. There would be revenge.

Another loose horse shot past him, a knight's destrier, and he tried unsuccessfully to catch the reins. A second captured horse would be valuable, even if the owner of it had got away. But as he looked at the animal, his heart faltered in its rhythm. He knew that mount. That saddle. Reginald. His blood turned to ice.

The victorious regent was surrounded by cheering men. John Marshal looked on as the old man was congratulated by his compatriots, the Earl of Chester being among the first to shake his hand. Chester's arrival at the Stonebow gate had certainly been timely, but John Marshal couldn't help but wonder whether it had been staged that way, so that the earl should be the one whose intervention proved decisive. Had it really taken him all that time to break through from the north gate? But no matter, it was done now. The battle was over. The captured lords and earls – Saer de Quincey of Winchester, Henry de Bohun of Hereford, both the de Clares, Gilbert de Gant, whom Louis had had the temerity to name Earl of Lincoln, so many! – were making their submission.

It was still only mid-morning, so there was plenty of the day left. John Marshal took his contingent of men to find the rebel headquarters. There might be some important information there which would be of use in driving the French out of the rest of the country, but more to the point, there would be valuables to be seized. Such had been the speed of their retreat that they were bound to have left most of the treasures they'd stolen. He could do with some pecuniary gain: as a bastard son he'd inherited little of worth from his father, and he could

expect little from his uncle, who in any case had five legiti-
mate sons of his own to provide for. No, he had to make his
own way in the world and that suited him well, especially on
a day like this. He felt a glow of satisfaction as he remembered
the fight, and particularly the action around the siege engines.

On finding the French headquarters he was agreeably
surprised to find that there were even more goods than he'd
expected. Once he'd appropriated the best of them for himself
and on behalf of his uncle, he allowed his men to take the
remainder. As he looked about him he realised that he wasn't
the only one to have thought of plunder: others were allowing
their troops to loot as well. As he watched, a group of Chester's
men kicked in the front door of a house and started to carry
off goods from inside, to the screams of the inhabitants. A man,
presumably the householder, tried to stop them, but he was
knocked to the floor and beaten viciously before they made
off with his possessions.

Possibly this was going too far? He made his way back to his
uncle, temporarily installed in the minster yard, and reported
the situation to him. The state of affairs was becoming more
serious: as some men saw others starting to loot the houses,
they themselves joined in. But surely they had come to rescue
these people? Had they not suffered enough under the French
rule? He put it to his uncle. The other lords pressed around
eagerly like wolves, greed plain on their faces.

The regent was silent for a moment as he considered.
Then he pronounced judgement. 'I think we will allow this.
Firstly, the men will be difficult to stop now that they have
started and developed a lust for plunder. Better to let them
continue with our blessing than to try and stop them and let
them realise we have lost control. Secondly, they have just won
a battle for the king, so they must have their reward.' He paused
and chose his next words with care, looking at his nobles. 'It is
also possible that the citizens of Lincoln surrendered too easily
to the invaders and collaborated with them, so the stripping of

their town will serve as an object lesson to other places which may be attacked, to encourage them not to submit so tamely.'

It would be impossible to argue with him, and of course he was talking great sense. The only thing John Marshal should do would be to ensure his own personal share of the plunder – as some of the others were obviously about to do, slipping away surreptitiously from the gathering – and yet he hesitated. He had seen something else out of the corner of his eye, which made even him balk. He tried one more time. 'But my lord, they are even starting to loot the cathedral, the house of God.'

Even the regent looked taken aback by this, but the papal legate, hovering at his elbow, bent down to whisper in his ear, and then stood to address the gathering in his reedy voice. Men strained to hear.

'As the representative of the Holy Father it is my decree that the clergy of Lincoln did not do enough to fight the invaders in the name of their true king, and so they are to be considered as enemies and excommunicates.'

So that was that. Encouraged by their leaders, the victorious army started to attack and steal from the town they had come to save. John felt ambivalent – taking the French treasure was fair game, but the trinkets and possessions of the citizens was another matter. And yet, could the victorious men be denied? They'd fought hard, after all. He decided that he wouldn't take any more for himself – what he had taken from the French would be plenty – but he wouldn't seek to stop anyone else from gaining, either. Fair was fair. He rode through the streets, watching. All around him soldiers were entering houses, carrying off anything they could find and beating down anyone in their way. Women's screams started from many places – there would be more crimes than robbery this day. A group of Salisbury's footsoldiers broke into a tavern and rolled out the barrels of ale, which they smashed open in the street. Others joined them and soon the road was full of drunkards.

Amid the chaos he found one who showed distaste. Gilbert de l'Aigle joined him and they rode side by side through the madness. The other knight shook his head, indicating his disapproval as another shop was plundered in front of them, the owner beaten and kicked into the gutter as he sought to save his wares. 'I don't like this.'

John Marshal shrugged. It probably wasn't fair on the townsman but he had seen such things before, and he knew it wouldn't stop until the evil had run its course through men's veins, until they had gorged themselves on their crimes, until the city was stripped of its last silver halfpenny. He merely said, 'My lord the regent has sanctioned it.'

His companion did not reply but looked on tight-lipped as citizens started to flee their homes, carrying whatever possessions they could carry. They didn't really have anywhere to go – some sought to hide, others fled downhill towards the south gate, following the path of the invaders who had taken flight.

John Marshal watched them and didn't at first hear the other's question, but once it was repeated he was able to answer. 'Reginald le Croc? We were together by the siege engines, and then in the melee near here. I think I saw him heading off down that street there. He may have been following someone. I lost sight of him.'

Gilbert thanked him and departed, as John Marshal continued to watch the destruction unfold.

———

Edwin and Alys looked at each other over the dead body of the knight. Edwin had a sense of unreality, and he could see that she looked dazed as well. There was blood and broken furniture everywhere, the front door hanging crazily off its leather hinges, and, of course, three bodies on the floor and another in the kitchen. He sought to come to terms with what had happened. Vaguely, he became aware that the noise of battle had ceased;

men were no longer running in panic past the door. Carefully he moved his arms, laid Sir Reginald's head gently on the floor and rose. His whole body was stiff and aching. He was covered in blood which was drying on him and he was aware that he stank. But he was alive, and so was she.

He risked looking out of the door and stepping outside. The street was empty, although discarded weapons and the occasional corpse lay around. He sought to close the door as best he could, although it would need mending. He turned back inside, to see that she had mutely taken one of the pieces of cloth which littered the floor and was reverently covering the knight's face and body with it. She arranged it a little more carefully than was necessary, and stood. Still she said nothing.

He had to break the silence. 'I think it's over.'

She nodded. 'Yes.'

But he was wrong. From the higher part of the city came more shouts and screams, although this time without the clash of weapons. What was going on?

She knew, for she had been warned. 'They're looting.'

He was shocked. 'They can't be. We've won. We came to save you, not to destroy the town.'

But the sounds were coming nearer. Shouts. A door being kicked in. Gleeful calls. Dear Lord, the victorious army was breaking into the houses. How would he protect her? He looked futilely at his knife – it would be of little use if a gang of armed men broke in. But he had to try – he hadn't come this far to give up now. 'You should go and hide upstairs. I'll stay here to try and see them off.'

'You can't.' She was quaking, but firm. 'You came here to save us, at the risk of your own life. I can't leave you here alone to face them.' She looked around then picked her way through the debris to pick up Gervase's discarded and bloodied axe, which trembled in her hands. They stood side by side facing the door.

The looters had reached the empty house on the end of the block. Edwin could hear them crowing over their gains as they made off with whatever they had found. Then crashing and splintering coming from next door. A man's voice, shouting at them to stop. The sounds of a struggle, a thump on the floor. Then laughter. Footsteps outside the house. He braced himself and gripped the dagger. There was a scuffle outside the door, and then it was flung back, crashing into the wall as most of the remaining hinges gave way. Alys swallowed and raised the axe.

A man stood in the doorway, but as Edwin's heart lurched he recognised the figure. Dear Lord, it couldn't be. Were they to be this lucky?

It was Sir Gilbert. He looked around at the carnage in the room and at Edwin.

'I've driven them off, for now. I saw you outside the door a moment ago. Thank God I found you. You're injured?'

Edwin looked down at himself, realising how he must seem. 'No. It is not mine. Most of it is …' he looked down at the shrouded figure on the floor.

Sir Gilbert followed his gaze. 'Oh no. No. Please …' He stumbled over and drew the cloth to one side. He fell to his knees, then looked up, confusion turning to anger, fury blazing in his eyes. 'Who did this?'

Edwin backed away, afraid of the rage. 'It was him.' He pointed to the body of Gervase.

Sir Gilbert blinked as though he had noticed the other bodies for the first time. 'What in God's name has been happening in here?'

Edwin drew breath to answer but was interrupted by more shouts from outside. Sir Gilbert whirled around, sword drawn. Three men had appeared in the doorway, footsoldiers with some kind of livery which Edwin didn't recognise. He tried to prepare himself for a fight, but the men took one look at the gore-spattered knight, the blood-drenched man behind him, the carnage and the corpses on the floor, and fled.

Sir Gilbert spoke. 'No time now. Get upstairs, both of you. I'll defend the house.'

Alys opened her mouth but Edwin knew better than to argue. The knight was angry, and any potential looters would bear the brunt of his wrath. The house would be safe, but she probably didn't need to see the consequences. He took her arm and dragged her towards the staircase. 'Come!' Somewhat unwillingly, she allowed herself to be guided.

Edwin started up the stairs, but as he reached the top there was a sudden flurry of movement and he had a brief moment of warning as the knife came towards him. He ducked quickly back down and the weapon flailed over his head, the holder of it overbalancing. Edwin grabbed his assailant's foot and pulled him over, readying his own weapon, but Alys screamed at him to stop and wrenched at his arm. He looked properly at his attacker and realised it was a small boy. It must be one of her brothers. Quickly he ascended the last few steps to allow Alys entry to the room, where she immediately grabbed the boy and held him close. He was obviously frightened out of his wits, but he had been ready. Over in the corner two other children huddled on the bed, looking in terror at him. He must look like a figure from their worst nightmares. Alys stumbled over to them and hugged all three children as they clung to her. Edwin stationed himself by the top of the staircase, dagger drawn, ready to repel any attack.

It wasn't needed. He stood unmoving for what seemed like hours, but the trouble in the rest of the street didn't bother them, the sight of the armed knight standing guard at the door being enough to put off any looters. Eventually the worst of the noise passed and moved on, and he risked moving back from the steps and sitting heavily on the floor. He realised how exhausted he was.

Alys looked up from the children. She was still white-faced. 'I don't understand.'

He realised that she didn't know who either of the knights were who had come to her aid. 'They are companions … friends of mine.'

She shook her head. 'No. I mean … I don't understand how Gervase could do those dreadful things. I've known him for years, he was a friend of our family, and yet …'

He wanted to comfort her, but he didn't know how. 'He's dead. He will harm you no more.'

She nodded and fell silent. But after a few moments she spoke again. 'When he said …' she swallowed her next words, aware that the children were listening, 'when he was saying those things downstairs, about what happened to Nick and to Papa. He must have had someone else. He didn't say "I did this", but "we". Who was he talking about?'

Edwin reached forward and took her hand. 'There's something I have to tell you.'

Chapter Twelve

It was late in the afternoon, and the last sounds of looting in the street had been some time ago. Alys sat on the bed in the chamber, with the children draped round her. Edric was still watchful, and hadn't let the knife fall from his hand through all the day, but now it drooped as he fought against exhaustion. Margery and Randal were fast asleep, Randal's hand clutched around a fistful of her gown even as he slumbered. Next to the bed Edwin lay sprawled on the floor, exhaustion having eventually overcome him too, but he still gripped the dagger in his hand as though ready to wake and defend them if the need arose. She wasn't sure he would be able to, though, even if something did happen, for he was so deeply asleep that she'd felt obliged to check several times to make sure he wasn't dead. From downstairs came the sound of the knight as he paced. He had stood guard at the door without flagging for many hours, and she'd heard how he'd been forced to drive away drunken thieves and looters several times. Gratitude to him – and to Edwin, and to the dead knight downstairs, and even to Aldred – penetrated every bone in her body. She touched each of the children in turn, stroking their faces, and knowing that they wouldn't be here alive had it not been for the efforts of brave men to protect them.

The noises from downstairs changed – no longer a pacing but a kind of dragging – so she decided to go and see what was afoot. He'd told them all to stay upstairs, but surely the danger was past now. Gently she disentangled Randal's hand from the skirt of her gown, and shifted quietly so as not to disturb Margery. Edric too had nodded off, so she laid his head down on the pillow. With a final look at them and at the slumbering Edwin, she moved towards the steps.

She was tentative as she neared the bottom, not wanting to startle the armed man, so she waited and coughed loudly before attempting to set foot off the stairs. He heard her and came through, bareheaded now and having laid down his sword and shield. Sweat streaked his face, but at least it was the one part of him not covered in dried blood, so he looked a little less nightmarish. He too looked exhausted and she felt a pang that he'd given up his chance to rest in order to protect them. His face was sombre and stern, and she was a little afraid. She had never spoken to a knight before – how was she supposed to address him?

When he saw who was standing on the stair, he softened and held out his hand to help her down. 'Come. There is no danger.' His voice was hoarse and his English accented.

She took his hand and stepped down. 'Sir, I …'

He led her through to the shop and released her hand before turning to face her. He spoke gently. 'My name is Gilbert. And you must be Alys.'

'Yes, but how did you know?'

The corners of his mouth made an effort to turn upwards. 'Edwin spoke of little else once he had returned to pass on your message.'

She didn't know what to say, but was saved from replying by a look of some consternation on his face. 'Is he …?'

She hastened to reassure him. 'He's asleep. As are the children.'

He nodded. 'Ah, yes. Edwin said you had a family. Well, while they're resting, perhaps you could help me. I'm trying to create some order down here.' He gestured round the room, and Alys could see that he had already righted the damaged counter, and had moved Aldred's body in from the kitchen. He saw her looking and spoke again. 'I don't know much of how you live in this house, but I thought if I cleared the kitchen then it might be better for when the children come down, so I moved him in here.'

She nodded her thanks. 'Perhaps we should lay them out.'

'Very well. Although I don't think this one –' he kicked Gervase, scornfully – 'is worthy to lie with the others.'

Alys looked down at the man she thought she had known, who had been her neighbour since she was a little girl. As she surveyed the twisted face she felt anger rising within her. Until now it had been masked by the fear and tiredness, but it was hardening into revenge and she was surprised at her own vindictiveness. 'I would throw him out into the street.'

He nodded his appreciation and heaved the body on to his shoulder. He carried it out of the front door, barely hanging on its last hinge, and disappeared out of sight down the hill for a moment. She heard a thump and then he returned. 'He lies in the gutter, where he belongs.' He took hold of the door and shut it with care, wedging it in place and barring it with the remains of a broken chair. 'That will hold it for now, until something better can be found. Now, to work.'

Together they laid the bodies of Aldred and the other knight next to Nick, and straightened the limbs. She couldn't work out how she felt about Aldred. She'd always disliked him, and even feared him a little, but he had died trying to save her, which surely made him a hero? Maybe one day things would be clearer, but just now she concentrated on trying to block out the sight of the huge wound which had left his head half hanging from his body.

The knight asked what had happened and she explained it as best she could, although she couldn't account for Edwin's almost miraculous timing. Once the bodies were laid decently, the knight made as if to cover them with some of the bloodstained cloth which littered the floor, but she put out her hand to stop him, thinking that they deserved better. He watched while she dragged out two unmolested bales of fabric, and cut a piece of fine serge for Aldred and one of the precious twilled silk for the knight, which she draped reverently round him. He looked at her in gratitude and knelt to pray.

After a few moments he arose, wincing as he did so, and she realised that she had failed in a duty. 'You're wounded!'

He shook his head. 'No, just the stiffness setting in after such a day.' He looked down at himself and flexed his hands and fingers. 'I'm weary, no more. But perhaps you might have some water in which I could wash?'

She took him through to the kitchen and poured water into a basin, watching it turn red as he washed his face, head and hands. He looked ruefully at his armour and surcoat. 'I'd better leave these on for now – I might need them as I go back through town.' He saw the expression on her face. 'Yes, I must go back, and I must take Edwin with me. But fear not, I'll put some of my men to patrolling your street, so you should see no more trouble.'

She allowed herself to sink on to one of the stools, but jumped up again as she heard a strange noise from the yard, and something bumping against the kitchen door. After the events of the last day and night she was ready to fly into a panic, looked desperately around her, but the knight put up his hand to calm her. 'It's only my horse. I'm afraid I put him in your yard so as not to leave him on the street, and he has doubtless eaten your vegetables or trodden them into the ground.'

She brushed aside a consideration which might under normal circumstances have been serious. Right now she had other worries. 'But sir, how can we ever thank you? How can we repay you? After all you've done for us ...'

He looked steadily at her. 'Thanks are appreciated, but not needed. Seeing you and your family alive is all I need. But perhaps you would say a prayer for the soul of my friend. I will send men to come and collect him later. And in the meantime, perhaps you would go and wake Edwin for me – I wouldn't like to go upstairs myself for fear of frightening your children.'

She nodded and moved towards the stairs, but he forestalled her to finish speaking. 'And don't worry. I've heard him speak of you, and I know he'll come back to you before we have to leave the city.'

Edwin was dazed as he followed Sir Gilbert through the bloody remains of the city. Everywhere he looked there was more devastation – contorted bodies in the streets, blood in the gutters, wreckage strewn from the doorway of every house. Edwin put one foot in front of the other over and over again, the sound of weeping in his ears. But more than this, over and above and through it all, was the pounding thought that he had killed a man. He had deliberately stabbed another living person with a weapon, and that person was now dead. No matter that he was a murderer, a traitor – he now lay dead because he, Edwin, had killed him. How would the Lord ever forgive him for that?

'You could have done nothing else.'

The voice broke through into the emptiness of his mind. Had he been speaking aloud? Or did Sir Gilbert have some sense which told him what he was thinking about? He didn't know. It didn't matter.

The voice came again. 'If you hadn't done it, you would be dead now. And Alys, and probably the children as well. You had to.'

Edwin said nothing, concentrating on putting one foot in front of the other. If I keep looking at my boots, I won't have to see the evil around me; I won't have to see the bodies of people who are dead, dead like the man I killed.

He felt his shoulders being grasped, was forced to stop walking. 'Do you hear me? Did you want her to be murdered? You saved her, and in doing so you killed a man. It happens often. Him or her; him or you. These are the choices we have to make.'

Edwin looked up at him, numb. 'If those are the choices, I don't think I want to be here. I don't want to do this. I want to go home.' He walked on, stepping round the body of a man who was surrounded by a weeping woman and several children. The sound of hooves started again as they continued, and the knight drew level with him.

'So, tell me how you knew. Alys told me about her father and what happened today in their home, but she didn't know why you had arrived in such a timely fashion.'

Edwin tried to get his tired mind to function. Why had he been there? What had happened? He had helped open the gate, and then … 'It was several things, but mainly it was the wounded man at the castle.'

Sir Gilbert looked at him enquiringly, and Edwin forced the words out, telling him in a hoarse voice of his encounter with the injured Stephen. 'It was something he said which set me on to the right track. He was talking about dying, and saying that he would recognise his brother when he saw him.' He looked up and realised that he was making no sense. 'What I mean is, Alys had told me all about what happened, and it was not until that moment that something leaped out at me. When she was returning from her father's funeral, they were in danger of being attacked by a party of French, but as soon as they saw the neighbours with them, the French backed away. Why would they do that? They can have felt in no danger from one man and his mother, but they left them alone. They must have recognised them as the people who were working for them, and left them in peace. And when her brother's body was dumped at the door – who would know who he was and where he lived except for someone who knew the family well? And the night when her father and brother both went missing – it seemed clear that there must have been two people following them. Otherwise the boy would have got away and got home while the assailant was striking his father down. No, the two of them must have followed both of them and then split up as their prey went separate ways. I would guess that the boy was too quick for the woman to follow, so Gervase probably did that while his mother followed Alys's father and knocked him down. She didn't do it overly well for he survived, long enough to pass his message on to Alys.'

'And thank the Lord he did, and that she passed it to you, for who knows what might have happened had he not. And here are plenty of others who will be grateful to you as well.'

Edwin looked around him and realised they had reached the minster yard, where the nobles of the regent's party were gathered, together with men who looked to be their prisoners. John Marshal hailed Sir Gilbert by waving his arm and hurried over. He spoke even more quickly than usual. 'Where have you been all day? My lord the regent has already left with the papal legate to go and inform his Grace the king about our great victory – he didn't even stop for anything to eat, so keen was he. I swear that today has taken twenty years off him. The regent, that is, not the legate. Well, obviously. He is … but wait, weren't you away after Reginald le Croc when I last saw you? Did you find him?'

Sir Gilbert merely looked at him. John Marshal seemed to understand straight away.

'My condolences. I know you were brothers in arms and you will feel his loss.'

Sir Gilbert bowed his head, and Edwin felt a deep chasm of sadness opening up within himself which he didn't think would ever close.

John Marshal was continuing. 'But I must tell my lord of Chester, who leads us now my uncle is gone. It's already rumoured that he will be named Earl of Lincoln for his day's work.' He strode off towards the knot of men vying for the earl's attention.

Edwin and his companion stood in silence for a while. There seemed little to say. Edwin stared at the cathedral, his eye wandering over the ornate west front without really noticing. Some of Sir Gilbert's men, obviously relieved to see him, arrived to take his horse. They also brought over a knight whom Edwin did not recognise, and who carried no sword.

After a while the Earl of Chester stood to address the assembled throng of nobles and others. Raising his hands for silence he spoke in a commanding tone. 'My friends, by the grace of God we have today won a great battle. By our deeds we have struck a great blow against the ambitions of the French pretender, and the Lord was with us. I charge you all to return to your lands with your prisoners, and there to keep them in close custody until you should learn the king's pleasure regarding them.' There was a murmur at this, but Edwin didn't understand why. He listened as the earl continued. 'The taking of so many prisoners is surely a sign of God's countenance being turned towards us today. Our foes lost only the Count of Perche, and I can tell you that despite all today's combat, we have lost but one man, the knight Reginald le Croc. Let us give thanks for our victory.'

Edwin couldn't believe what he'd just heard. One man? He himself had just walked through a city littered with bodies, both combatants and civilians. How could this be? The earl had got it wrong. But then he looked around him, saw the nobles with their self-satisfied smiles, their rich prisoners, their baggage horses loaded with gold, silver, jewels, clothes, all stolen from the innocent people of the town, and he understood. They hadn't got it wrong; they just didn't care. Anyone who wasn't one of them simply didn't count. All the brave souls who had died defending their city, their homes and their families counted for naught as far as these men were concerned. He felt queasy. He backed away from the congregation, turned and fled until he found himself a quiet corner in the lee of one of the cathedral buttresses, where he fell to his knees and was sick, retching until long after his stomach was empty. Afterwards he staggered away, collapsed again, put his hands on the wall, and sobbed until he thought his heart would break.

After a while he felt hands upon him, lifting him with care to his feet. He looked up into the gaunt face of Master Michael. The hollows under the eyes looked even darker than they had before, but the expression was one of sympathy.

'Come. Come away from my wall before you damage it, and sit over here.'

Edwin let himself be shepherded, half carried. He thought again of all that had happened, and realised something which should have been blindingly obvious all along. 'You were helping to move the masonry, weren't you?'

Master Michael nodded. 'They wouldn't have got far without me. You can't just pick up large stones and move them, especially if you want to do it quietly. You end up making too much noise, or worse, causing a rockfall which can crush you or make moving everything else too difficult.'

'But William suspected you to be on the side of the French.'

Master Michael sighed. 'It is always difficult to be a stranger in a town, although I have been here some fifteen years now. But yes, in my youth I worked in France, on some of the great cathedrals there, so I was always going to have people look askance at me here, especially when Frenchmen invaded. But they didn't understand my motives.'

'Your cathedral.'

'Yes. This is the love of my life, it *is* my life. I couldn't stand by while it was in danger – and it would have been in danger if the siege had continued. Nobody would want to work here; my skilled masons would leave in search of better work and food elsewhere; and once they had gone, people would start stealing the stone, and the whole project would be forgotten.'

'So why not just help the French? If they'd taken the castle then the siege would have stopped.'

Master Michael shook his head. 'You still don't understand me. There are two main reasons why: firstly, the French were on the verge of taking my stone to use in their damned siege engines, and I couldn't side with anyone who would perpetrate such sacrilege. This stone has been cut, shaped and blessed to be used in the house of God, not for killing and maiming.'

'And the second reason?'

'This – this is my home. I have worked in many places, and Lincoln is the place where I feel that I belong. I love every stone and building in it – if not all the people – and I couldn't see it in the hands of enemies. So I banded together with other men: Alan, Aldred, Nicholas and his son, and a few of my local masons. Also initially with William, although he was so distrustful of me that it was difficult to work together as he was convinced I must be some kind of spy. We knew that the key to salvation might well be the western gate: the castle wouldn't save us on its own, there would need to be outside aid, but they couldn't help if they couldn't get into the city. And the western gate is so close to the castle that the French didn't often patrol there. So we cleared away the rubble while trying to make it look as though it was still blocked.'

He paused, his skeletal face sombre. 'Unfortunately, though, we didn't succeed in making those inside the castle aware of what was going on. We tried three times, as Alan, Nicholas and Nick tried to get there, but then we realised it was just too dangerous. Even after what happened to them, Aldred wanted to try again, but he couldn't get close enough.'

'Someone was trying to stop you.'

Master Michael sighed. 'Yes. And I still don't know who, but if I find out then I will see justice done.'

'Justice – if you can call it that – has already been partly done.' Edwin filled in the details of what he knew, striving not to think too much about how Gervase had died, lest he be sick again. He tried to concentrate on what might have happened to Mistress Guildersleeve, determined that he wouldn't be party to another murderer escaping justice, not after what had happened at Conisbrough.

Master Michael nodded slowly. 'This all makes sense – a wonder I didn't see it before. I was desperate to know if Nicholas had lived long enough to pass any message on, or if he could say whether he had told the French any secrets, but I couldn't find out. Of course he would tell his daughter if he was on his deathbed, but I just didn't think of her being the link – she's only a girl, after all.'

Edwin said nothing, thoughts of Alys playing through his mind. But the master mason was continuing.

'As soon as I met you, I knew you were the key. Appearing out of nowhere like that? Nobody in control of their wits would come to Lincoln at a time like this. You are, if I may say so, not a very good spy.'

Edwin wasn't sure whether to take that as an insult or not. He had never wanted to be a spy, but he *had* managed to work out what was going on, after all. He opened his mouth, but was forestalled.

'Ha, I thought that would wake you up a bit. Look, we've succeeded in our task. The town has been rescued, and yes, there have been losses and looting, but the city still stands, and can be rebuilt. William is still alive – I've seen him – so we still have a mayor who loves the city, and we'll be safe under the protection of the king and of Dame Nicola. Nicholas spoke often of her with affection: I think they might have known each other when they were younger. That's part of the reason he was so desperate to help. But for me, it was my cathedral. People come and go and change their minds, but stone is eternal.'

Edwin shook his head to try and clear it. How could Master Michael think that the buildings were as important as the people? All that death …

'But listen, I have a proposal for you. I was only speaking half in jest a few moments ago – you will never be a good spy, as your heart isn't in it. But I saw you in the market the other day when the Peters were trying to catch you out, and I have never seen anyone reckon so fast. Why don't you stay here and work for me? You have an innate mathematical skill, and with a bit of teaching about types of stone and how much is needed for different parts of the cathedral, you would make an excellent marshal of my works. Things will be more peaceful here from now on, I promise you.'

Edwin's heart beat faster. To stay here in Lincoln. Near to … and to have a job which involved no war or bloodshed. A real chance to be part of something big, something glorious …

But then he remembered. His life wasn't his own to dispose of as he saw fit. He had spent his whole life in the service of the earl in one way or another, and he couldn't imagine himself asking to be released from that service. Still less could he imagine the earl agreeing, certainly not now that he had proven himself 'useful'. He held his arms out in a gesture of helplessness, then slumped back with a huge sigh.

'You can't know how much that means to me, Master Michael, but regretfully I will have to turn your offer down.' The mason nodded, as if he had expected such an answer, and Edwin stood and turned to go. As he began walking he spoke over his shoulder. 'But just one more thing – thank you for pulling Gervase off me the other night. I think you probably saved my life.'

Master Michael acknowledged him with a gracious nod, and raised his arm in farewell.

———•◦•———

Sir Gilbert watched Edwin run, but didn't follow. No doubt he wanted some time to himself to take in all that had happened. He turned to Fitzwalter, of whom he had heard but who he had never met. He indicated that the captured knight should walk with him.

'Is there anyone to whom you would like to send a message?'

Fitzwalter nodded gratefully. 'To my wife, if you please. If you would be so kind as to fix my ransom then I can also inform her of that so that she may begin raising the money.'

'I am not sure yet whether you will be permitted to remain in my custody or whether his grace the king will insist on all prisoners being made over to him. Until we know, you may remain my guest if you will give me your word that you will not try to escape.'

Fitzwalter nodded and held out his hand. 'I give you my word.'

Gilbert shook it. 'Good. Now, walk with me a while and tell me how you came to be here and what happened.'

They began to amble in no particular direction, their steps taking them round the outside of the cathedral. Fitzwalter ran his hand through his hair as he began to speak. 'As to how I'm here – well, the Lord only knows. It seemed so clear that we didn't want John as king any longer, so I agreed to oppose him, but somehow this turned into having the French as our allies and by then it was too late to back out. I only wanted what was best for the realm.'

Gilbert raised his eyebrows but said nothing.

'And so here we were, trying to break down those strong castle walls before the regent could get to us – how in God's name did he get here so quickly with such a host? It was I who saw you approaching, so I fetched Saer de Quincey and we rode out to watch. We thought you not too numerous and wanted to attack you over the open ground, but de Quincey thought we'd better ask the comte de Perche. I rode back to find him, and by the time we came outside the city again, you'd started to muster on the ridge. I urged him to attack you while you were out on the open ground, as I thought we could destroy you before you even came near to the city.'

He became more animated. 'I thought I would be able to participate in a true knightly pitched battle. Such occasions happen so rarely that they are bound to go down in history

– minstrels would sing of the deeds. There would be glory and fame to be won. How much better to fight like that than in the cramped streets of the city …' His eyes shone as he gestured, but then he looked at Gilbert and stopped.

'But I digress. Anyway, as we watched you forming up, your second force came into view over the ridge, waving more banners. The breeze had dropped again so it was impossible to see who they were, but there were certainly a goodly number. De Quincey started to lose some of his enthusiasm.'

He stopped and turned. 'The comte continued to watch the new arrivals for a few moments more, making some calculations; then he spoke, saying that you were too numerous, and that it would be folly to attack you out on the open ground – we would be surrounded. So he said we would return to the city and make ready to defend ourselves there. I was disappointed, but the decision was the correct one once we'd seen how many men you had. Attacking a superior force like that in the open would be suicide, and I wasn't so keen to take part in a pitched battle that I wanted to lose my life in it. So we turned our horses and returned to the city. And of course now I wish we *had* charged out in the open.'

Gilbert looked at him. 'Truly? Even though now we will throw the French pretender off our shores, and the true king can reign?'

'Well, when you put it like that …'

Gilbert almost allowed himself to smile. It was the first time in many hours and it made his face hurt. 'Come. We will return to my men and I will have a messenger dispatched to your wife.'

Once the arrangements had been put in place, Gilbert returned Fitzwalter to his men, bidding them help him disarm, and summoned Richard, his most senior sergeant. While he was waiting for the man to arrive he had his squire disarm him. All his muscles were screaming at him, and he wanted nothing more than to lie down and sleep until tomorrow, but there were more important matters to attend to. Leaving the boy to sort out the bloodied armour and equipment, he satisfied himself with a draught of wine from a skin as he waited for Richard to arrive. When he appeared, Gilbert issued brisk instructions to him to send a party of men to the house in the Drapery, some to bring back Reginald's body and some to stay and guard the house until the morrow. He also issued a command that a carpenter be commandeered in order to make a coffin as soon as possible.

Richard was a man of few words, but he took in all the instructions, nodded and turned to leave. Gilbert stopped him. 'Oh, and while you're about it, send someone to find young Edwin and bring him back here safely. I don't want him getting in any more trouble.'

Looking at his sergeant's departing back, Gilbert took a last swig from the wineskin, handed it to a nearby man, and set off to find John Marshal.

He encountered him on the other side of the cathedral, overseeing his men as they sorted through the piles of goods and treasure which he had evidently captured. He smiled thinly at Gilbert. 'Maybe not enough to make up for being a bastard, but a pretty good haul all the same, eh?'

Gilbert ran his eyes over the goods. There was certainly plenty there, and a very small part of him wished he could have made similar gains. But he had been about more weighty matters, so there was no use sighing over it. He got straight to the point. 'My lord, I crave your permission to leave the city tomorrow to return Reginald's body to his family.'

Marshal nodded. 'Of course.'

'And if I may, I will take the man Edwin with me and return him to my lord the Earl of Surrey.'

Marshal thought for a moment and then nodded again, more slowly this time. 'Yes. He has done well and deserves to return home in safety. And Warenne will no doubt do well out of this. I will ask my lord the Earl of Chester what message you may take to Warenne, but I would imagine that he will be welcome to join the king's party once more.'

It still hurt his face, but he couldn't help it. Gilbert smiled.

———◆———

Edwin didn't know who the man was, but he followed him anyway, and was rather dazed when he was led back to Sir Gilbert. He didn't know what to think, but on facing the knight one thing was uppermost in his mind. His fingers slipped as he tried to loose the scabbard from his belt, but he managed it eventually and held the dagger out, the words tumbling from his lips. 'It was his. He said he would leave it with me until after the fighting was over, but now I need to give it back, so you must have it.'

Sir Gilbert looked at him long and hard, but Edwin didn't drop his gaze. 'Please, take it from me.' His hand was starting to shake.

The knight spoke. 'No, you should keep it.'

Edwin opened his mouth but was forestalled. 'I was his brother in arms, so his military fortune, which is not much, comes to me. The dagger is now mine, and I say you should keep it.'

Edwin stood, still holding the weapon out rather forlornly, but the knight took it from him and belted it back around his waist. 'Keep it in remembrance of him, and of this day.'

Edwin nodded. There didn't seem to be much else to say.

Sir Gilbert continued more briskly. 'Now, tomorrow we will leave, and after returning Reginald's body to his family we will travel to see your lord and tell him the news.'

'News?' Edwin's mind was still dulled.

'Yes, the news. You have succeeded in your task, the battle is won and the great lords are reconciled. The earl will no doubt be pleased and will wish to give you some reward.'

Edwin shook his head and thought of graves, and of missed opportunities. 'There is nothing I need – nothing that he can bestow, anyway.'

'Money? A home for your mother?'

Edwin hadn't thought of that. A tiny shard of brightness pierced the clouds which were fogging his mind. Yes, he was alive and he would see his mother again. And ...

Sir Gilbert seemed to have an uncanny knack for reading his thoughts today. 'We'll leave one hour after dawn, but perhaps you would like to be the one who goes down at first light to tell my men in the Drapery of this.'

Edwin tried to smile, but he didn't think he'd ever be able to again.

———

She was surrounded by panicking women. Along with many others she'd fled southwards with as many of her possessions as she could carry, down to the river. There, many of the women had taken to boats, thinking they would be safe from attack once they were out on the water. But the river was fast flowing, and the boats were difficult to control as they span and eddied through the water. There were now soldiers fleeing the city, the French and their allies. She couldn't believe how it had all gone so wrong. She and Gervase had thought there would be no chance of rescue so they'd happily sided with the invaders, hoping this would ensure them better treatment when they controlled the castle as well as the city. Indeed, they'd gone further and tried to stop those who wanted to work against the invaders. It hadn't escaped her notice that Nicholas Holland was one of these, so she'd started to pay him special attention, bringing food for his family, letting him think that she might let her Gervase marry that daughter of his. She almost laughed at the thought – her beautiful boy allying himself with the likes of her! She wasn't nearly good enough for him, and neither was anyone else. She alone knew him, knew what was best for him. But anyway, she was aware that Nicholas Holland and his cronies were up to something, but despite her best efforts at wheedling and cooking meals for his family, she couldn't find out.

They'd grown more desperate; they couldn't find out what the insurgents were doing, so they agreed on a secondary plan – at all costs they had to stop any message reaching the garrison. Gervase had killed the man who was to have been the contact and handed the body over to the French, and she herself had followed Nicholas that fateful night and had struck him down. But she hadn't hit him hard enough and he'd survived long enough to pass the message on to his blasted children. Gervase had taken the boy Nick and they had tried their best to extract the information from him, but he was loyal to his father, damn him.

But what son wouldn't be? She was so proud of hers. Her hope now was that they would both live through this day and that they could return to their lives in the city with nobody any the wiser. There would be opportunities in the ruined town for those clever enough to take them; together they would become rich and successful.

As she thought fondly of her son, she became aware that the boat was rocking dangerously. There was nobody in it who knew how to control it, and many of the other women were panicking and throwing themselves about, which was just making matters worse. She shouted at them to stop, but they were in the grip of terror and couldn't hear her. She tried to hold on, but the boat swayed ever more danger-ously and the shrieking rose in pitch. She started to panic and thrash about, hearing herself scream as she desperately tried to hold on to the boat and her bag of possessions at the same time. The rocking became more violent and finally the boat tipped up. She scrabbled frantically to hold onto the side but she couldn't, and she was thrown into the cold water.

The shock made her numb. She couldn't swim; none of them could. She thrashed her arms and legs uncontrollably, her heavy clothes weighing her down and trying to pull her under. In a desperate attempt to stay afloat she dropped her bag and watched it sink, taking all her wealth with it. But it was no use, the water was in her mouth and nose, choking her, and her last thoughts as she sank were of her beloved son, and the successful future which awaited him. Then the black waters closed over her and claimed her, and she thought no more.

Epilogue

It was just after dawn. Edwin sat in the kitchen of the house, looking at Alys and the children. A bright fire burned in the hearth, and the furniture had been put straight again. Four soldiers had stood guard throughout the night, and no harm had come to any. They and their shattered city were safe, although the price had been high.

They sat in silence, he looking at her and she at him. At last Alys roused herself and gave the children some bread and water. 'Take this out to the men with our thanks. Tell them we're sorry we have nothing better, but we hope they will take it to line their bellies before the start of the journey.'

All three children slipped out without a word, and then they were alone. Edwin took a step forwards. He reached out his arm, raised his shaking hand until it nearly touched her, but let it drop. There was so much he wanted to say, but how could he? He could make her no promises, for he was the earl's man and bound to do as he was commanded.

She too held out her hand, paused, and then laid it very lightly on his arm. 'Words are not enough to say what we all owe to you, but for what it's worth, I thank you from the bottom of my heart.' Her eyes, as blue as the summer sky, met his for a long moment. Slowly, very slowly, he brought up his hand and put it on top of hers for the lightest, briefest moment. Then, as the children returned, they stepped away from each other and he turned and left the house.

ḥistorical ṇote

The Battle of Lincoln took place on Saturday, 20 May 1217. It is normally referred to as the Second Battle of Lincoln, in order to distinguish it from the earlier encounter which took place there in 1141.

Towards the end of King John's reign, the nobility of England had rebelled against him and invited Prince Louis, the son of the king of France (later Louis VIII), who was married to John's niece, to invade and take the crown. However, during this invasion John died unexpectedly, leaving as his heir his nine-year-old son, Henry III. This caused many of the barons to undergo a change of heart, and by early 1217 many of the lords had defected back to the Royalist party, which was led by William Marshal, the regent, and by the Earl of Chester. However, Louis still had the support of a number of English nobles, as well as the French lords who had invaded with him, and his army was in control of most of eastern England. One of the most important strongholds in the region was Lincoln.

In 1217, Lincoln was one of the largest cities in England; a bustling and prosperous place whose wealth was built upon the wool trade. Wool and cloth had been exported from here to Flanders for many years, and the weavers of Lincoln had established a guild as early as 1130. Most of the people who lived in the city would have been engaged in some kind of trade, rather than being involved in the agricultural work which characterised rural areas of the country. The basic unit of currency – and the only coin in general use – was the silver penny, which could be cut into halves or quarters for small change. Twelve pennies made up one shilling; twenty shillings made one pound, and thirteen shillings and four pence, one mark. Cloth was measured either in yards (36 inches) or, for larger quantities, in ells (45 inches), and one may surmise that those who bought and sold goods must have had a good grasp of some fairly complex arithmetic.

Among the citizens of Lincoln in the early thirteenth century, according to the town's records, were William the nephew of Warner, who served several terms as mayor; Peter of the Bridge; Peter of the Bail; Ralf the son of Lefwine; and Master Michael, the master mason in charge of the cathedral works. Nicholas Holland and his family are fictional (although a 'Nicholas the son of Gunnilda' was living in Lincoln in the early thirteenth century), as are Mistress Guildersleeve, Gervase and Aldred. It was unusual at the time for anyone other than the nobility to have a hereditary surname: any second name which differentiated people with the same first name was likely to be either patronymic ('son of'), locative ('of Conisbrough') or occupational ('the baker'). However, some people were known by nicknames or by the names of their ancestors if they had been particularly noteworthy individuals, and it was about this time that some of those names started to become hereditary. Edwin's surprise at being called by his father's name is only to be expected, but the practice would become less unusual as the years went by.

The medieval city of Lincoln occupied a hill, with the castle at the top and the river at the bottom. The castle was originally built by William the Conqueror, on the site of a Roman fort, and consisted of two fortified mounds with a large bailey encircled by walls. It was in a prime position: to the south the defenders could command the steep descent towards the river, and to the west they could look out over the valley of the Trent and the highway. The castle had two principal gateways: one in the east wall (which is still in use) and the other to the west, giving access to the open country.

In 1217 the castle was under the stewardship of Dame Nicola de la Haye, a remarkable woman whose life story is worthy of a book of its own. She was the hereditary castellan, succeeding to her father's lands and duties after his death sometime around 1170. Although legally subordinate to her husband (she married twice) she played an unusually active role in running her own affairs. Indeed, on the two occasions when the castle needed defending she was in sole charge: her husband was absent during the siege of 1191, when the castle held out for forty days and nights against attack, and he died in 1215 before the events of *The Bloody City* took place. They had a son, Richard de Camville, who died in the spring of 1217, although there is no evidence to suggest that this was due to the invasion.

The city of Lincoln was not prepared for the large-scale attack which fell upon it in the spring of that year, and it capitulated quickly to the invading army. The castle, however, with its separate defences, managed to hold out. William Marshal knew that such a strategically important stronghold could not be left to fall into the hands of the invaders, so he gathered a force. They mustered at Newark before marching to the city via Torksey, to avoid using the main road which would have brought them directly into the path of the French.

The major contemporary narrative sources for the battle are the *History of William Marshal*, written in the 1220s, and Roger of Wendover's *Flowers of History*, which he completed in 1235; from these sources we can reconstruct a reasonable, if slightly confusing, account of what happened there.

Both sources agree that some form of contact was made with those inside the castle: according to Roger of Wendover, a messenger was sent out to tell the host of the situation inside and to offer them entry via the postern; according to the *History*, William Marshal's nephew, John, met outside the castle with Geoffrey de Serland, who told them of a door they could use; John was then attacked by a party of French as he tried to return to the host. However, the *History* then goes on to say that Peter des Roches, the Bishop of Winchester, managed to enter the castle and then the city, where he found a gate of great antiquity that was blocked but that could be cleared to allow the host entry.

The Marshal's army then entered the city via the north and probably also from the west, and from inside the castle, where their crossbowmen had been stationed. There was some fierce fighting in the narrow streets, and the Royalists drove the French southwards down the hill where they fled out of the city – those of them who managed to escape through the constricted gate, anyway. Both sources recount the death of the Count of Perche via a strike to the eye, although Roger of Wendover does not give a name to his killer, and the *History* attributes the fatal blow to Reginald le Croc, with William Marshal apparently attempting only a capture and feeling regret at the death of his cousin.

After the battle, the city was looted by the victorious army on the pretext that the citizens had collaborated with the enemy; the papal legate excommunicated the entire clergy of Lincoln, and the cathedral, too, was looted. So much plunder was gained by the Royalist army that the battle is sometimes also called 'Lincoln Fair'. Roger of Wendover recounts a sad addendum to the battle: 'Many of the women of the city were drowned in the river, for, to avoid insult, they took to small boats with their children, their female servants, and household property […] the boats were overloaded, and the women not knowing how to manage the boats, all perished.'

Finally, it is true that Roger states that only three people died in the battle: the Count of Perche, Reginald le Croc, and another unnamed knight. It is also true that this was a time when the deaths of commoners were not thought important enough to record, so, although the day might not have been quite as bloody as portrayed here, it is very likely that there were more than three casualties.

Edwin is a fictional character, but his lord, William de Warenne, was a real earl whose motives are open to question. When the civil war first broke out he had sided with John, and was one of the Royalists who were present at the signing of the Magna Carta. He later served as a Royalist commander, but in June 1216 the rebel army led by Louis was allowed to enter his castle at Reigate unopposed; later in the month, Warenne came to Louis and offered him his support. It is not clear why he changed sides, but whatever his reason, his rebellion was short-lived, and following John's death in October 1216, he wavered again. In April 1217, he entered into a truce with the Royalists; and then in May, the regent's summons was sent out. Warenne was still not trusted, however, and he and his men were not present at the Battle of Lincoln. Nevertheless, he was welcomed back into the fold almost immediately afterwards, and to this day nobody seems quite sure why.

Further Reading

Robert Bartlett, *England Under the Norman and Angevin Kings: 1075-1225* (Oxford University Press, 2002)

D.A. Carpenter, *The Minority of Henry III* (Methuen, 1990)

David Crouch, *William Marshal: Knighthood, War and Chivalry, 1147-1219* (Longman, 2002)

J.W. F. Hill, *Medieval Lincoln* (Cambridge University Press, 1948)

A.J. Holden (ed.), *History of William Marshal* (3 Vols, Anglo-Norman Text Society, 2002-2006)

Sean McGlynn, *Blood Cries Afar: The Forgotten Invasion of England 1216* (Spellmount, 2011)

Roger of Wendover, *Flowers of History: 1215 to 1235* (Llanerch Press, 1996)

Acknowledgements

The publication of this book would not have been possible without the help and support of many people, and I'm delighted to have the opportunity to thank them heartily.

Firstly I would like to thank Matilda Richards and Ross Britton of The History Press and its crime imprint The Mystery Press; their tireless efforts to improve, market and support my work are much appreciated (chocolate cake on the way next time I visit …).

I'd also like to express my gratitude to those who read early drafts of *The Bloody City* and offered extensive and incredibly useful feedback: Richard Skinner, Stephanie Tickle and Roberta Wooldridge Smith; and to Andrew Bunbury (a man who can spot a tautology at a hundred paces) for reading a later version. Thanks are also due to Adam Cartwright and Sumila Bhandari, who both had the misfortune to share an office with me at work while I was writing the first draft and who often found themselves drawn into impromptu conversations about plot, dialogue or background.

It's either a symptom of modern life or proof that I don't get out much, but I have a large and supportive community around me on the social networking site Twitter; some of these people I know personally and others only virtually, but they cheer my days with their wit and offer encouraging comments when I need it. I shall thank Andrew Buck, Kate Haigh, Julian Humphrys, Greg Jenner, Richard Sheehan and Jemima Williams by name, and hope that everyone else will realise that I'd list them all if only I had the space on this page. Keep it up, everyone!

Last but certainly not least, my thanks and love go to my husband James (for another super map as well as everything else) and our children. The fact that they put up with me at all is a source of constant wonder.

About the Author

C.B. Hanley has a PhD in mediaeval studies from the University of Sheffield and is the author of *War and Combat 1150-1270: The Evidence from Old French Literature*, as well as the historical work of fiction, *The Sins of the Father*. She currently writes a number of scholarly articles on the period, as well as teaching on writing for academic publication, and also works as a copy-editor and proofreader.

If you enjoyed this book, you may also be interested in …

The Sins of the Father: A Mediaeval Mystery

C.B. HANLEY

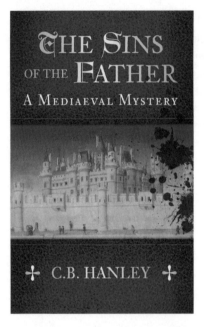

1217: England has been invaded. Much of the country is in the iron grip of Louis of France and his collaborators, and civil war rages as the forces of the boy king try to fight off the French. Most of this means nothing to Edwin Weaver, son of the bailiff at Conisbrough Castle in Yorkshire, until he is thrust into the noble world of politics and treachery: he is ordered by his lord the earl to solve a murder which might have repercussions not just for him, but for the future of the realm. Edwin is terrified but he must obey; he takes on the challenge and learns more until he uncovers a horrific secret which has been dead and buried for fifteen years, a secret which might kill them all – and realises there are some questions to which he might not wish to know the answers.

978 0 7524 8091 6

Visit our website and discover thousands of other History Press books.

www.thehistorypress.co.uk